To my dad, who taught me the art of silliness —E.C.B.

Dedicated to Stephanie Hays. A DRAGON-SIZED thank you for adding your unique sparkle with every step of this adventure. You're a true glitter-boost of inspiration to this art troll in his creative cave! —L.F.

Etch and Clarion Books are imprints of HarperCollins Publishers.

The Sparkle Dragons

For information address HarperCollins Children's Books,
a division of HarperCollins Publishers, 195 Broadway, New York, NY 10007.
clarionbooks.com

Library of Congress Cataloging-in-Publication Data has been applied for.

ISBN: 978-0-358-53809-7 hardcover
ISBN: 978-0-358-53808-0 paperback

The illustrations in this book were done in Photoshop with digital brushes
...and a dash of dragon sparkles too.
The text was set in Jacoby.
The display text was set in Maduki.
Cover and interior design by Stephanie Hays

Manufactured in Spain
EP 10 9 8 7 6 5 4 3 2 1
4500842198

First Edition

THE SPARKLE DRAGONS

BY EMMA CARLSON BERNE

ILLUSTRATED BY LUKE FLOWERS

Clarion Books
Imprints of HarperCollinsPublishers

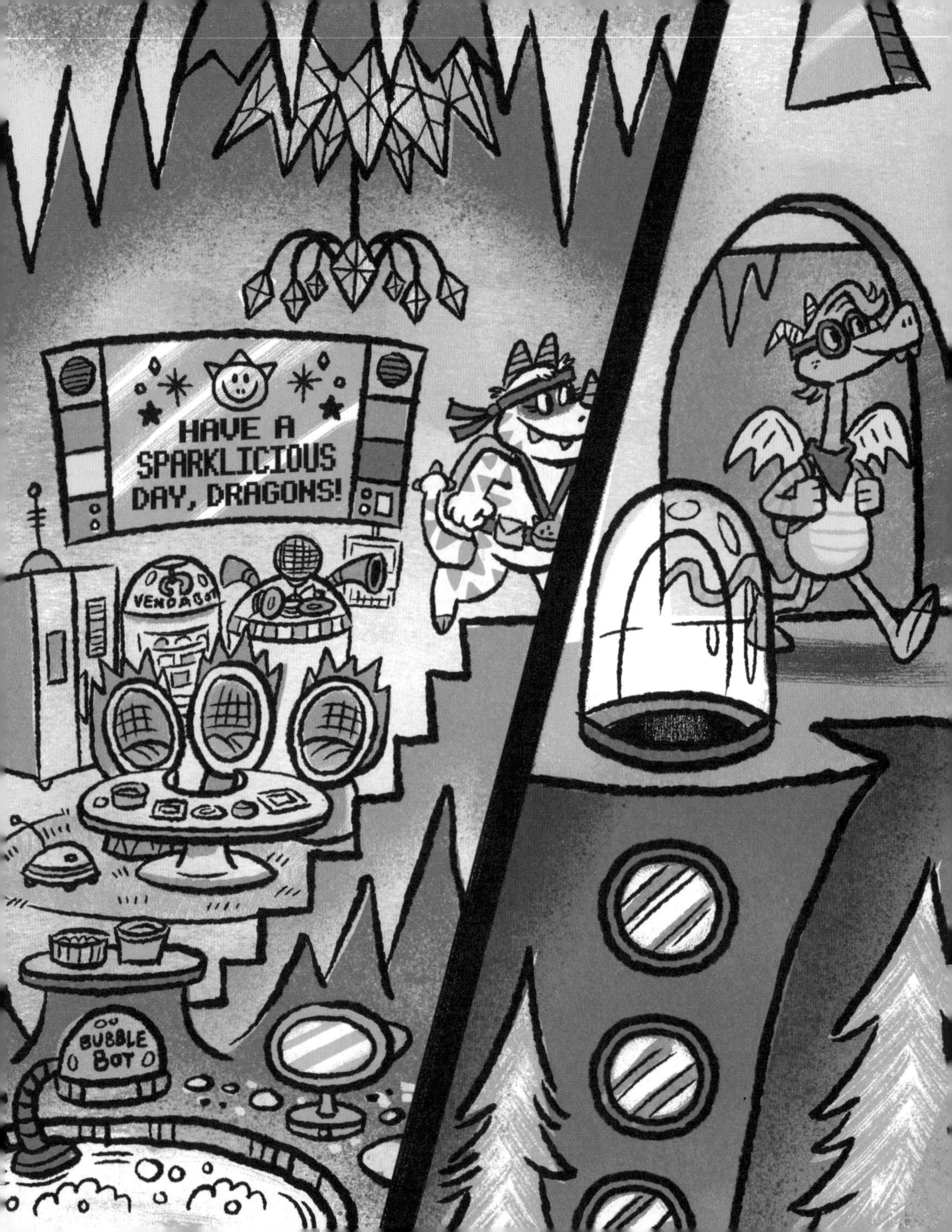
HAVE A SPARKLICIOUS DAY, DRAGONS!
VENDABOT
BUBBLE BOT

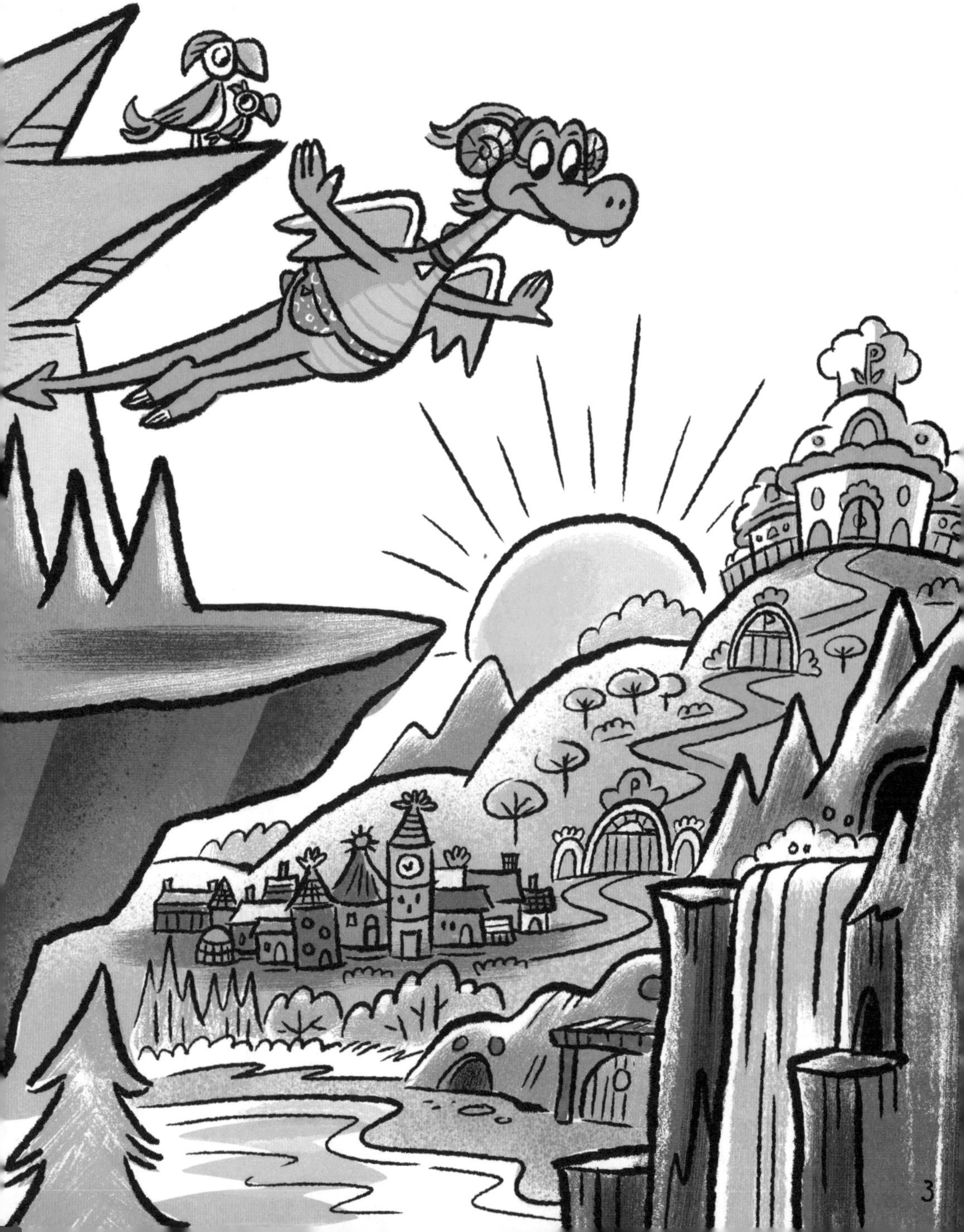

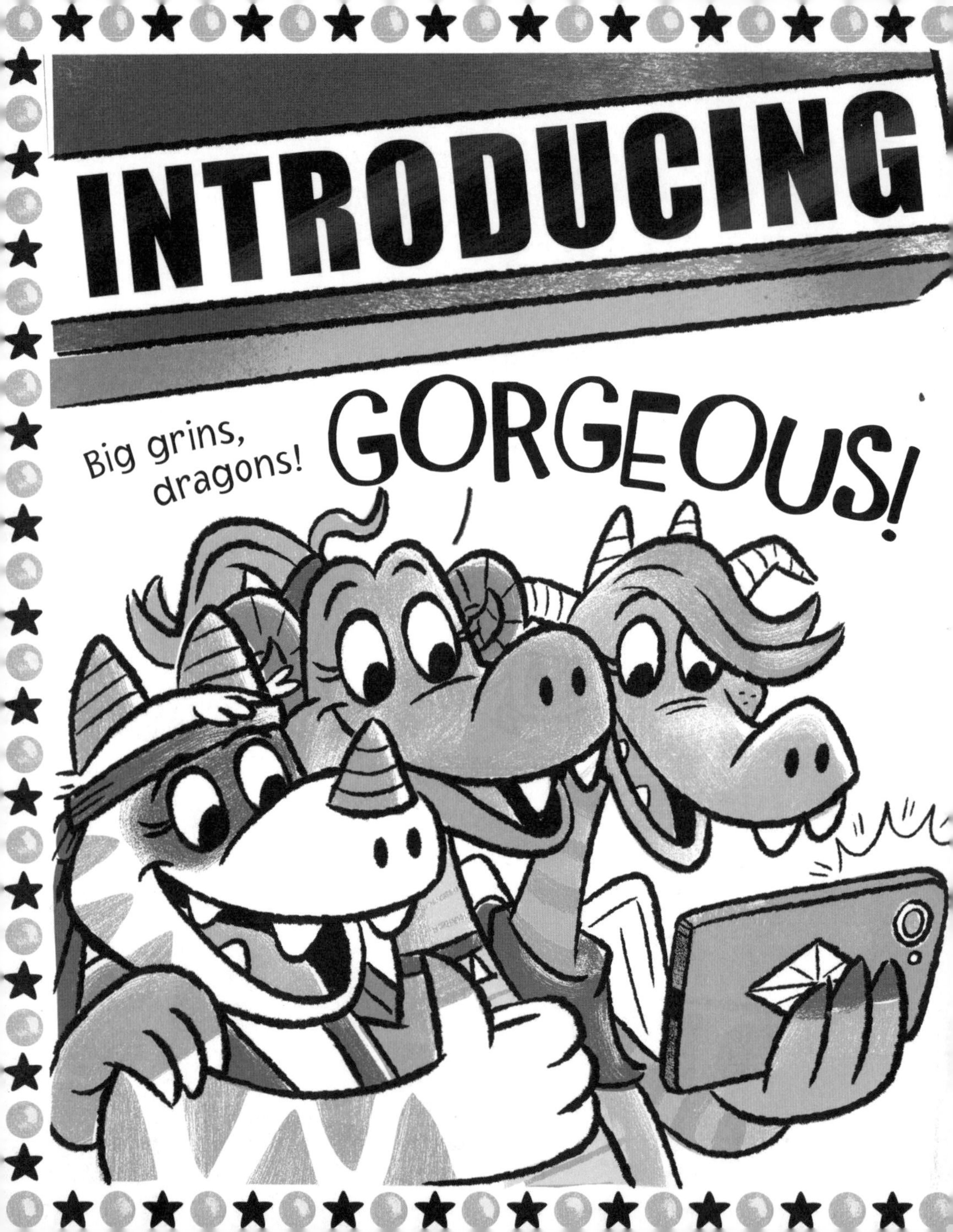
INTRODUCING
Big grins, dragons!
GORGEOUS!

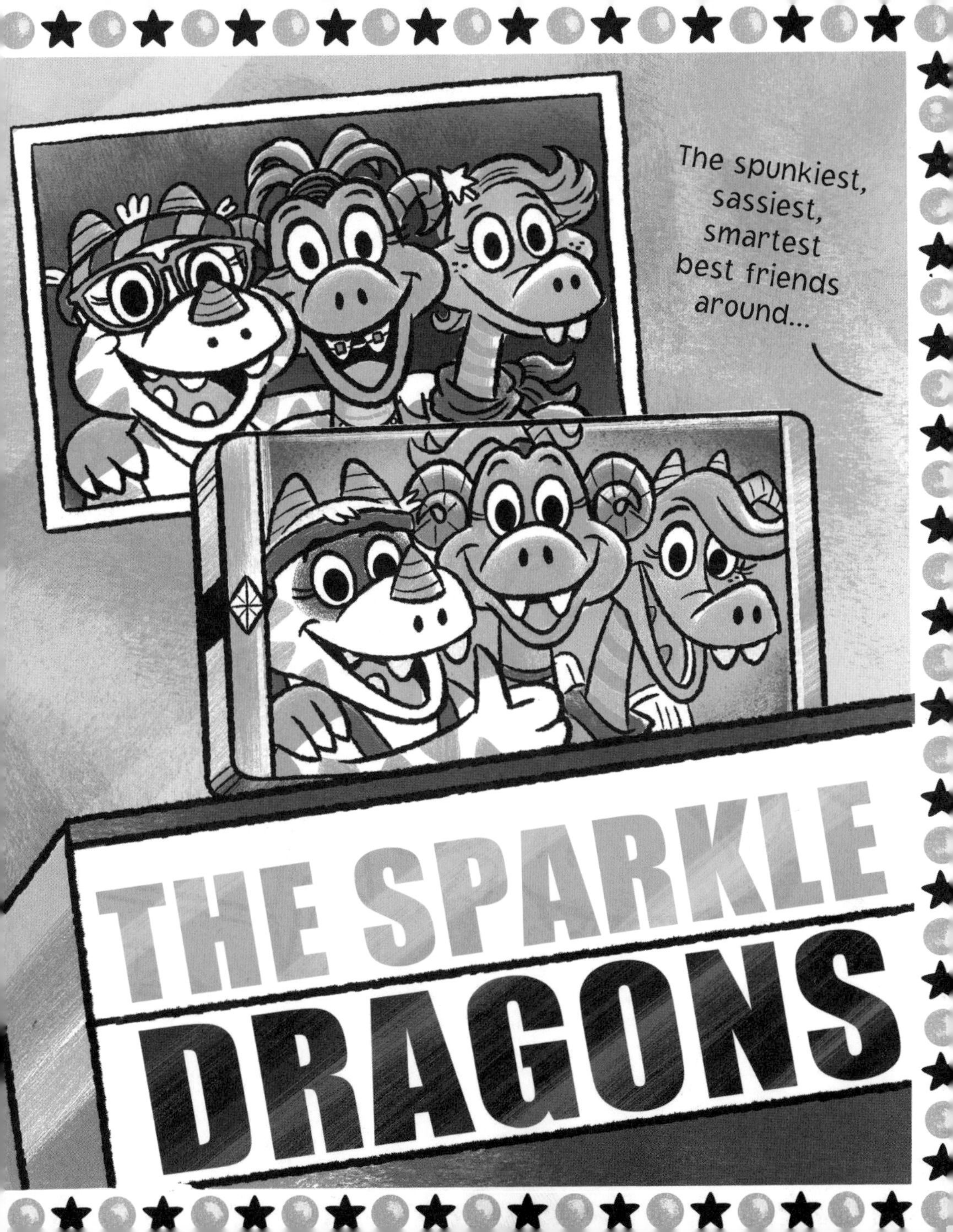
The spunkiest, sassiest, smartest best friends around...
THE SPARKLE
DRAGONS

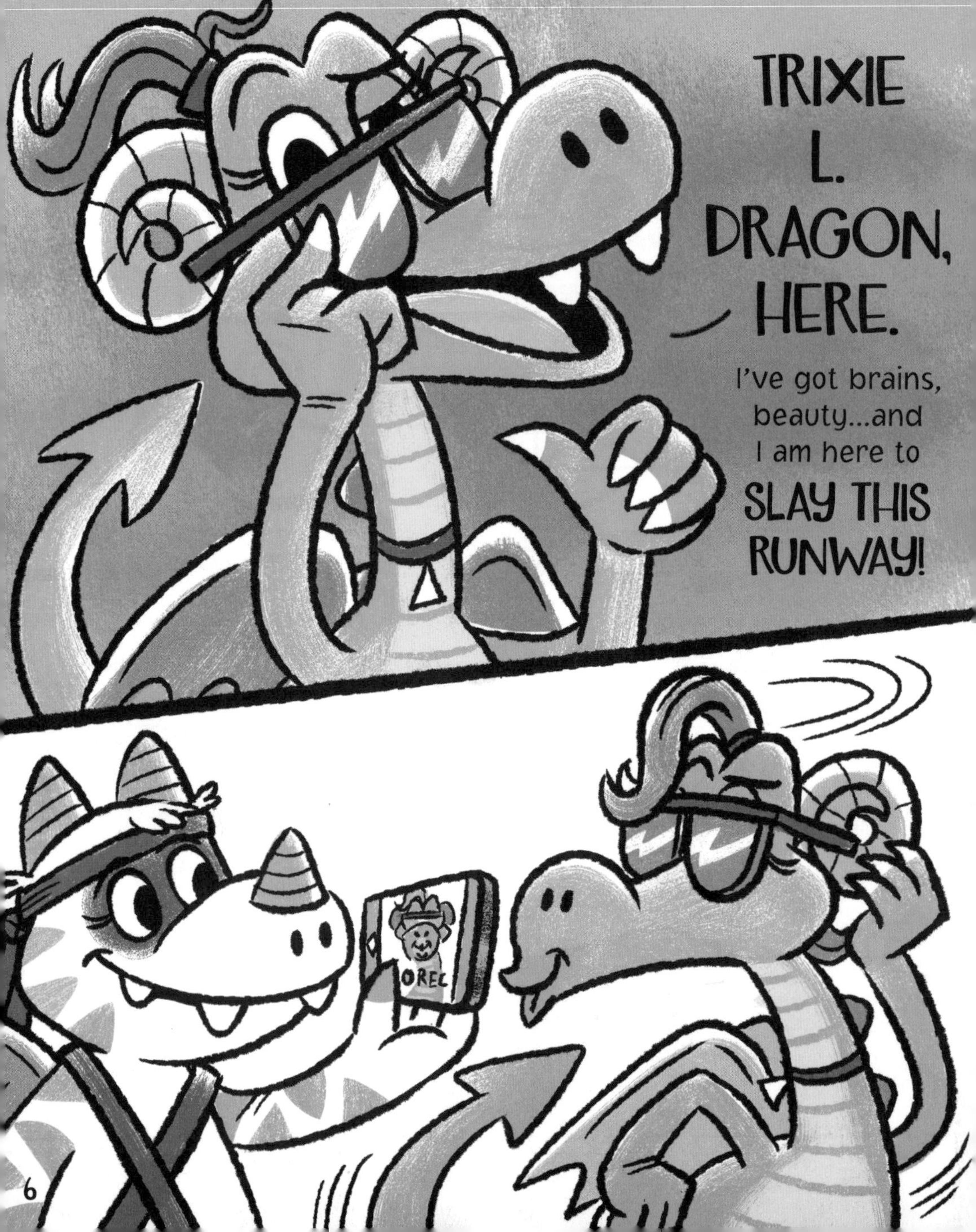
TRIXIE L. DRAGON, HERE.
I've got brains, beauty...and I am here to SLAY THIS RUNWAY!
REC

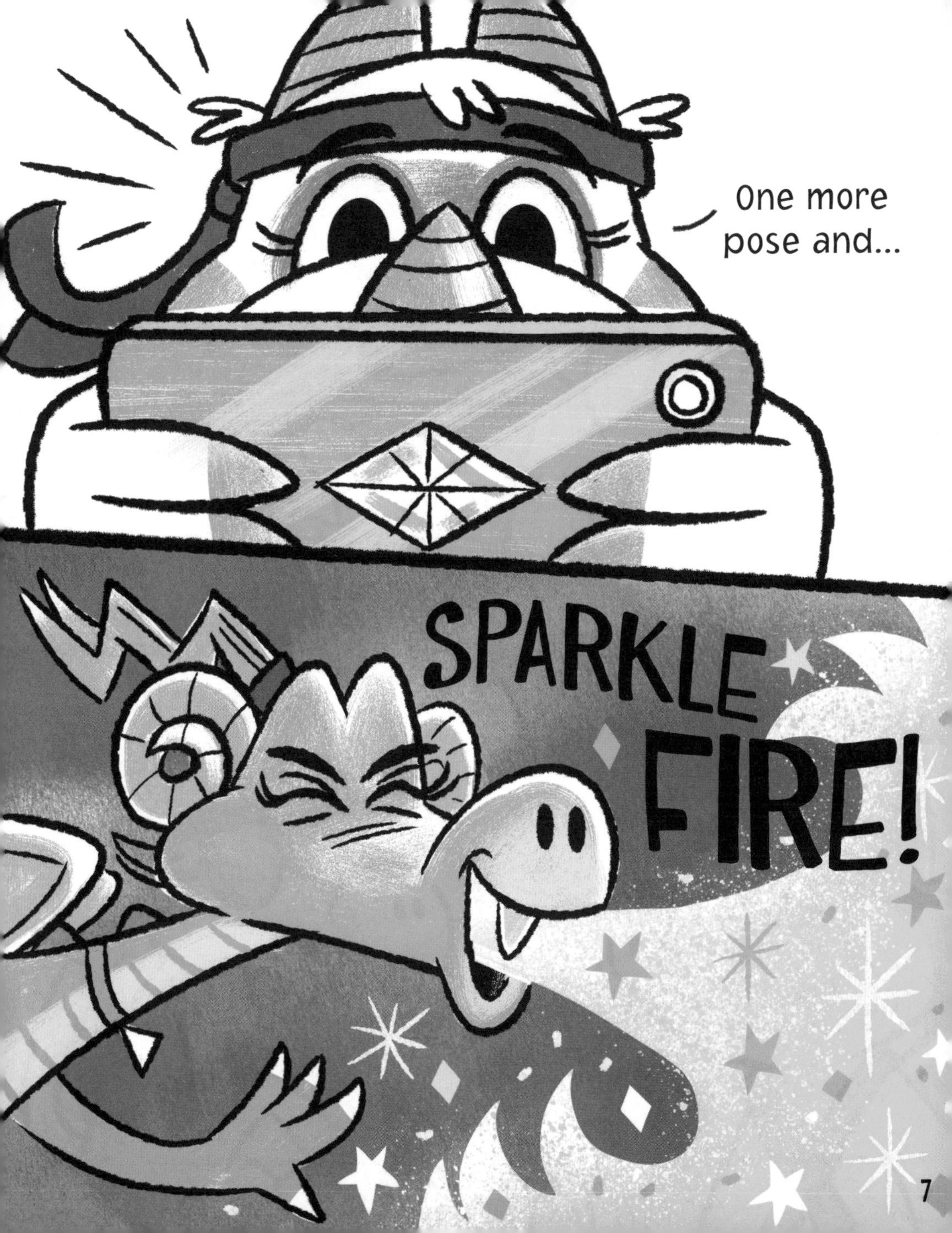
One more pose and...
SPARKLE FIRE!

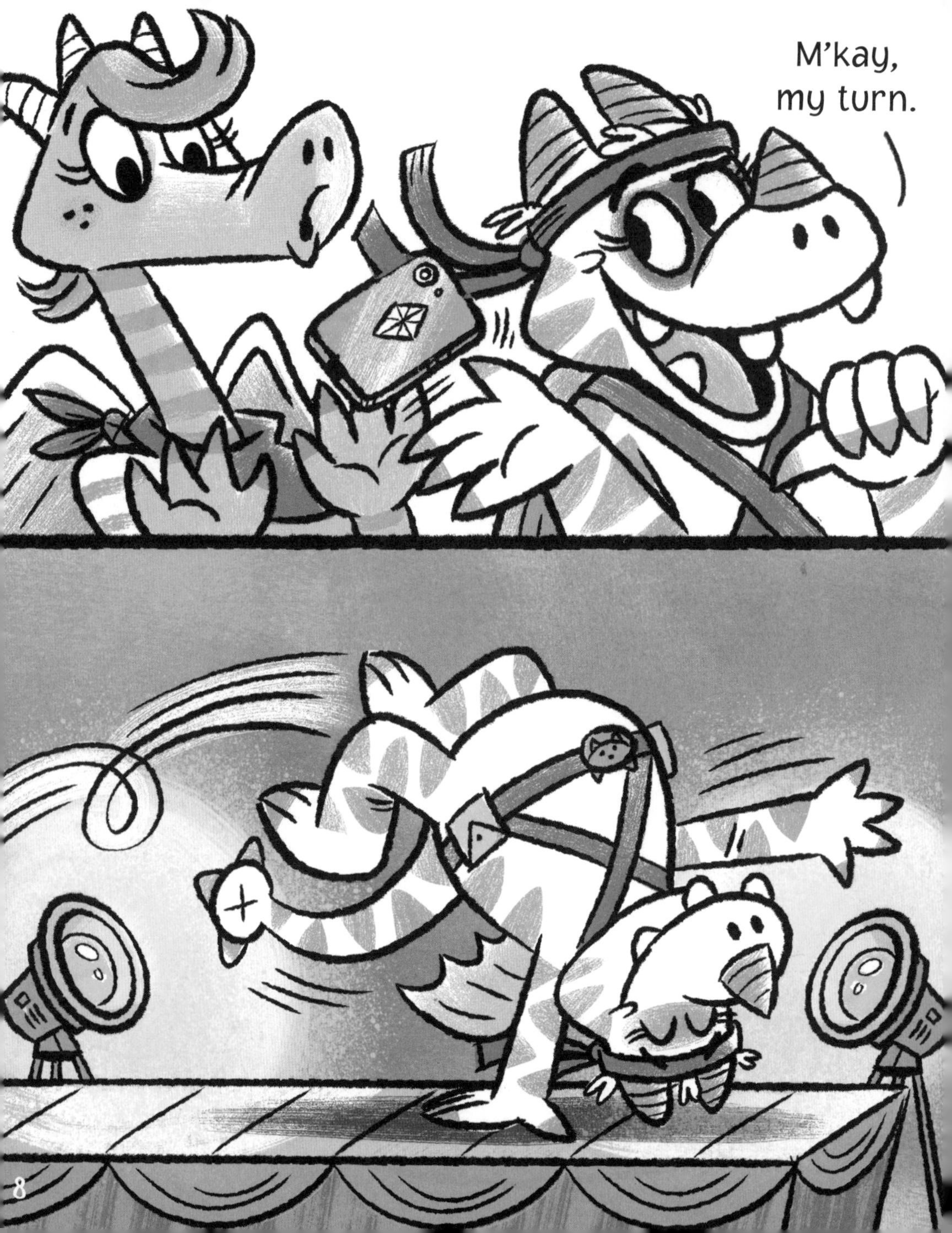
M'kay,
my turn.

HELLO, WORLD!

Rue here. I'm feisty, fierce, sharp as a dragon's tooth, and dedicated to fighting for good with my BFFs.

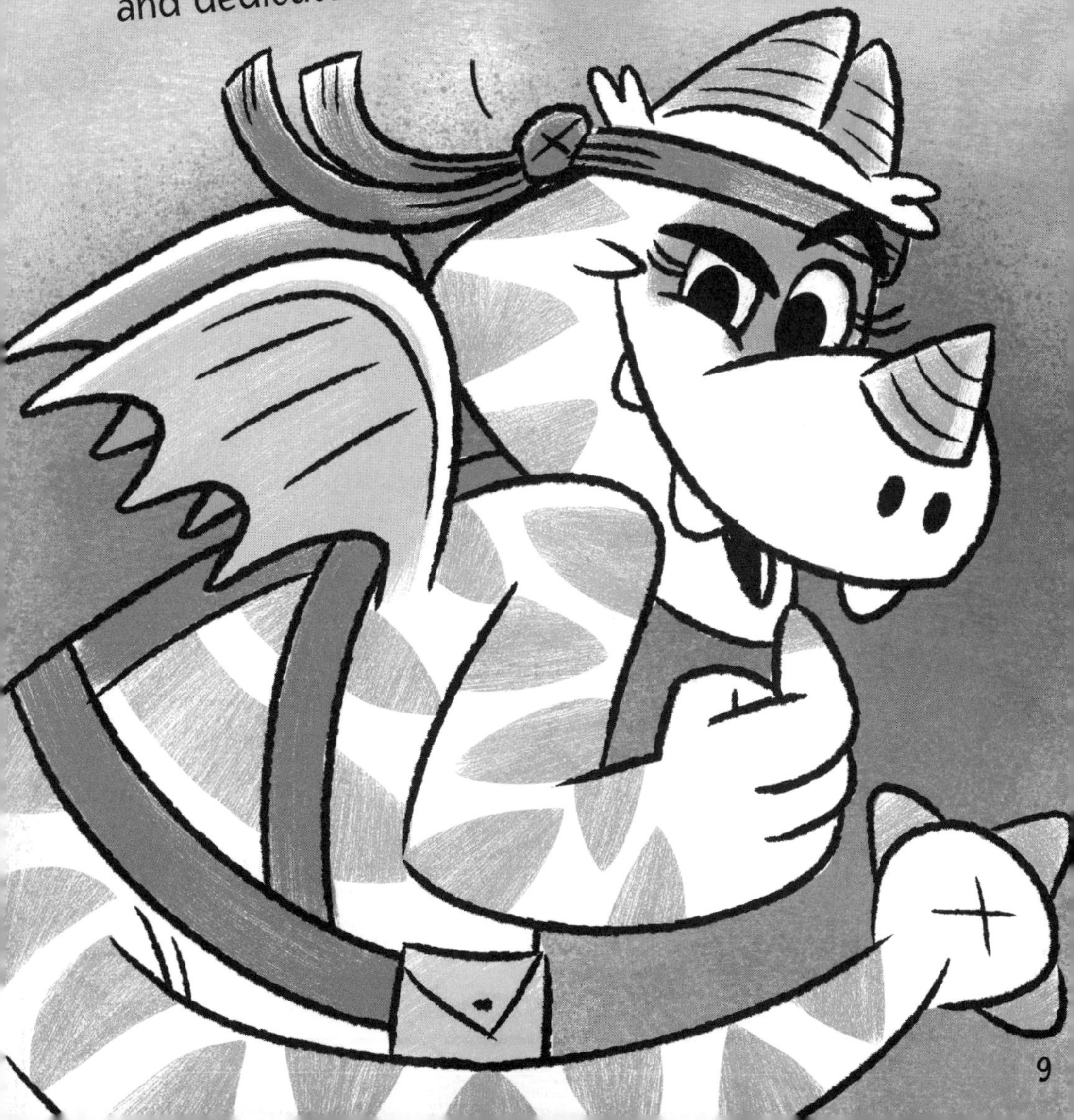

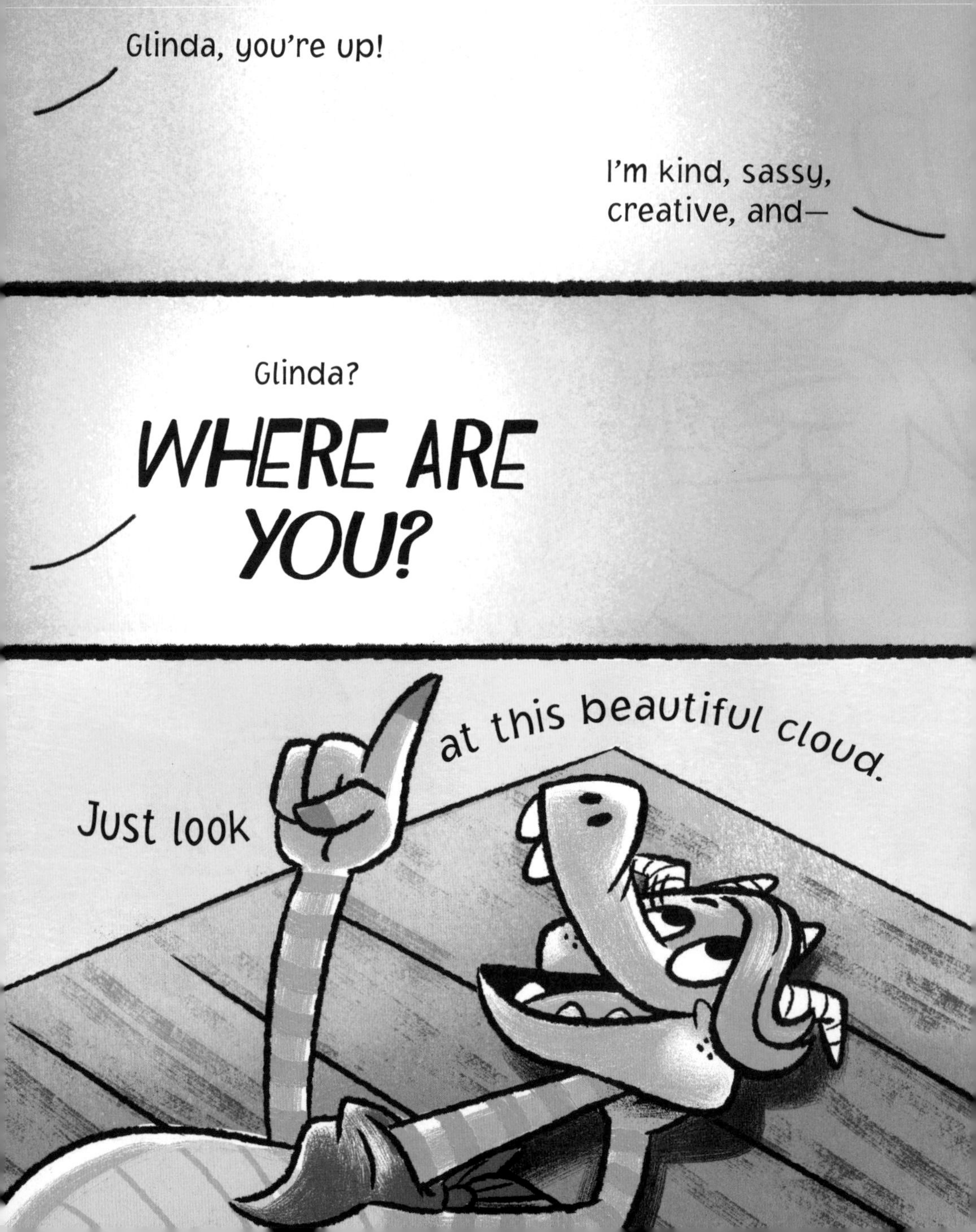
Glinda, you're up!
I'm kind, sassy, creative, and—
Glinda?
WHERE ARE YOU?
Just look
at this beautiful cloud.

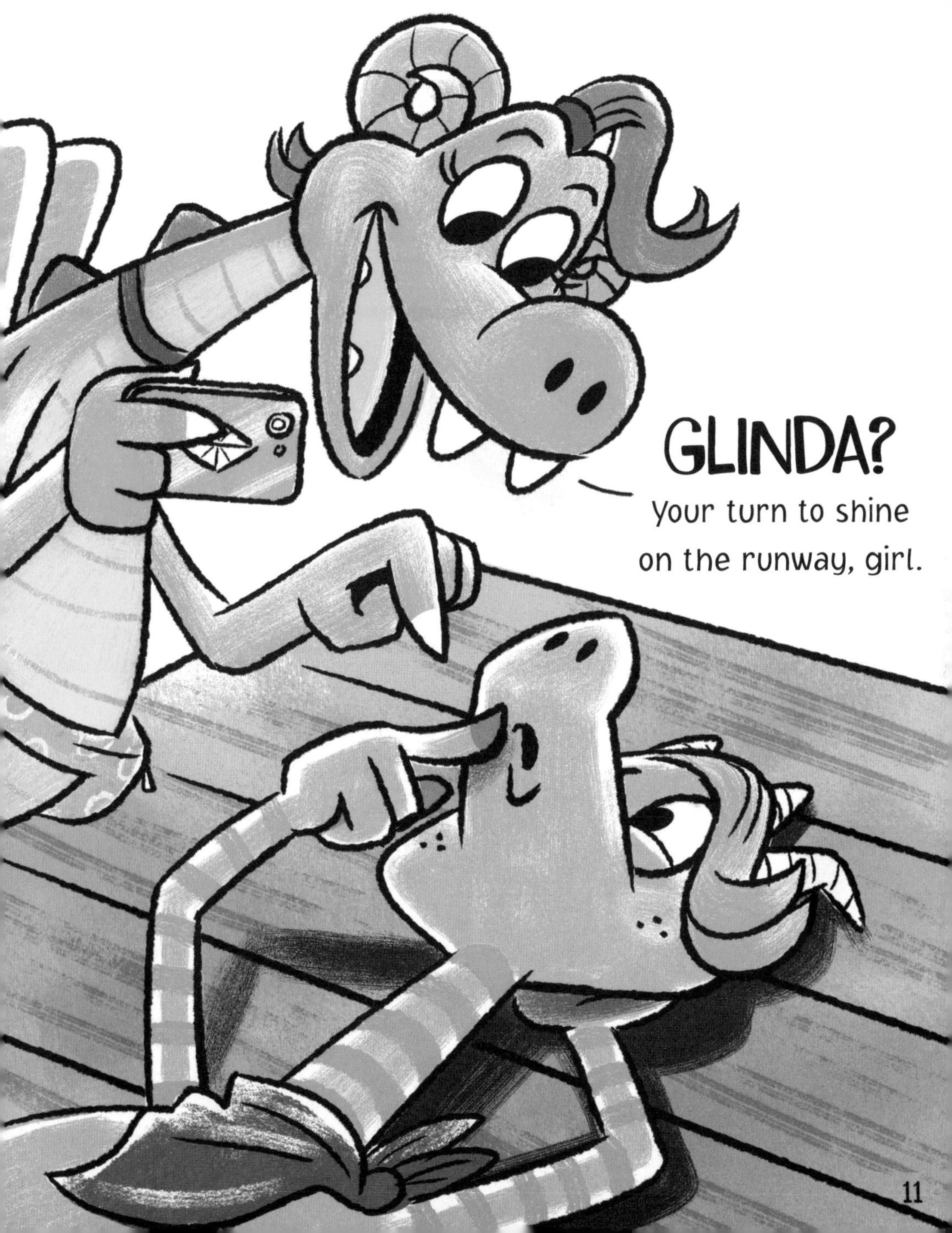
GLINDA?
Your turn to shine
on the runway, girl.

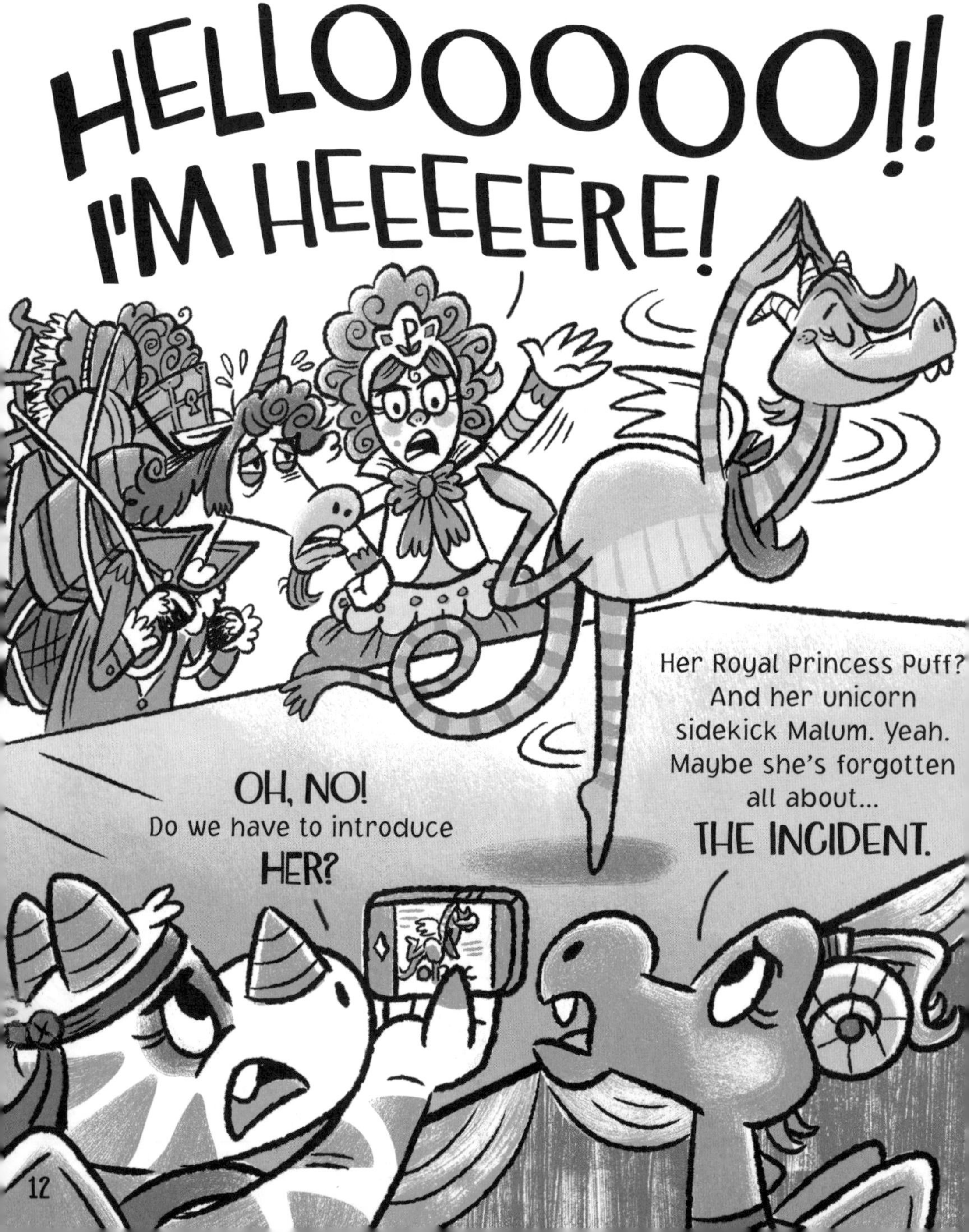
HELLOOOOO!! I'M HEEEEEERE!
OH, NO! Do we have to introduce HER?
Her Royal Princess Puff? And her unicorn sidekick Malum. Yeah. Maybe she's forgotten all about... THE INCIDENT.

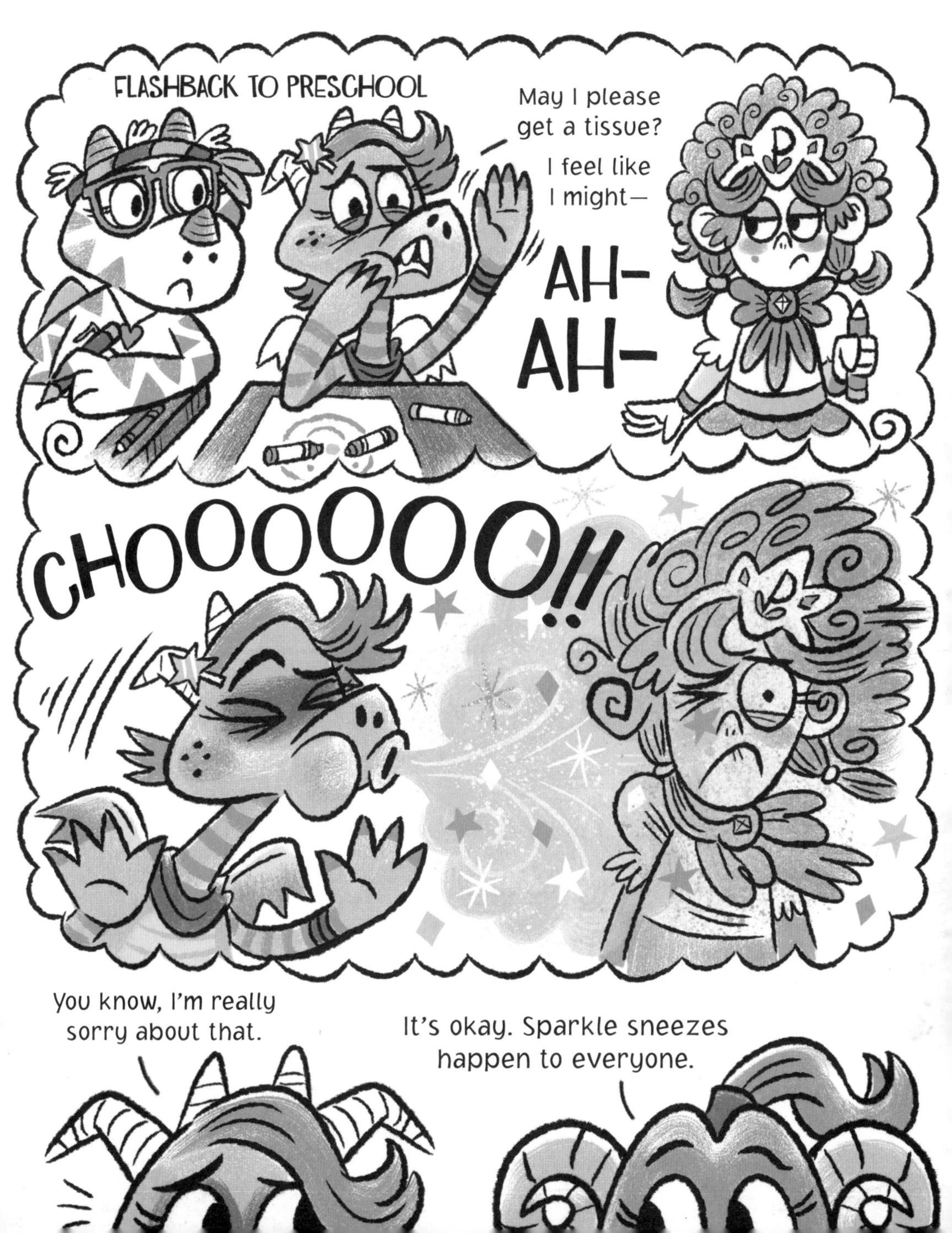
FLASHBACK TO PRESCHOOL
May I please get a tissue?
I feel like I might—
AH-
AH-
CHOOOOOOO!!
You know, I'm really sorry about that.
It's okay. Sparkle sneezes happen to everyone.

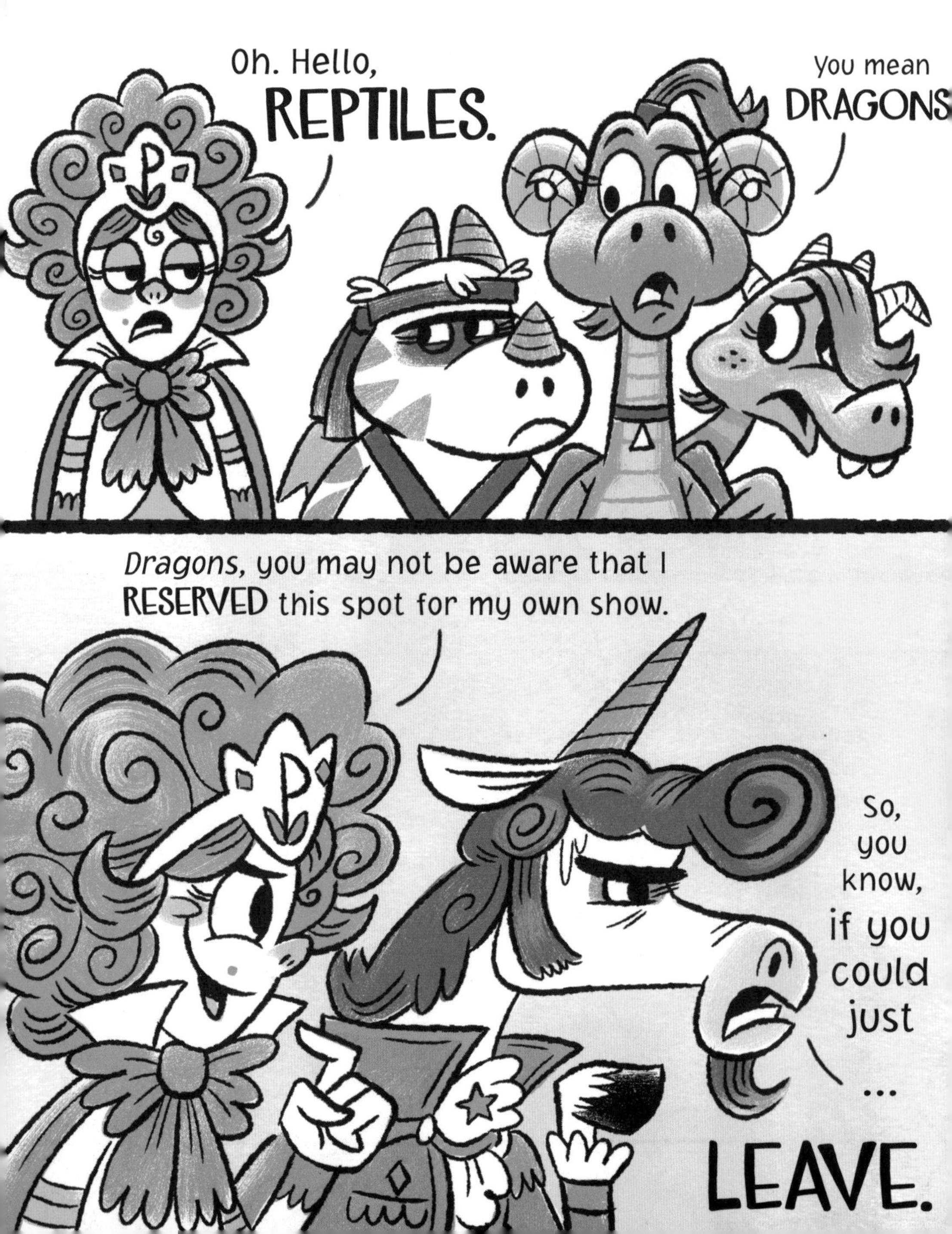
Oh. Hello, REPTILES.
You mean DRAGONS
Dragons, you may not be aware that I RESERVED this spot for my own show.
So, you know, if you could just ... LEAVE.

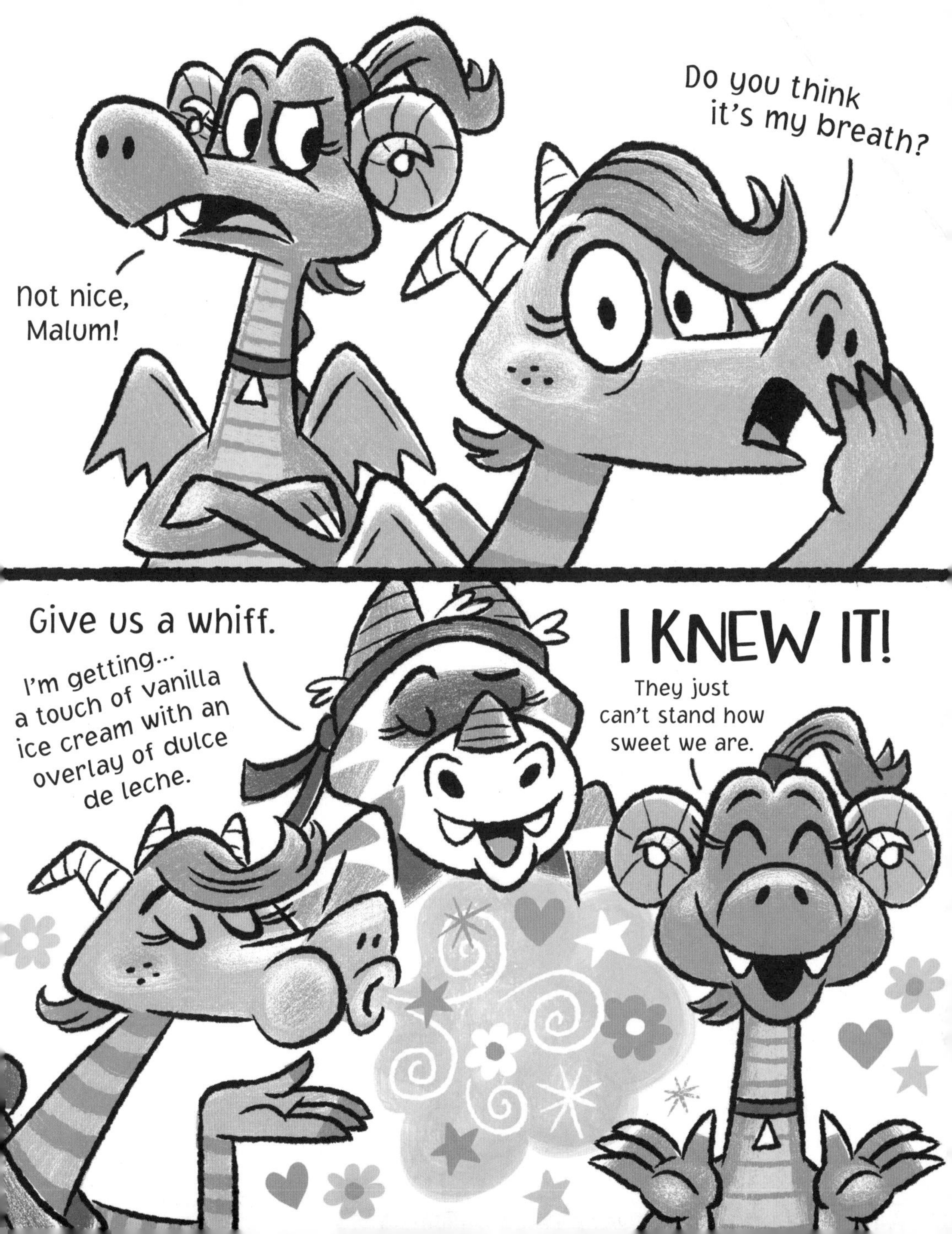
Do you think it's my breath?
Not nice, Malum!
Give us a whiff.
I'm getting... a touch of vanilla ice cream with an overlay of dulce de leche.
I KNEW IT!
They just can't stand how sweet we are.

CHAPTER ONE
A VERY PUFFY PAGENT

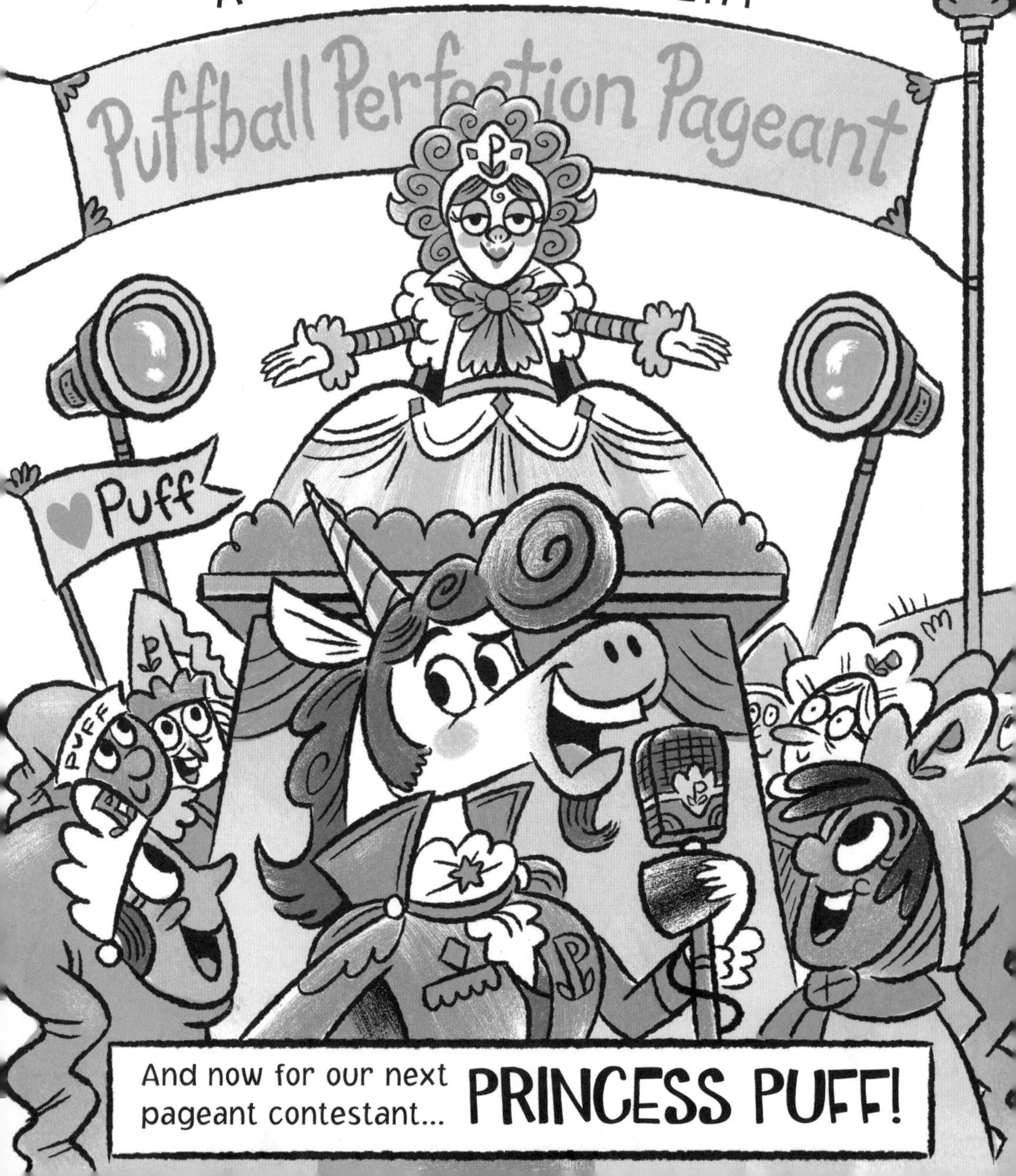
Puffball Perfection Pageant
Puff
PUFF
And now for our next pageant contestant...
PRINCESS PUFF!

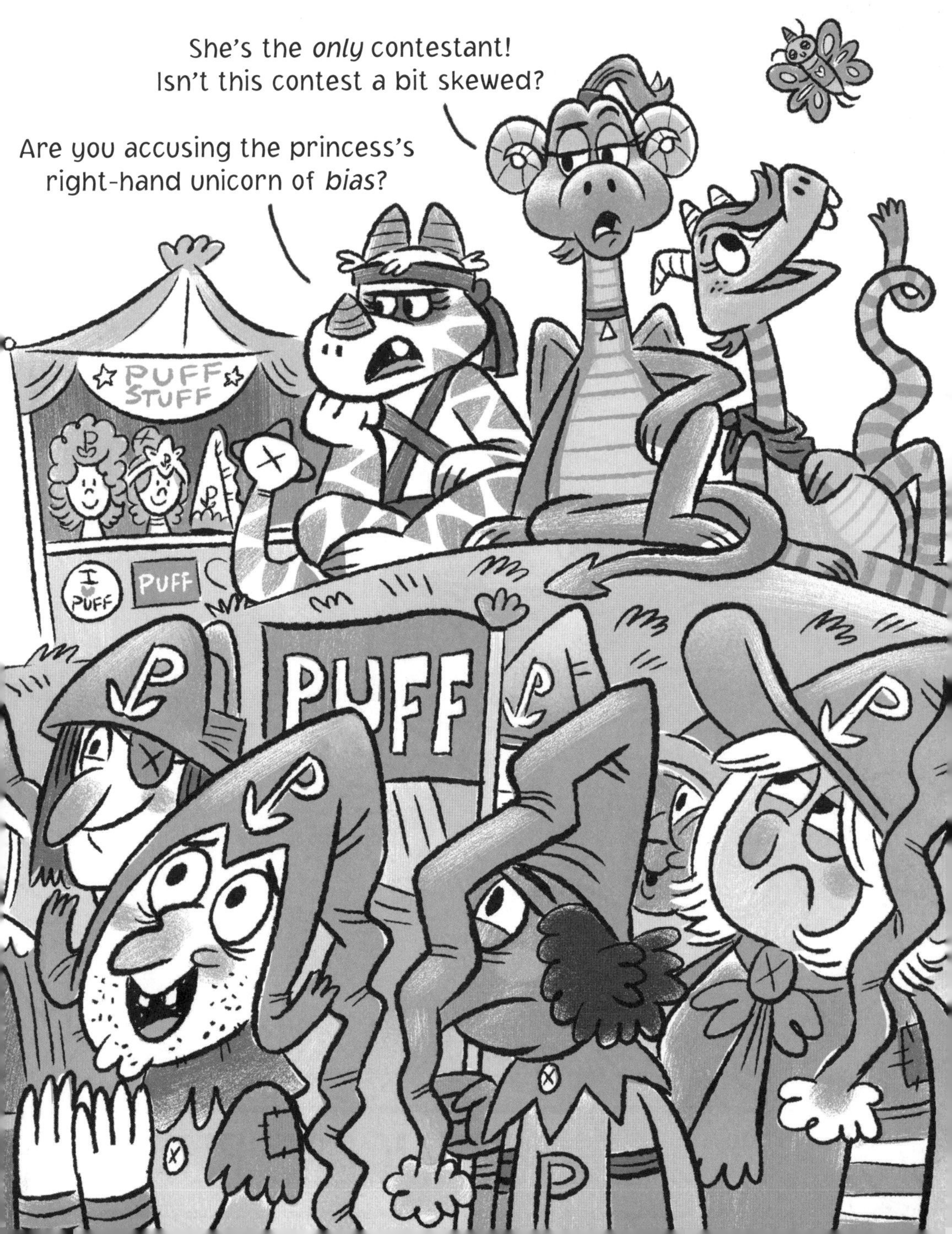
She's the *only* contestant! Isn't this contest a bit skewed?
Are you accusing the princess's right-hand unicorn of *bias*?
PUFF STUFF
I ♥ PUFF
PUFF
PUFF

And now we have...

PRINCESS PUFF!

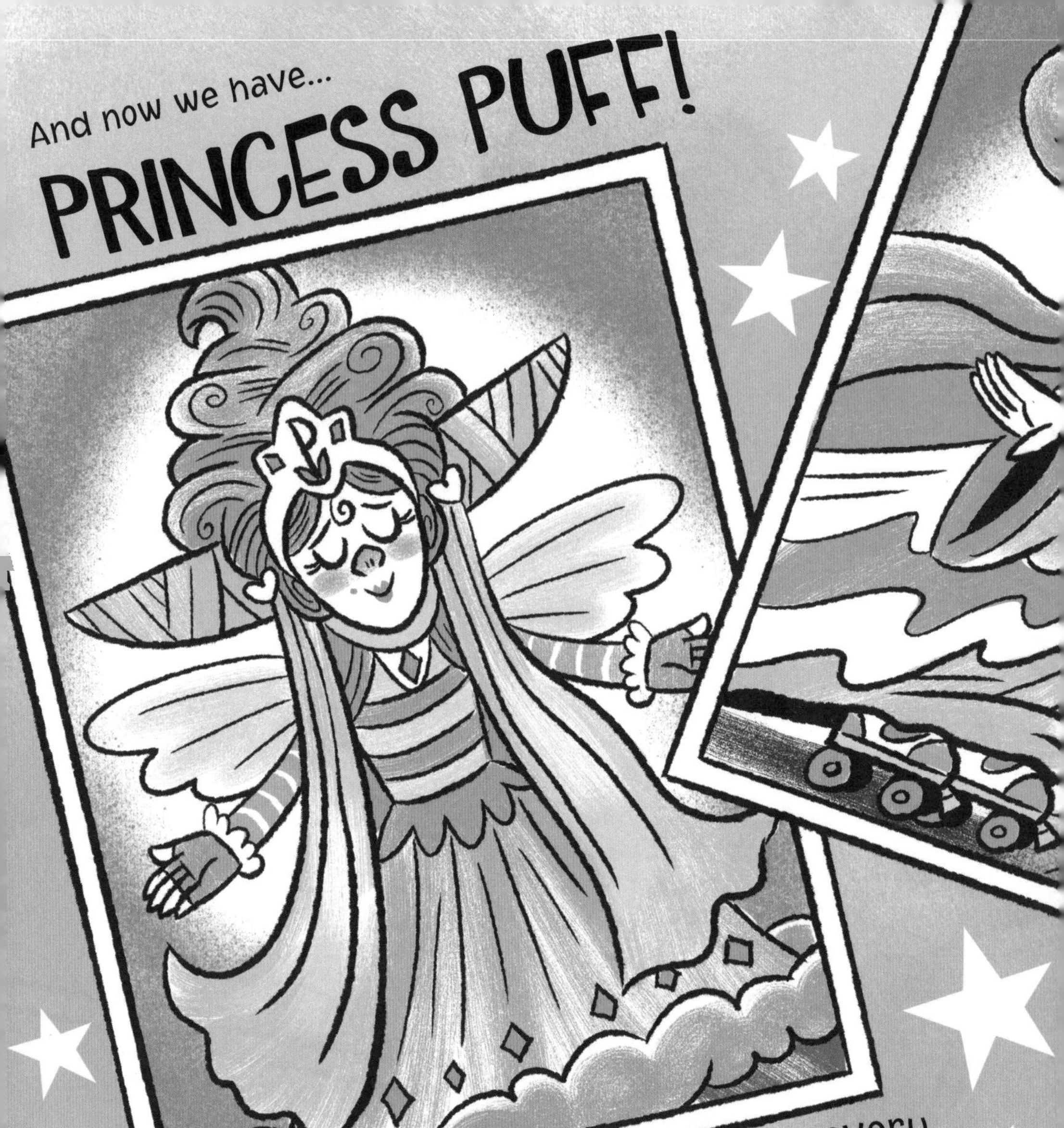

These scarlet gowns express every mood of our ruby-kissed royal!

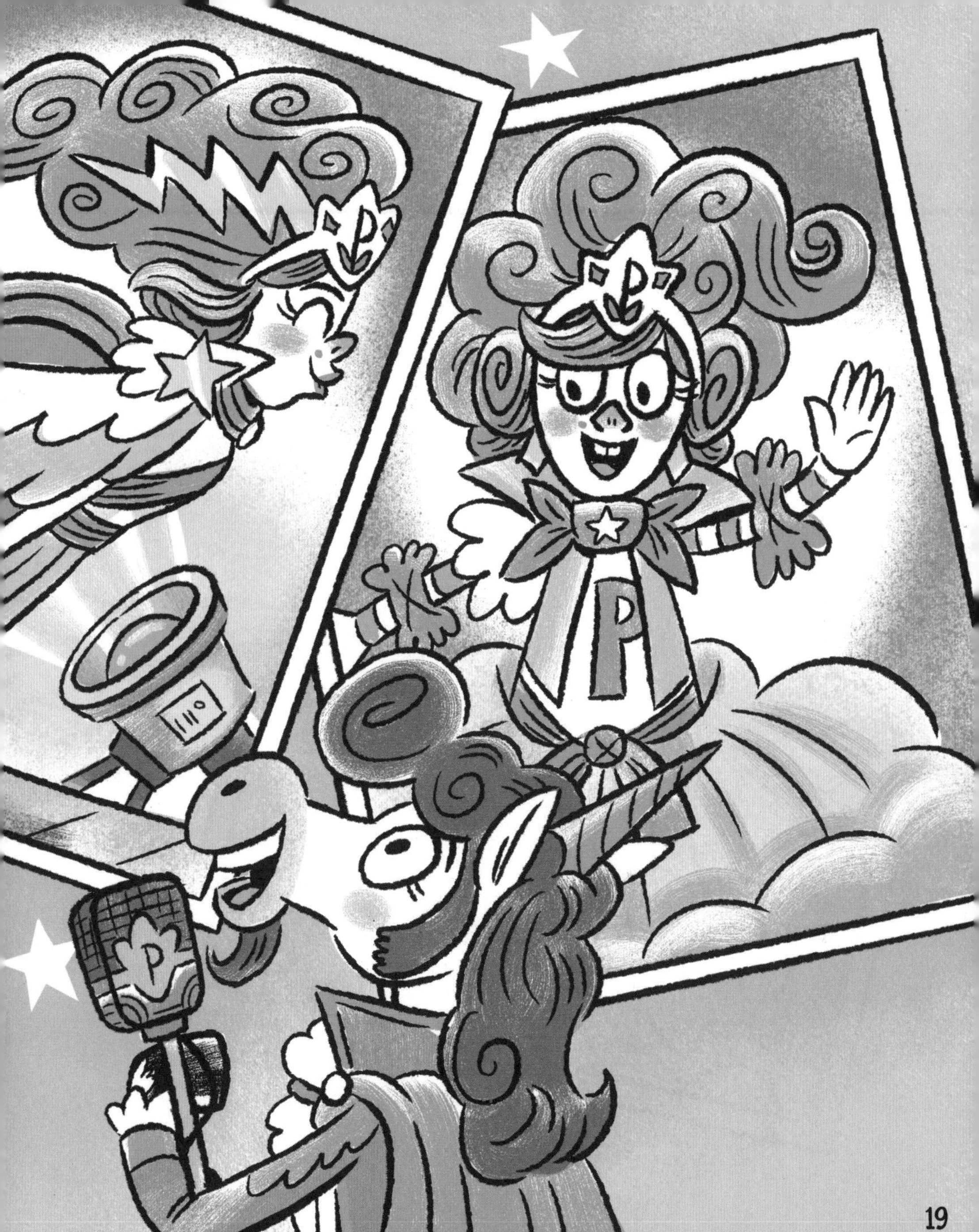

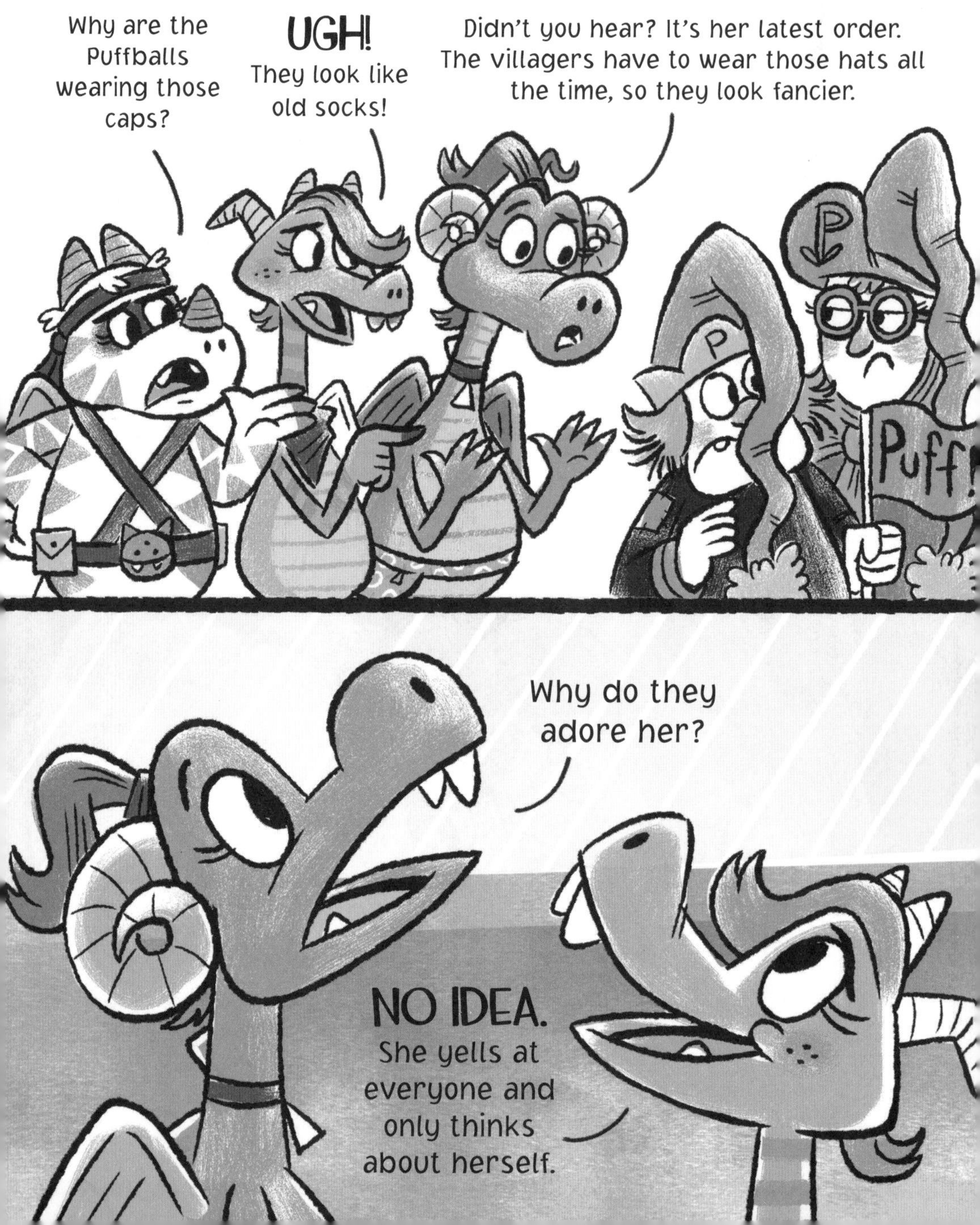
Why are the Puffballs wearing those caps?
UGH! They look like old socks!
Didn't you hear? It's her latest order. The villagers have to wear those hats all the time, so they look fancier.
P
P
Puff!
Why do they adore her?
NO IDEA. She yells at everyone and only thinks about herself.

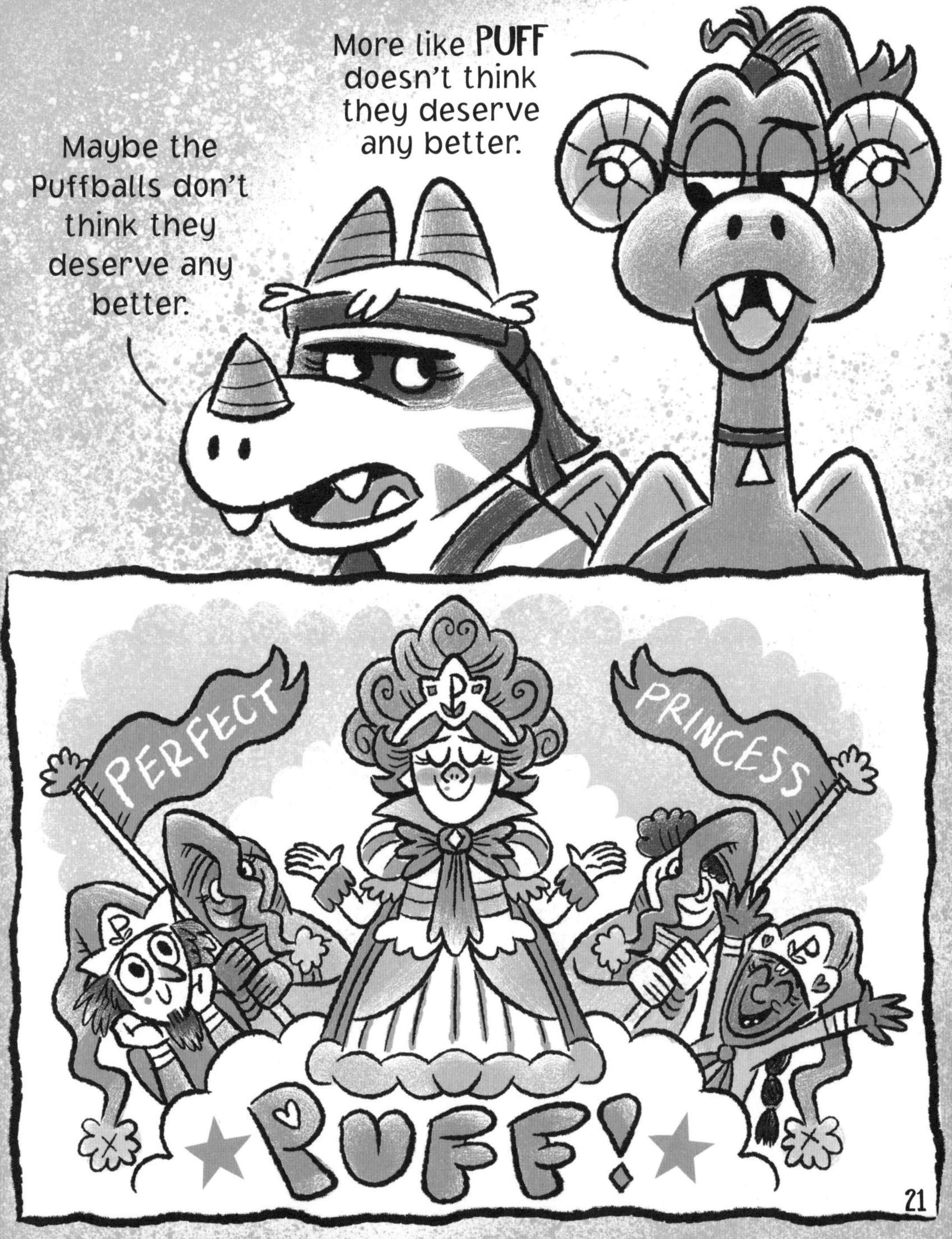
Maybe the Puffballs don't think they deserve any better.
More like PUFF doesn't think they deserve any better.
PERFECT
PRINCESS
PUFF!

CHAPTER TWO
WIGMANIA

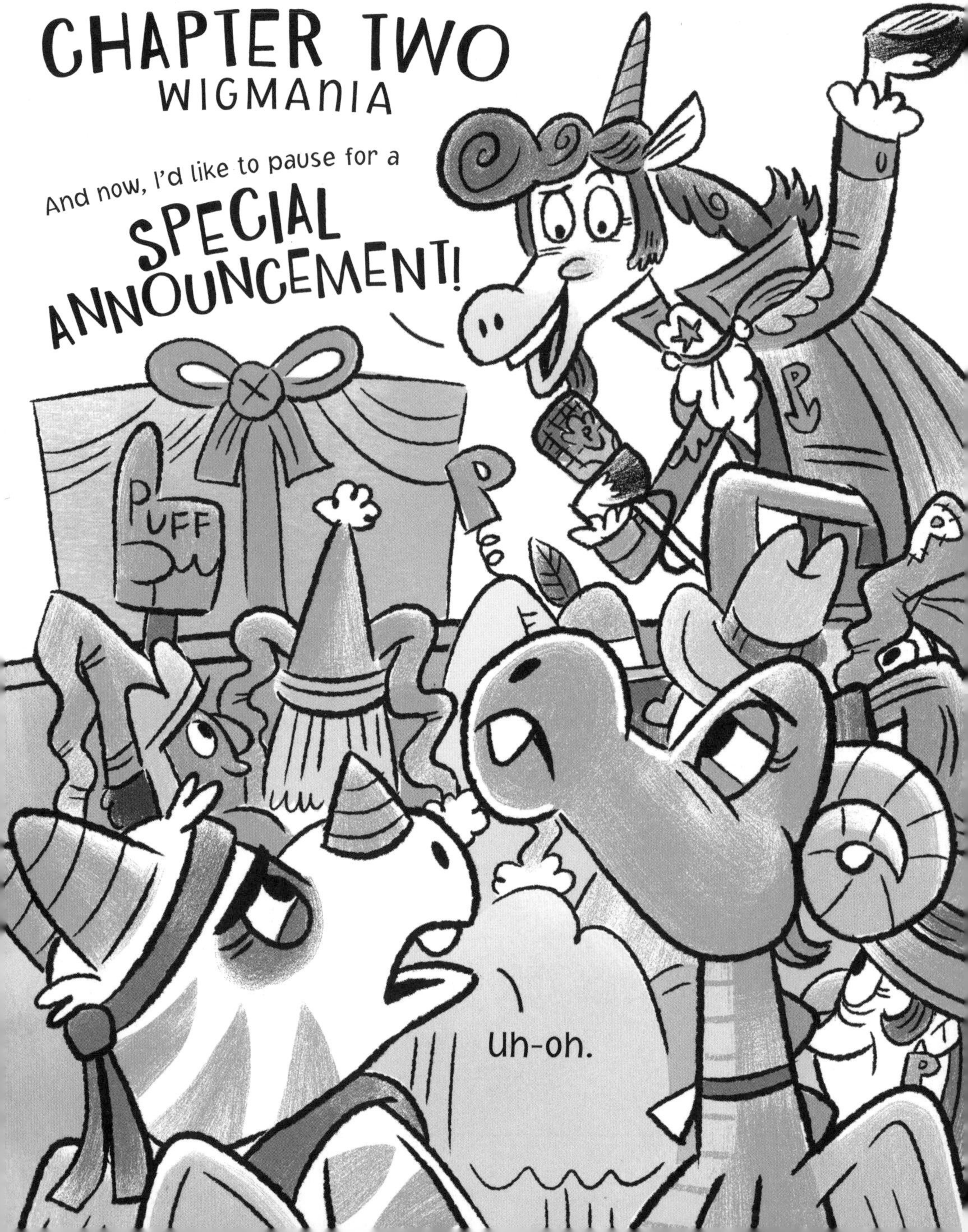
And now, I'd like to pause for a
SPECIAL ANNOUNCEMENT!
PUFF
Uh-oh.

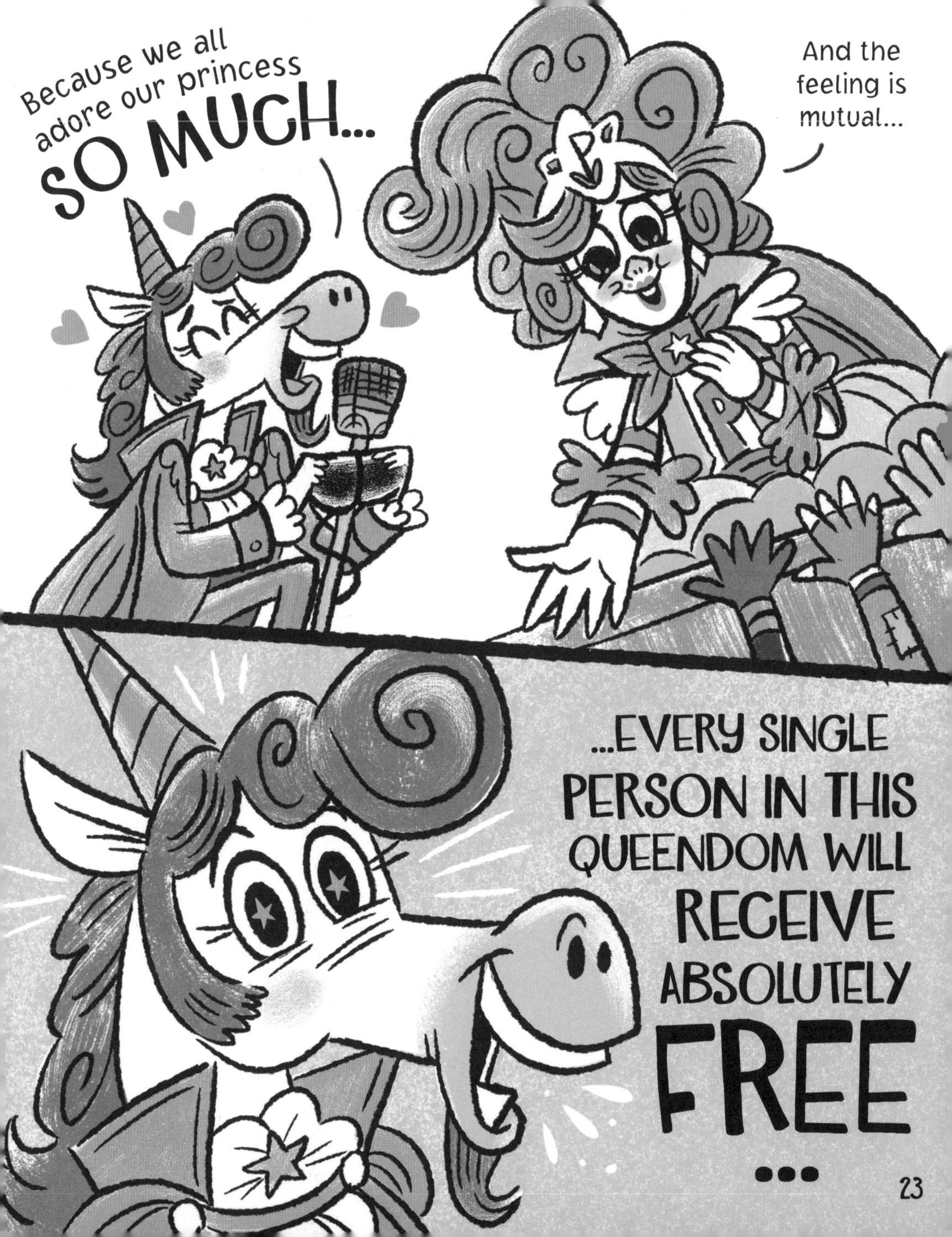
Because we all adore our princess SO MUCH...
And the feeling is mutual...
...EVERY SINGLE PERSON IN THIS QUEENDOM WILL RECEIVE ABSOLUTELY FREE
...

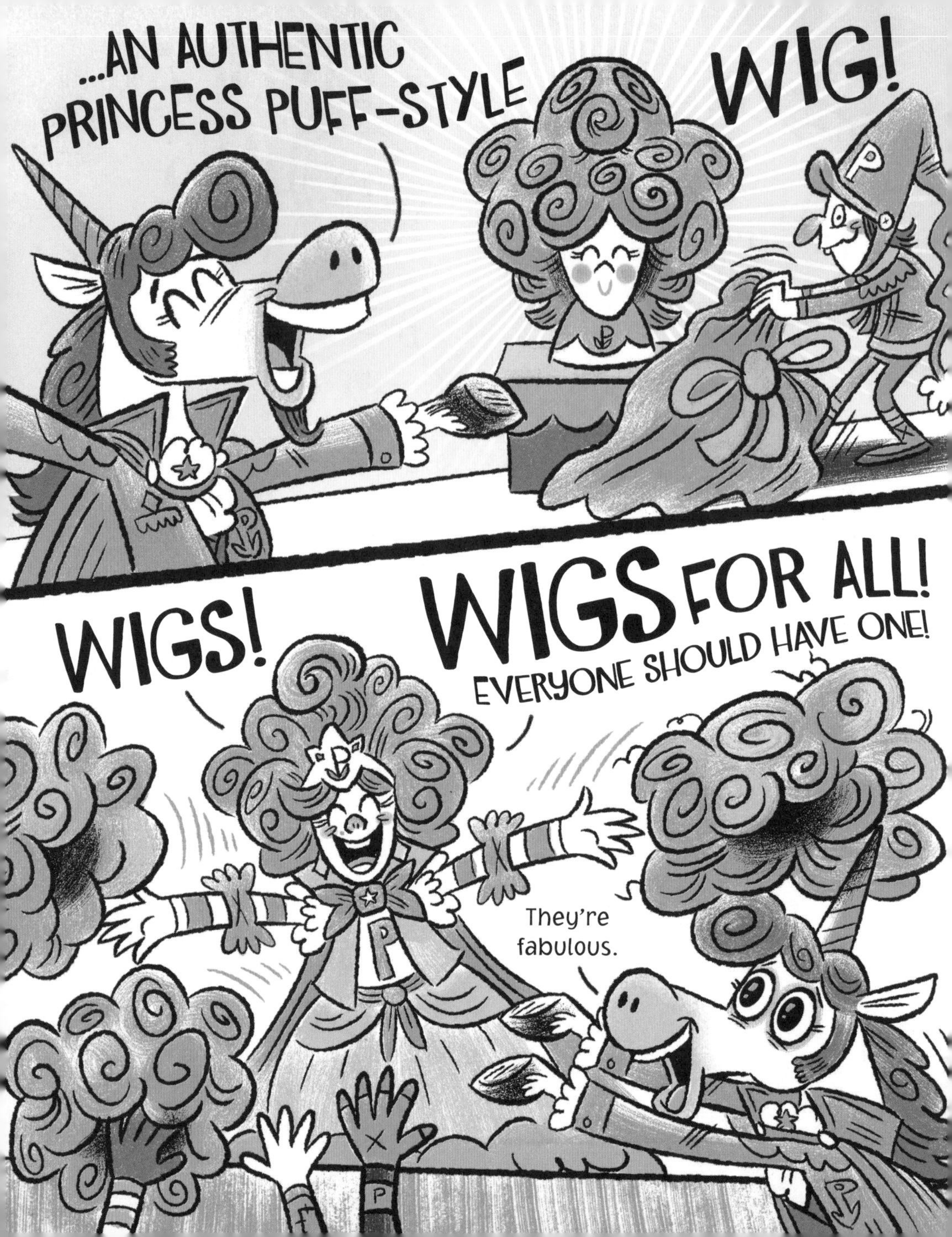
...AN AUTHENTIC PRINCESS PUFF-STYLE WIG!
WIGS! WIGS FOR ALL! EVERYONE SHOULD HAVE ONE!
They're fabulous.

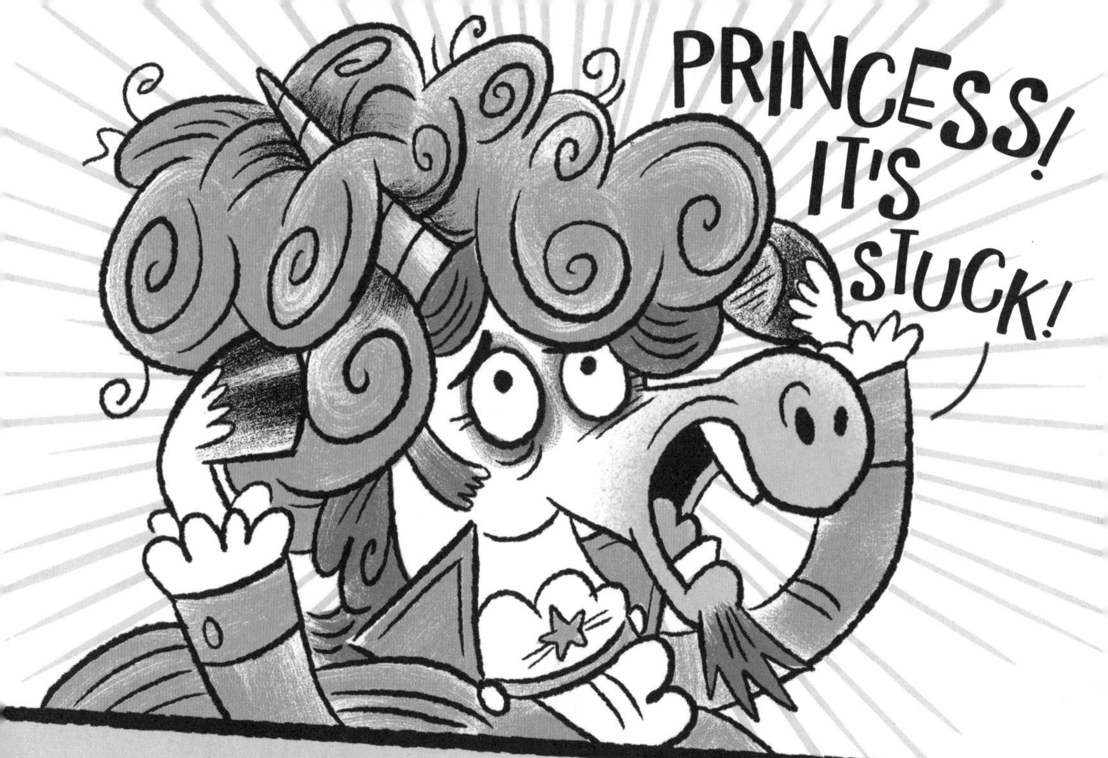
PRINCESS! IT'S STUCK!

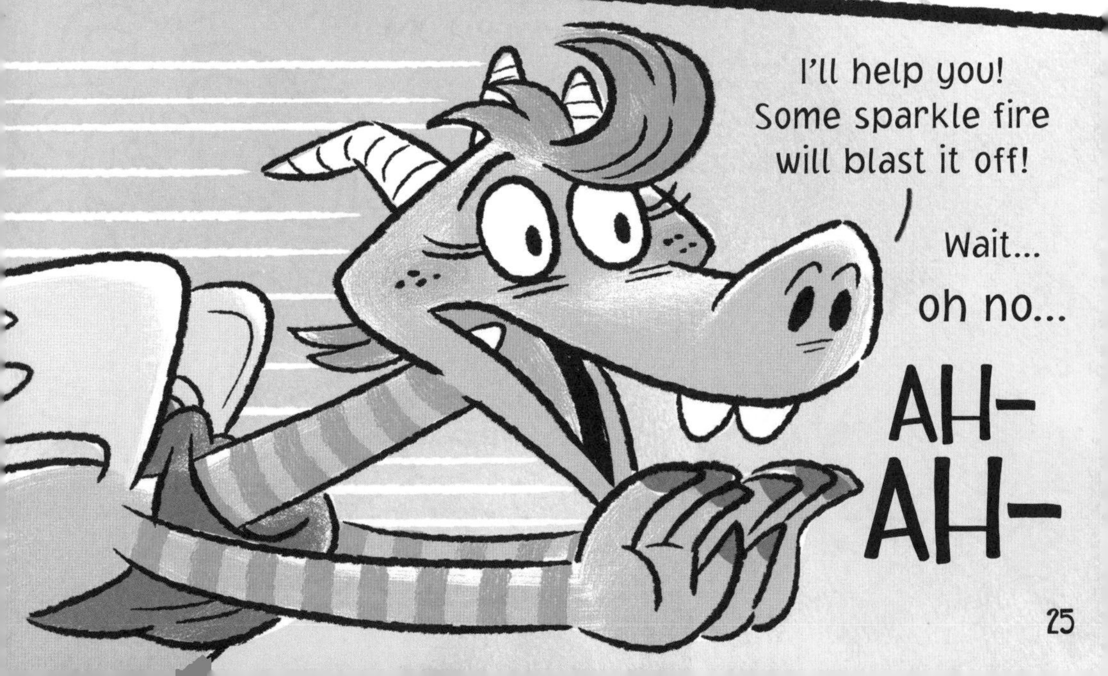
I'll help you! Some sparkle fire will blast it off!
Wait...
oh no...
AH-
AH-

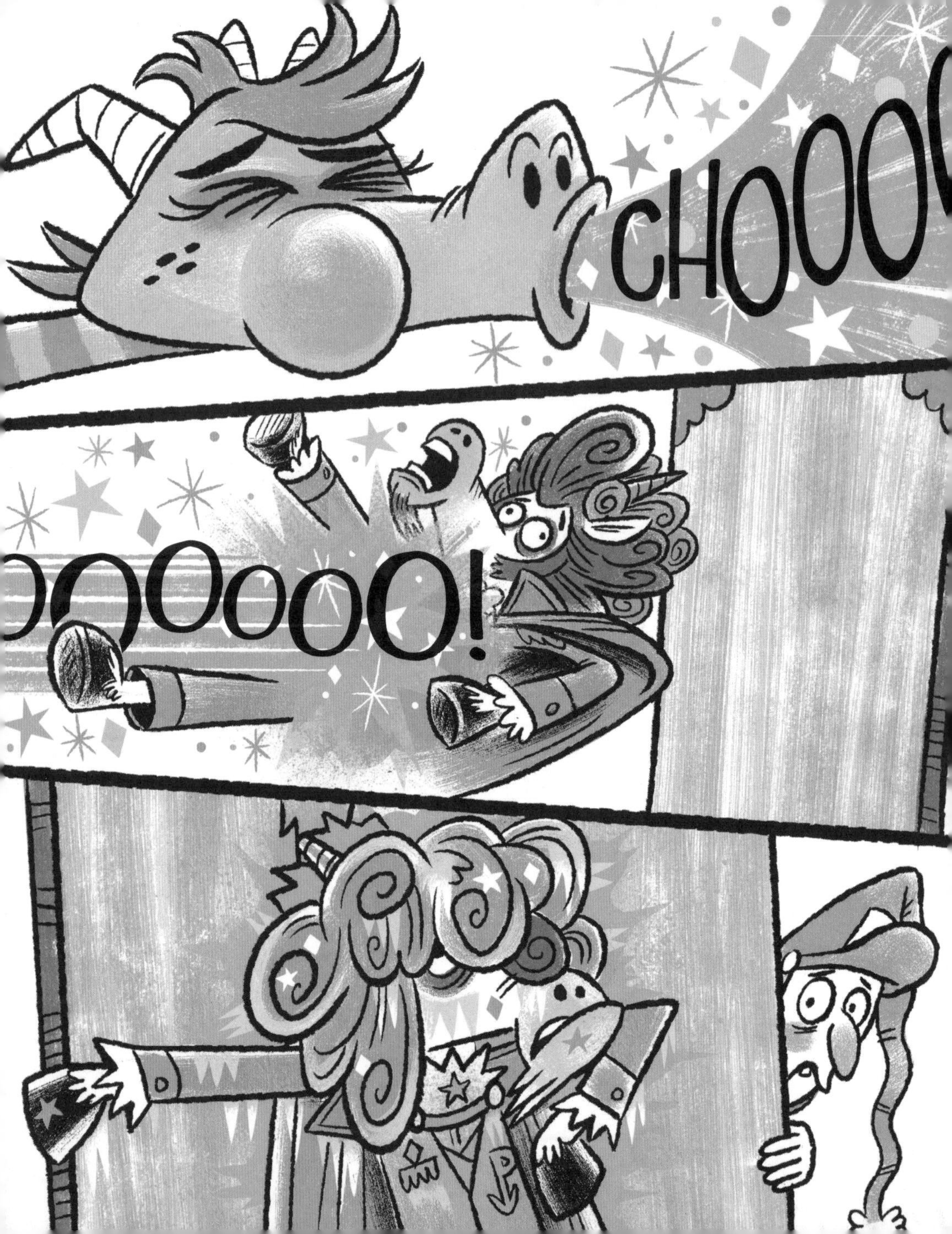
CHOOO
OOOOOOO!

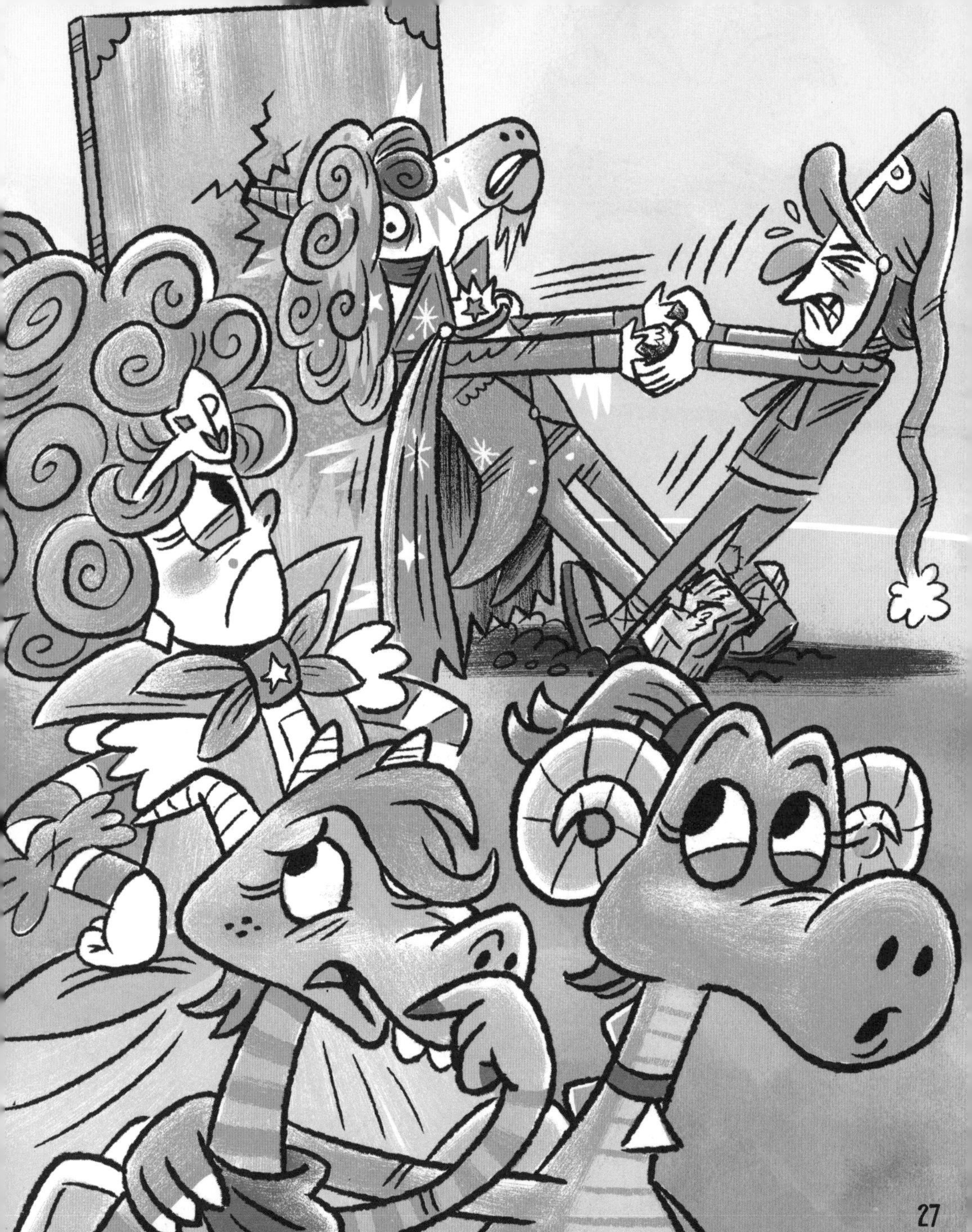

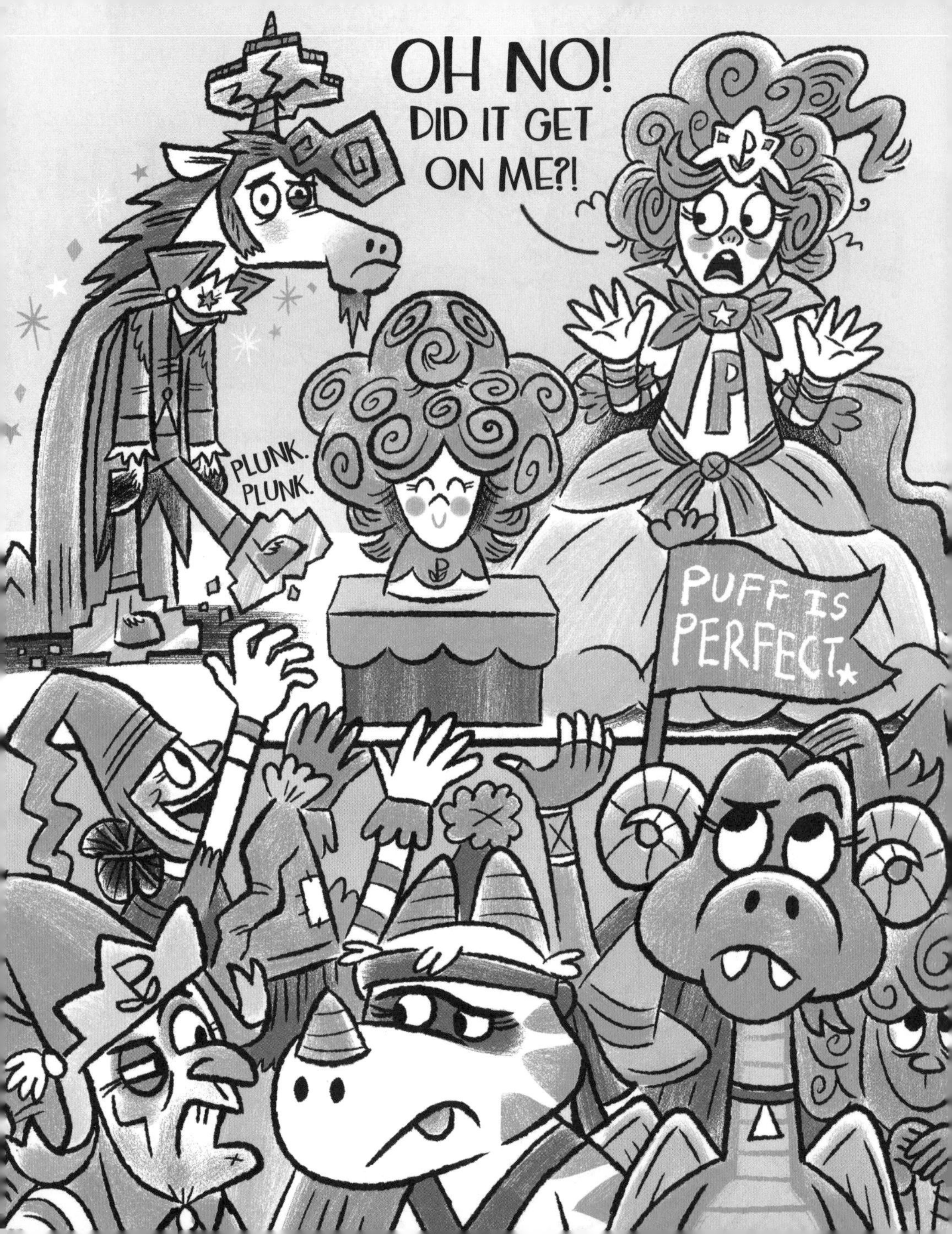
OH NO!
DID IT GET
ON ME?!
PLUNK.
PLUNK.
PUFF IS
PERFECT

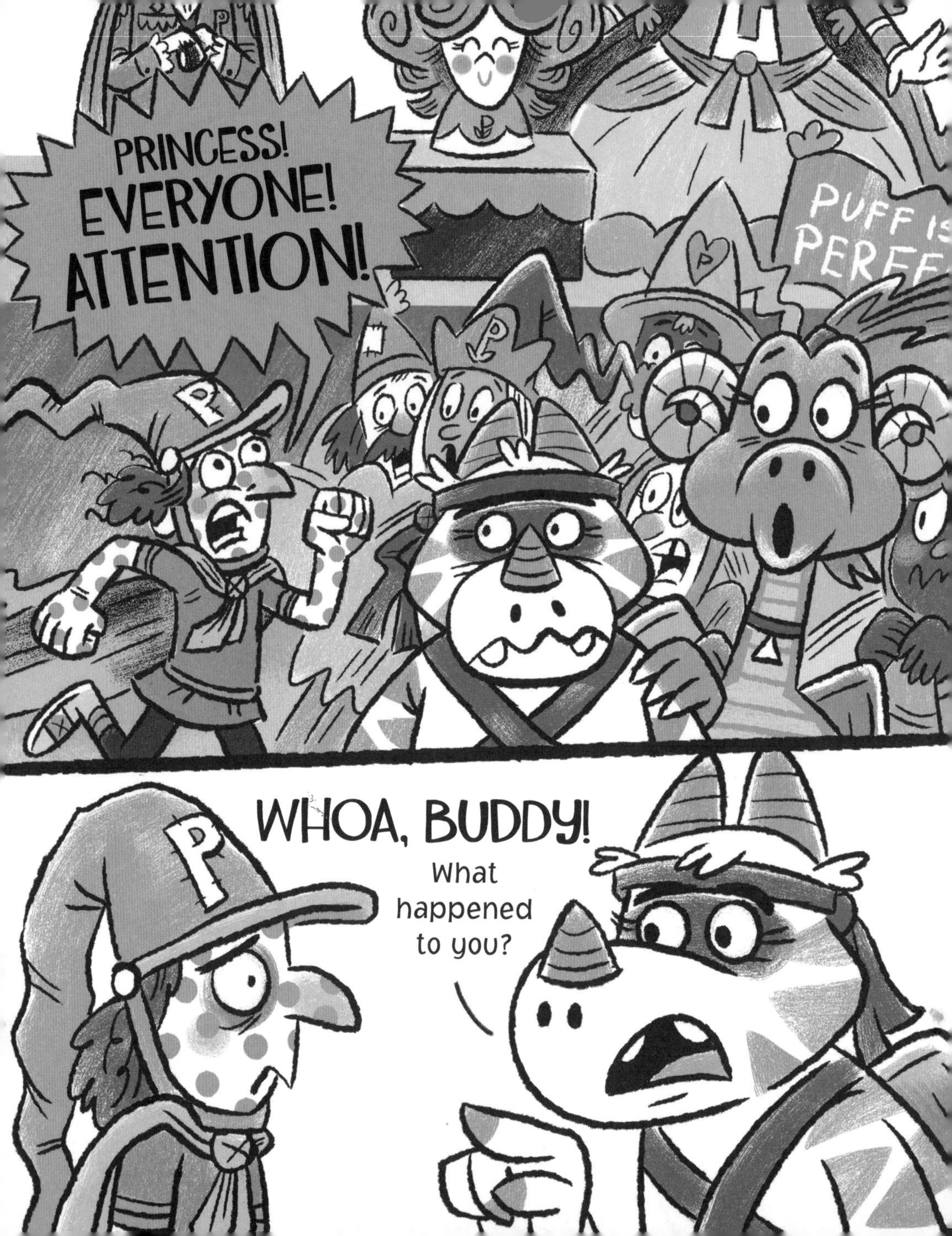
PRINCESS! EVERYONE! ATTENTION!
PUFF IS PERFE
WHOA, BUDDY!
What happened to you?

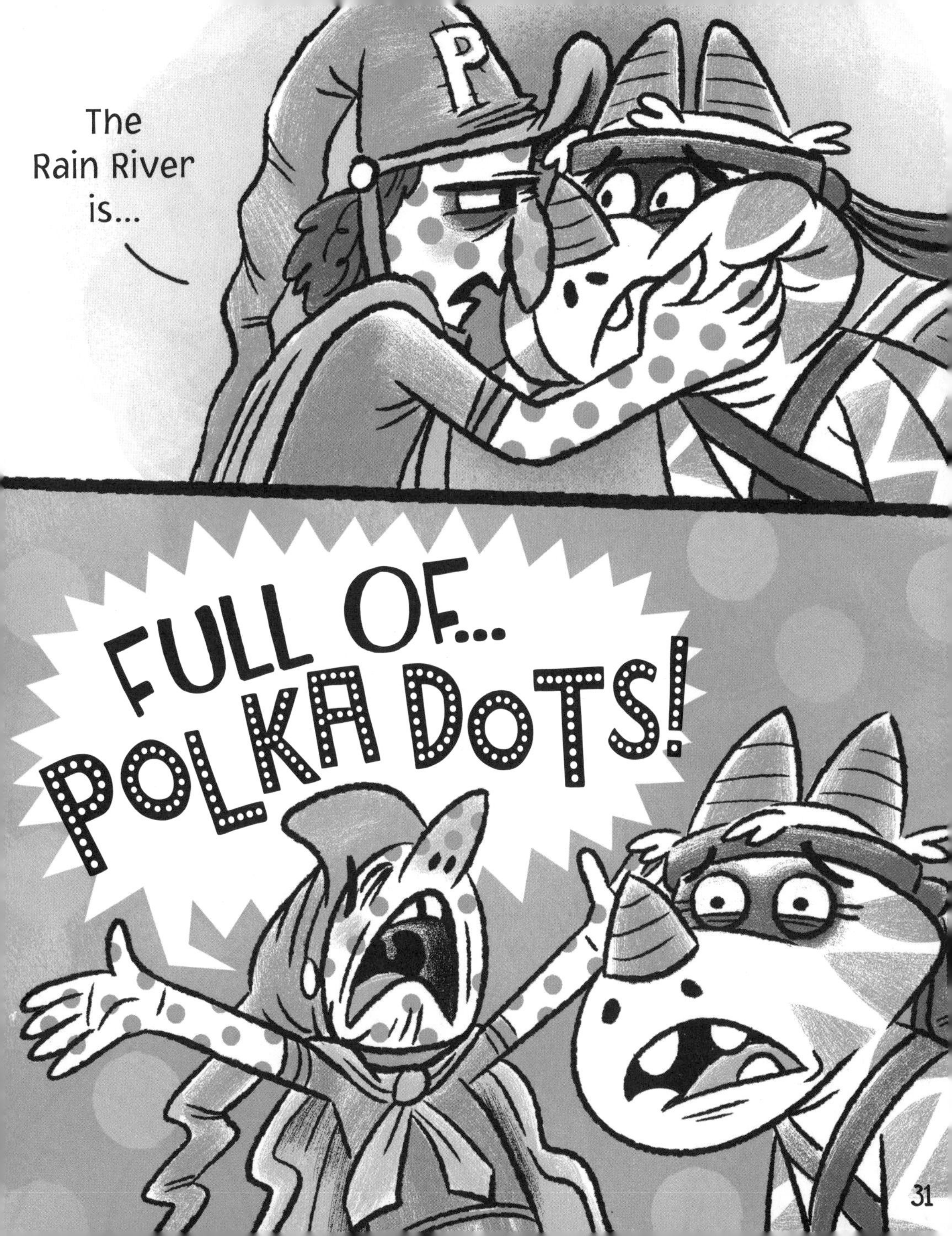
The Rain River is...
FULL OF... POLKA DOTS!

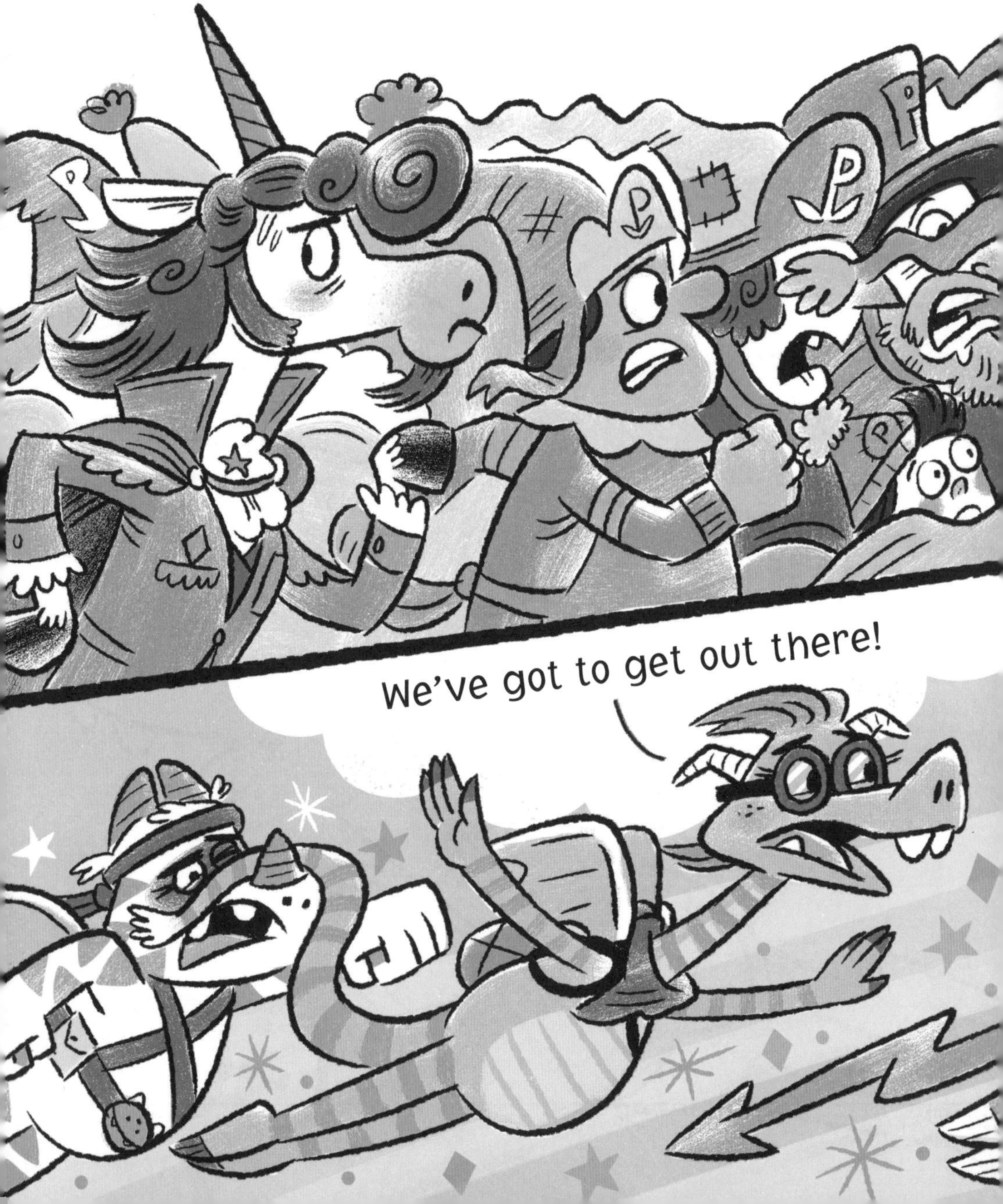
We've got to get out there!

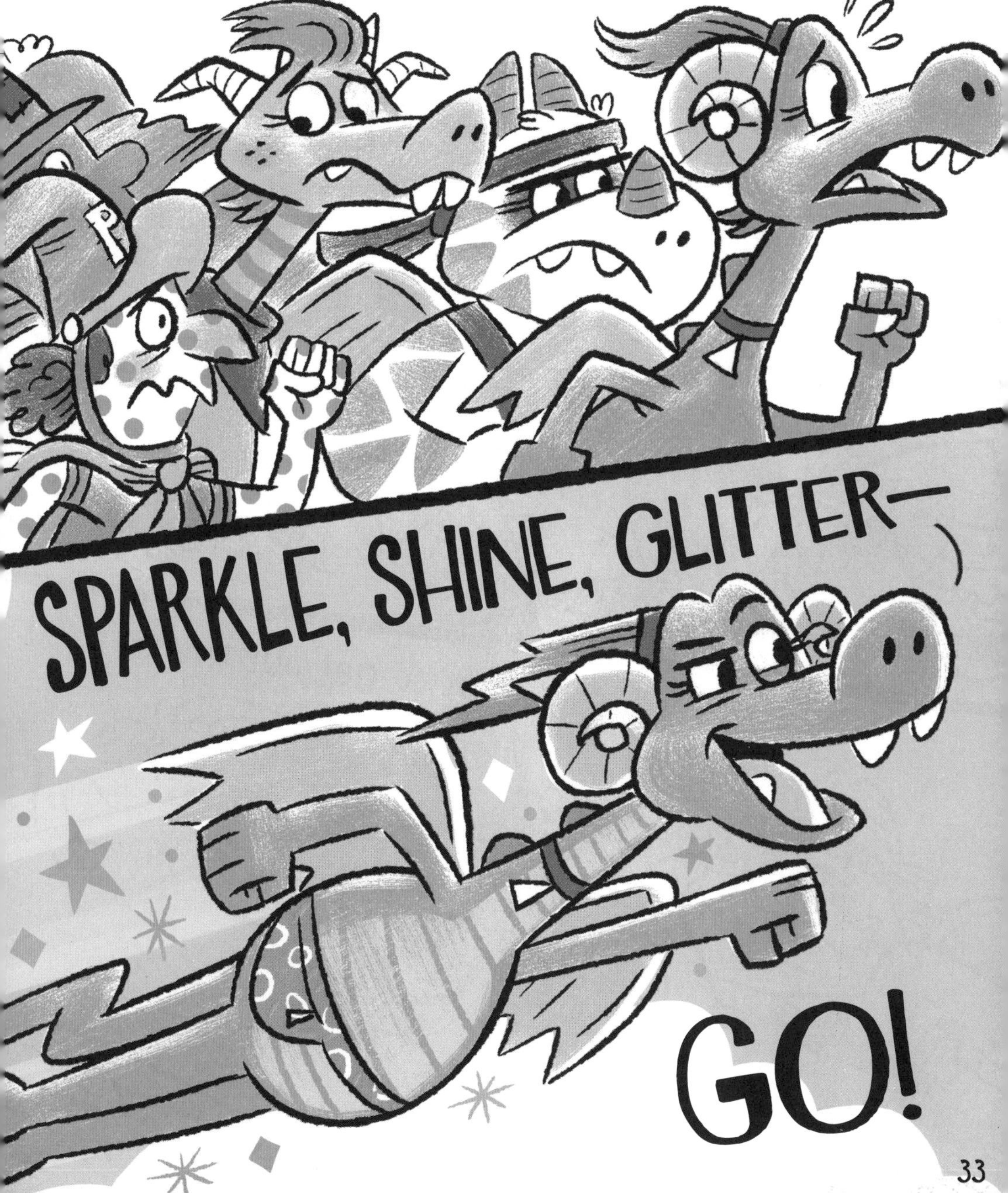
P
SPARKLE, SHINE, GLITTER—
GO!

CHAPTER THREE
DOTS, DOTS EVERYWHERE

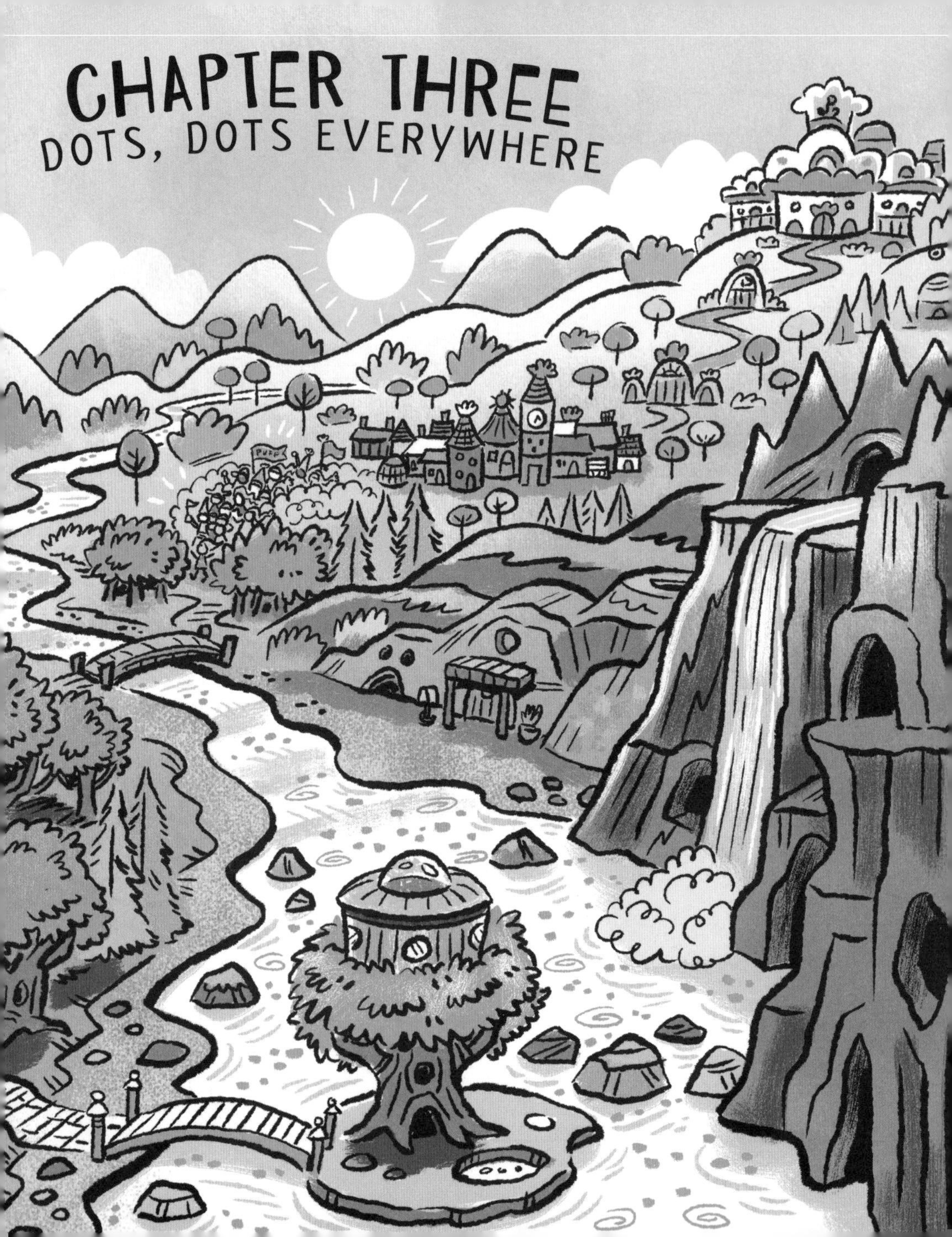

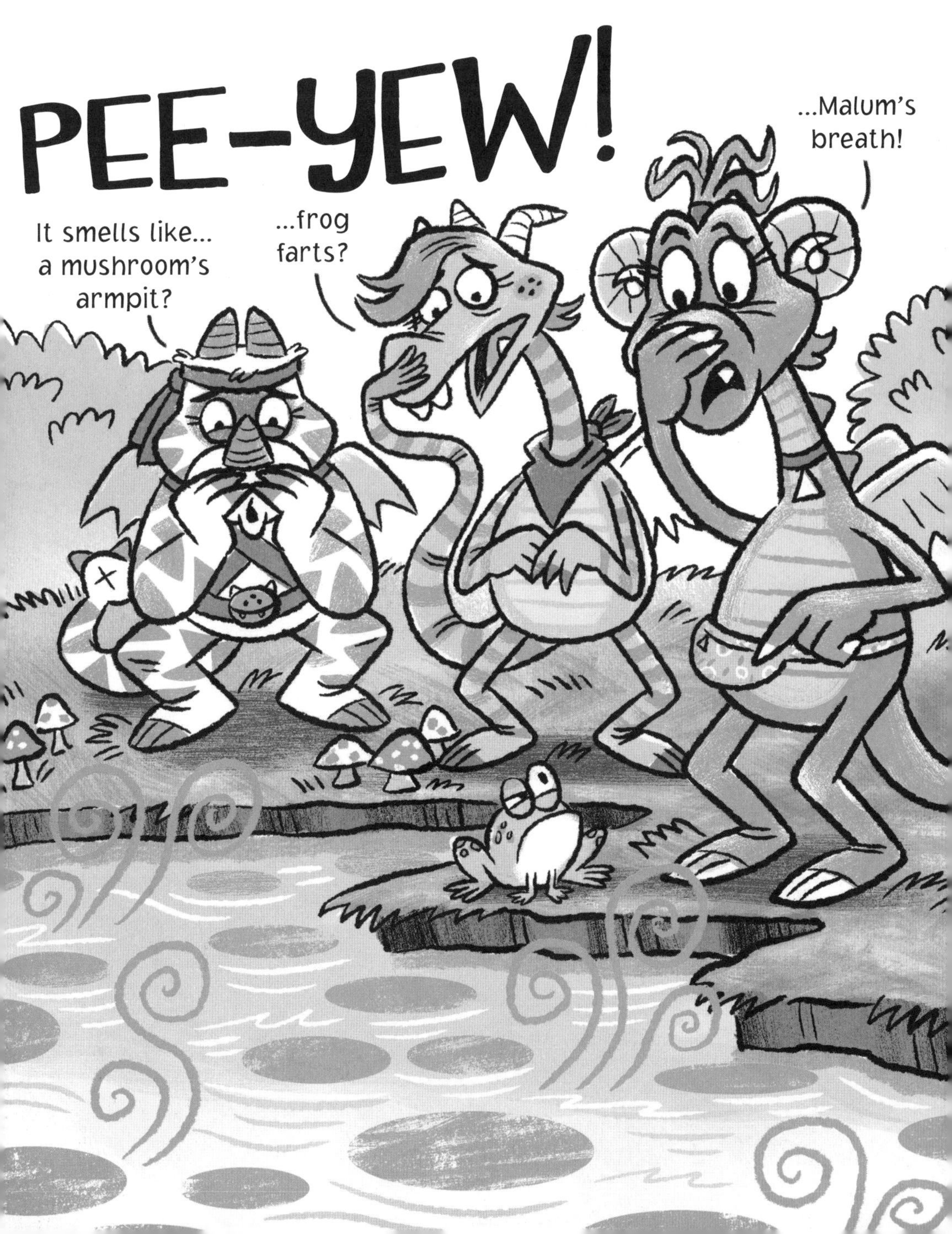
PEE-YEW!
It smells like... a mushroom's armpit?
...frog farts?
...Malum's breath!

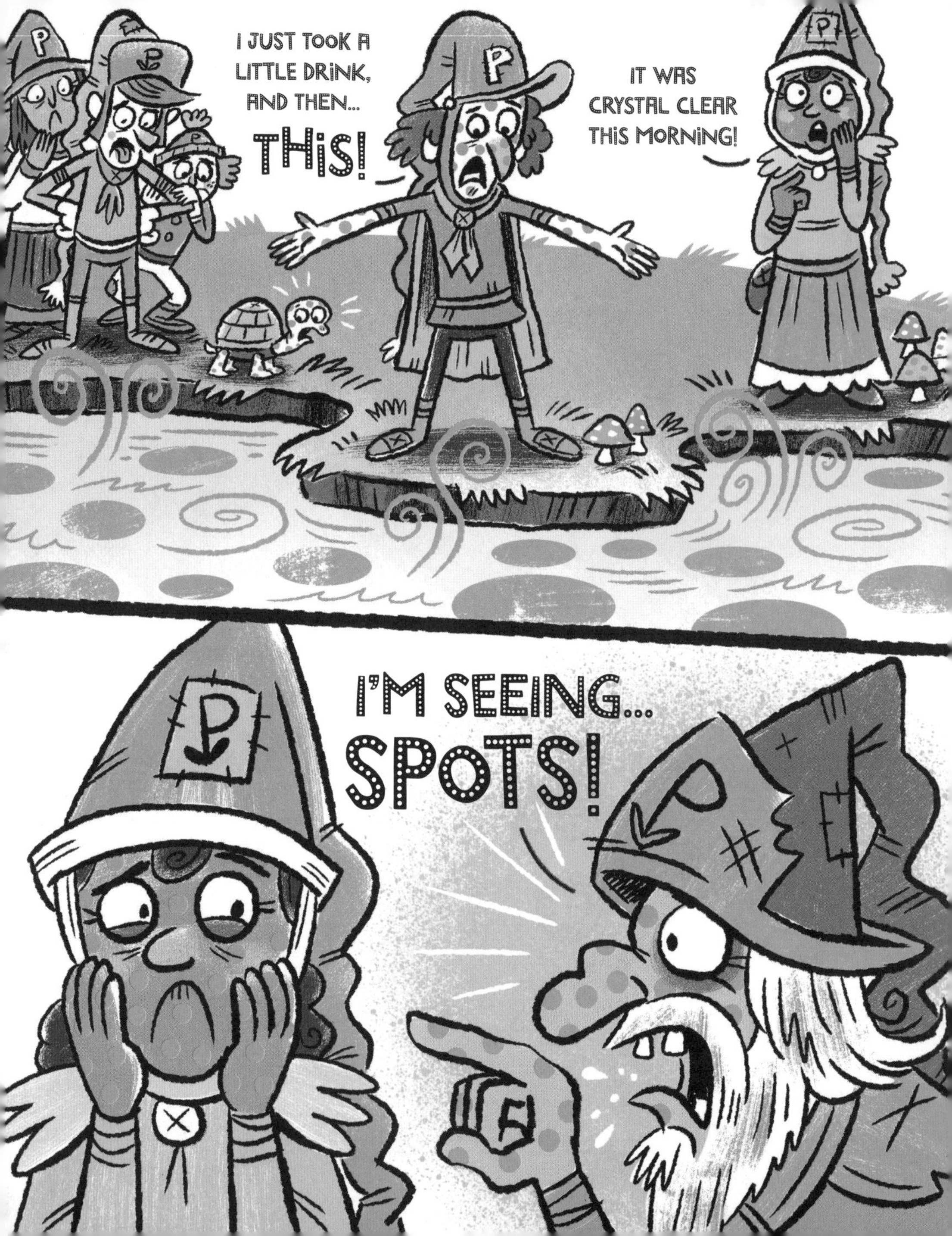
I JUST TOOK A LITTLE DRINK, AND THEN... THIS!
IT WAS CRYSTAL CLEAR THIS MORNING!
I'M SEEING... SPOTS!

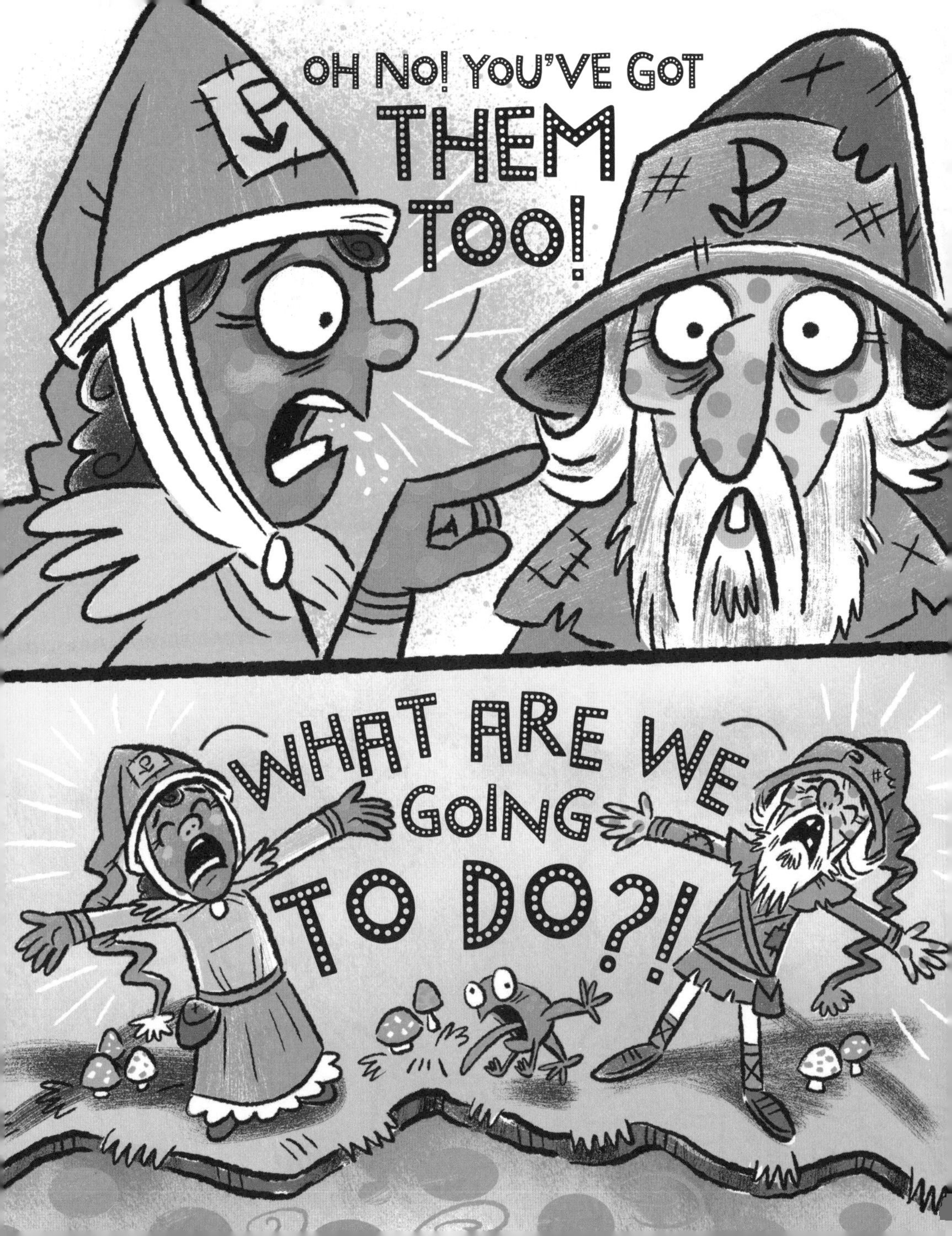
OH NO! YOU'VE GOT THEM TOO!
WHAT ARE WE GOING TO DO?!

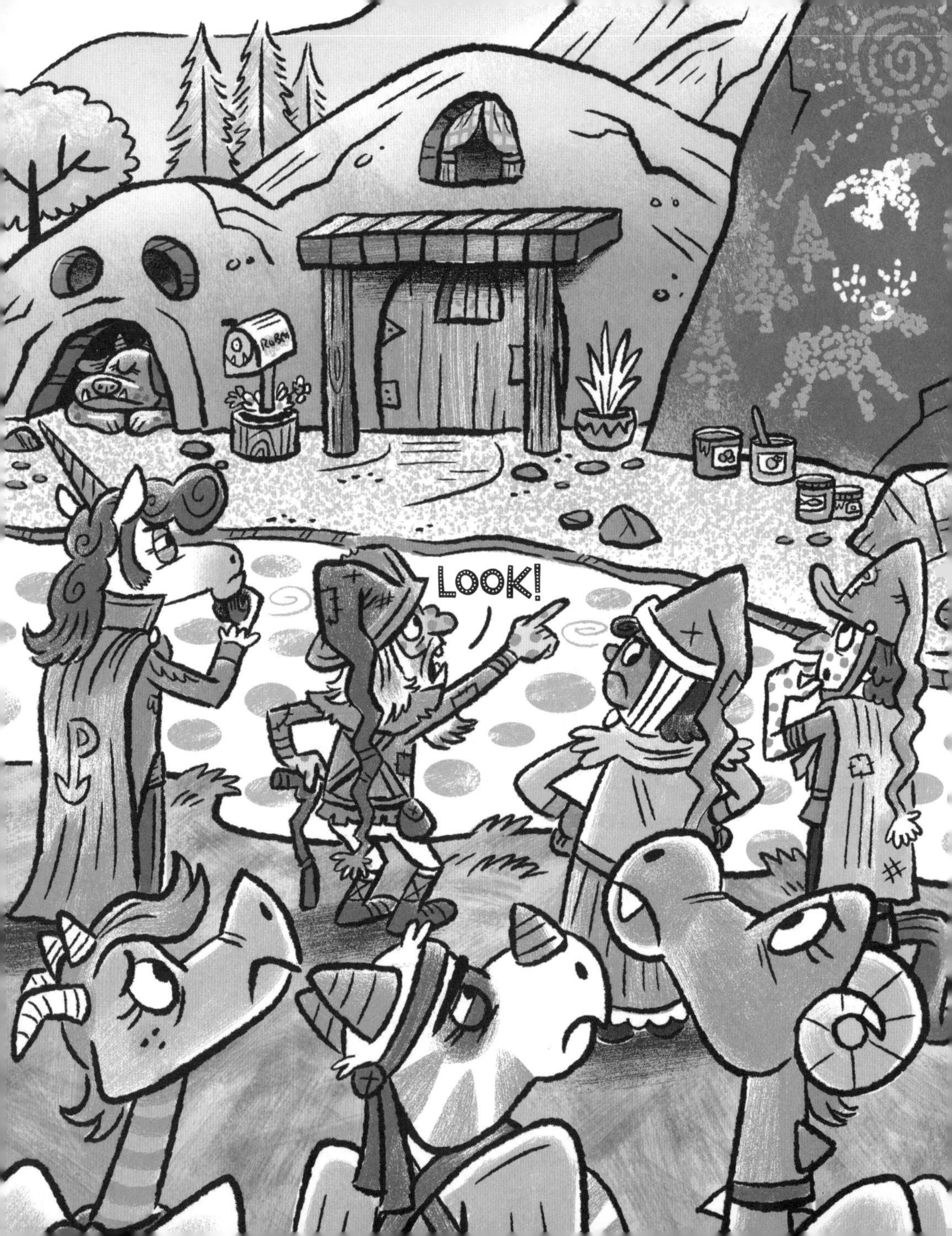
LOOK!

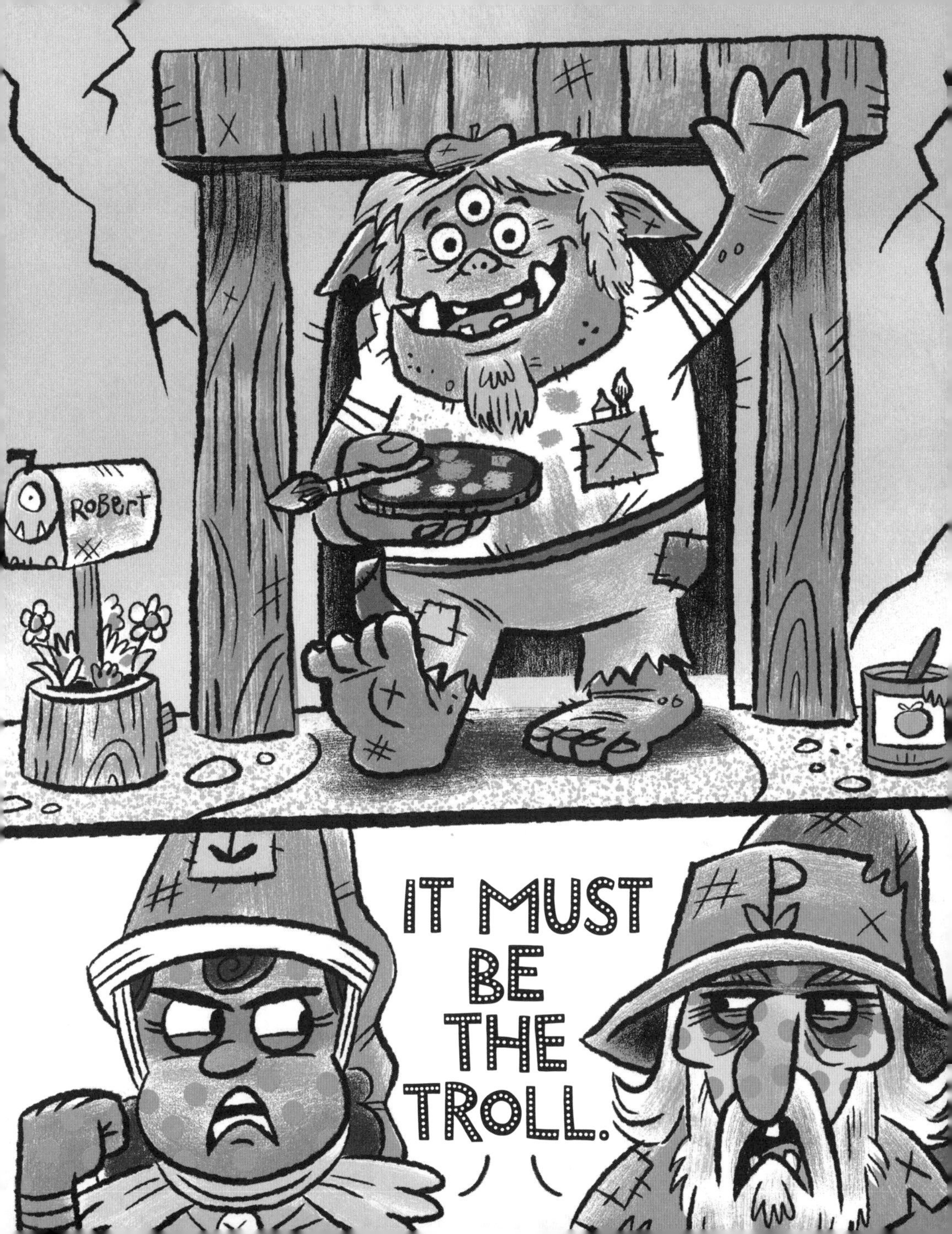
ROBERT
IT MUST BE THE TROLL.

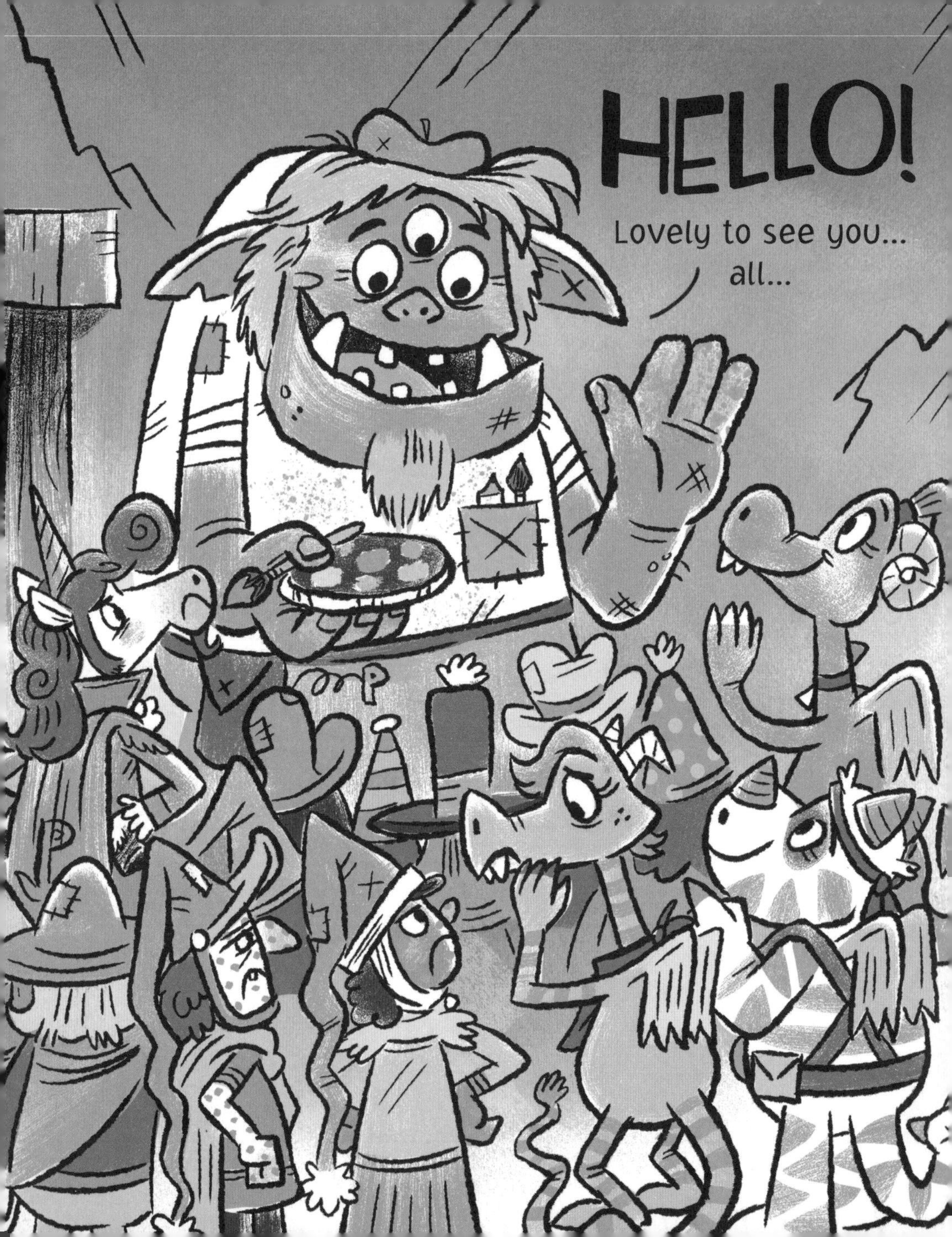
HELLO!
Lovely to see you... all...

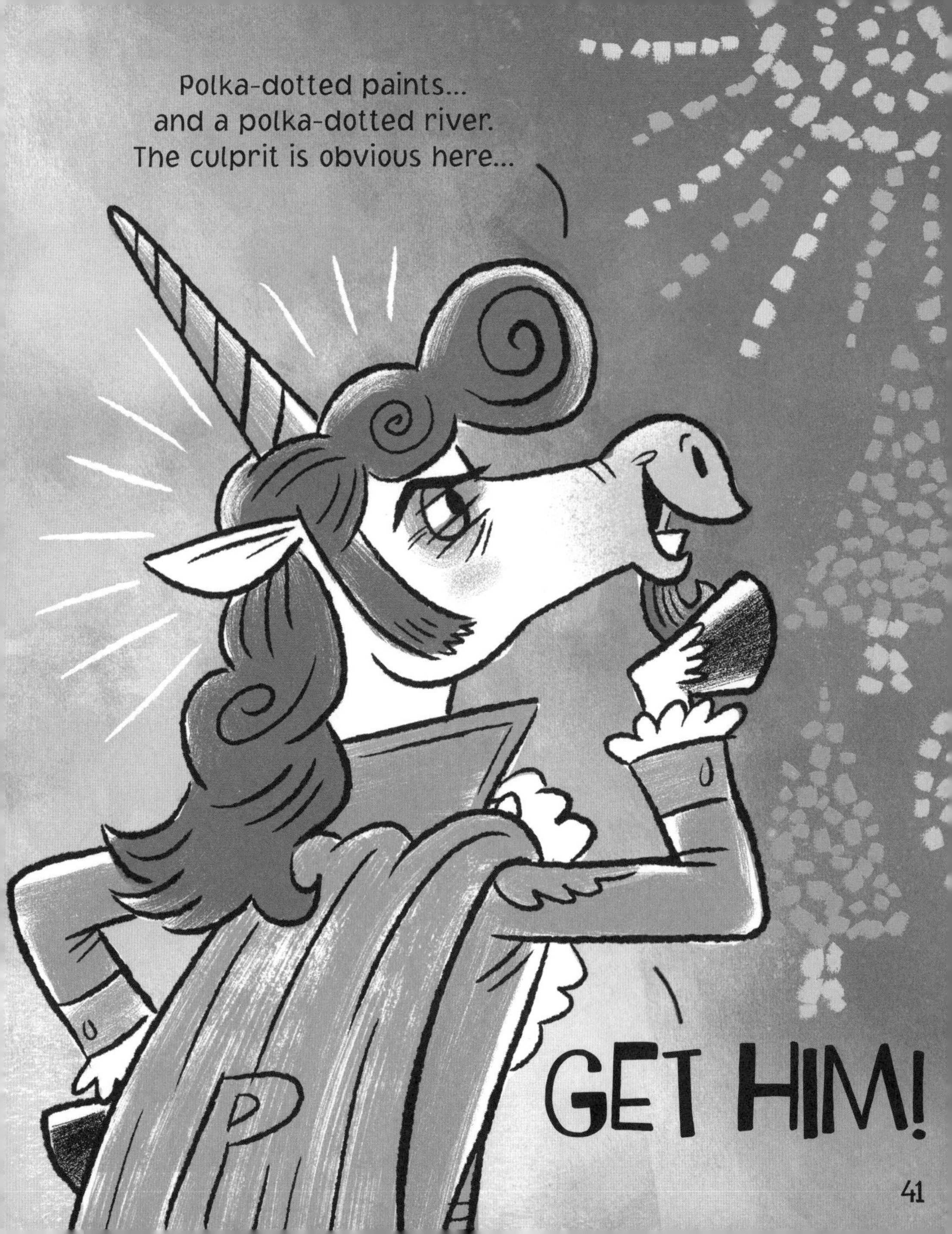
Polka-dotted paints...
and a polka-dotted river.
The culprit is obvious here...
GET HIM!

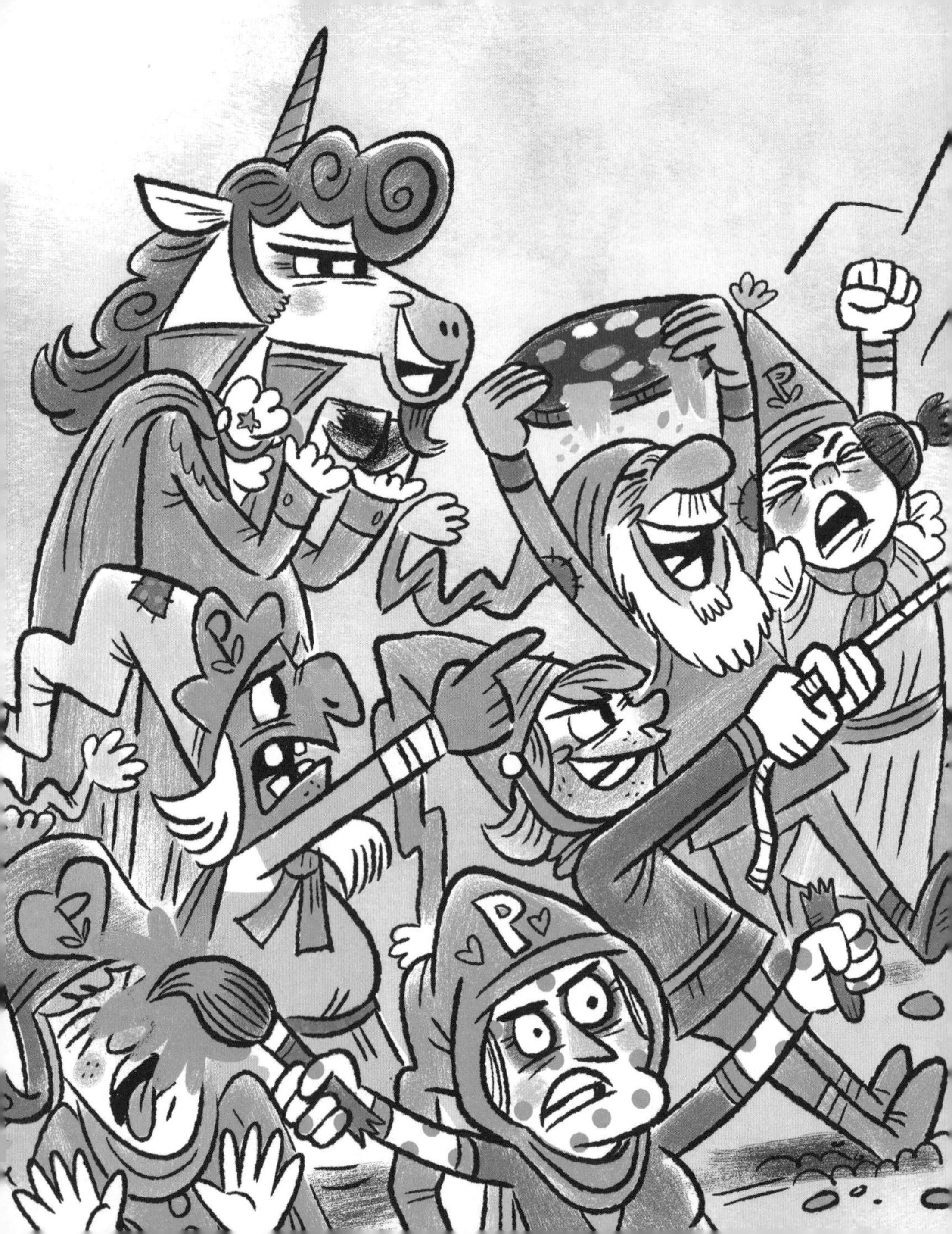

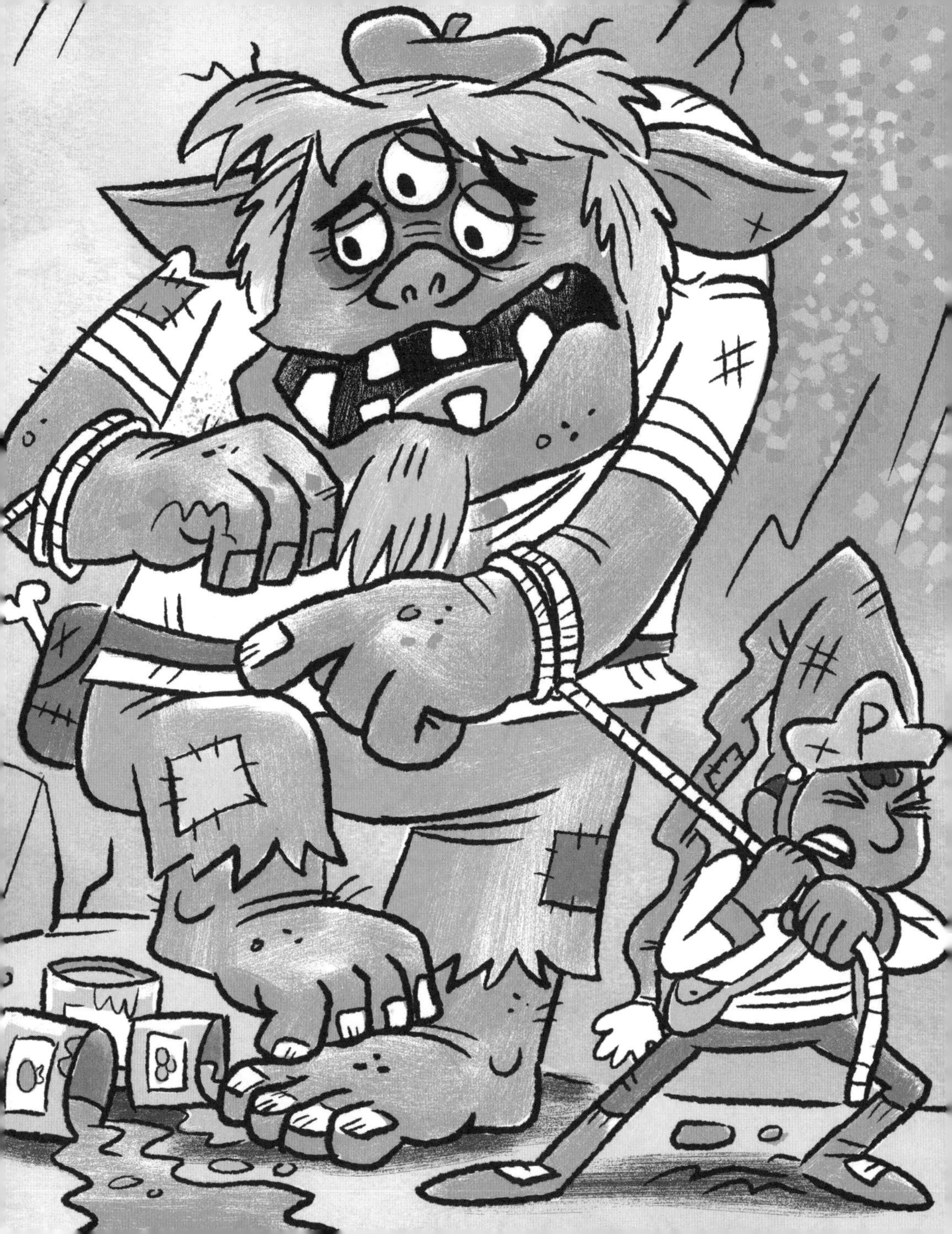
P

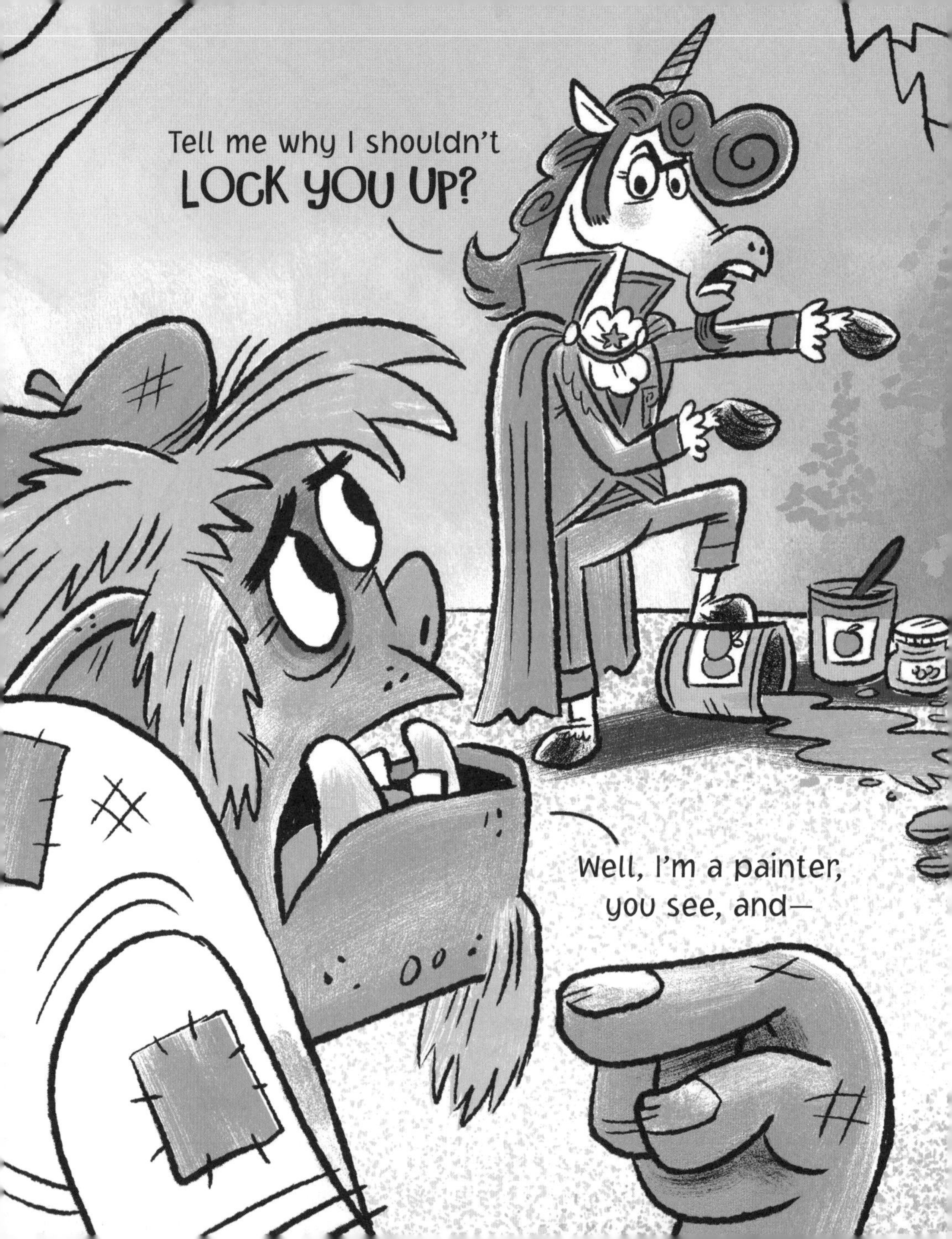
Tell me why I shouldn't
LOCK YOU UP?
Well, I'm a painter,
you see, and—

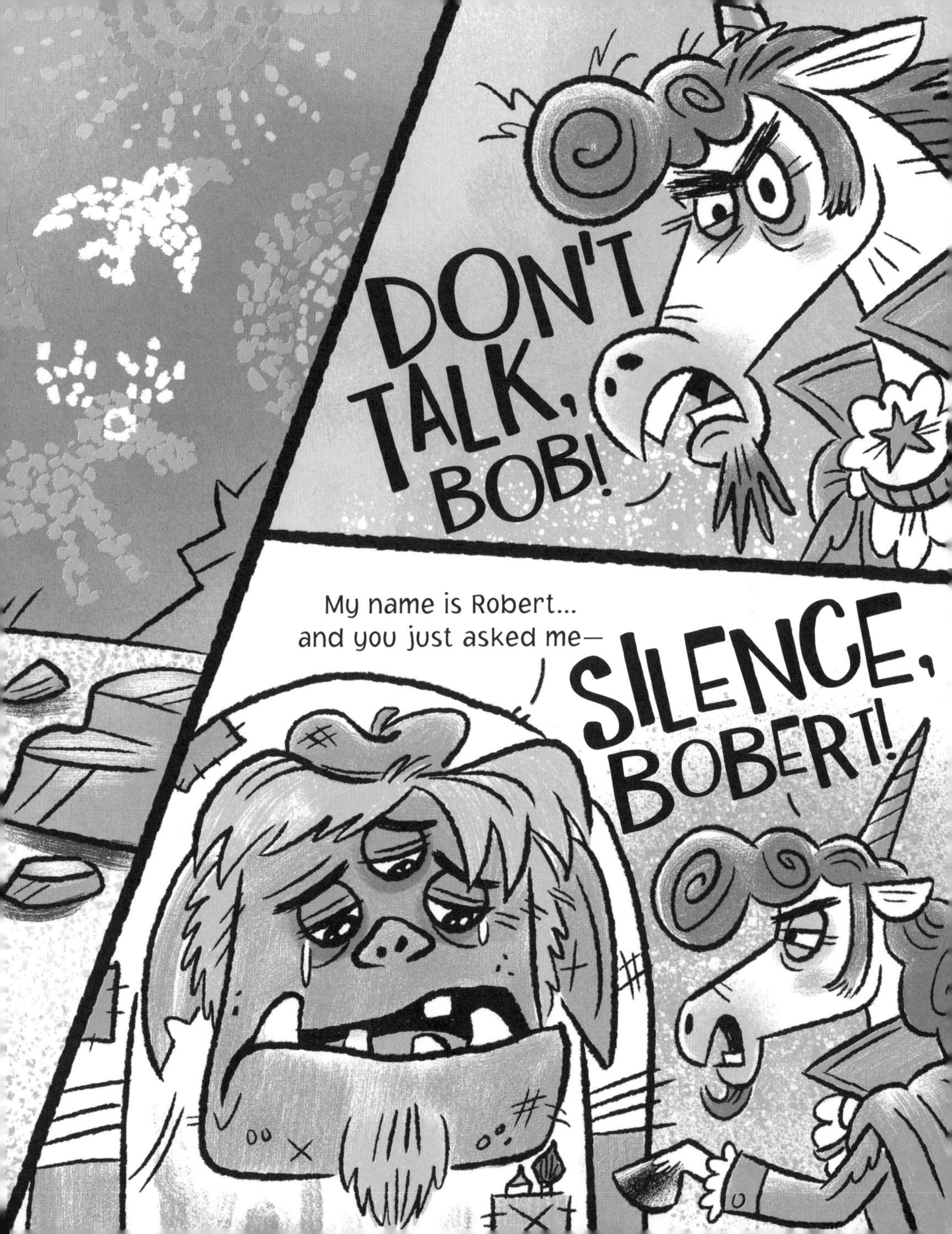
DON'T TALK, BOB!
My name is Robert... and you just asked me—
SILENCE, BOBERT!

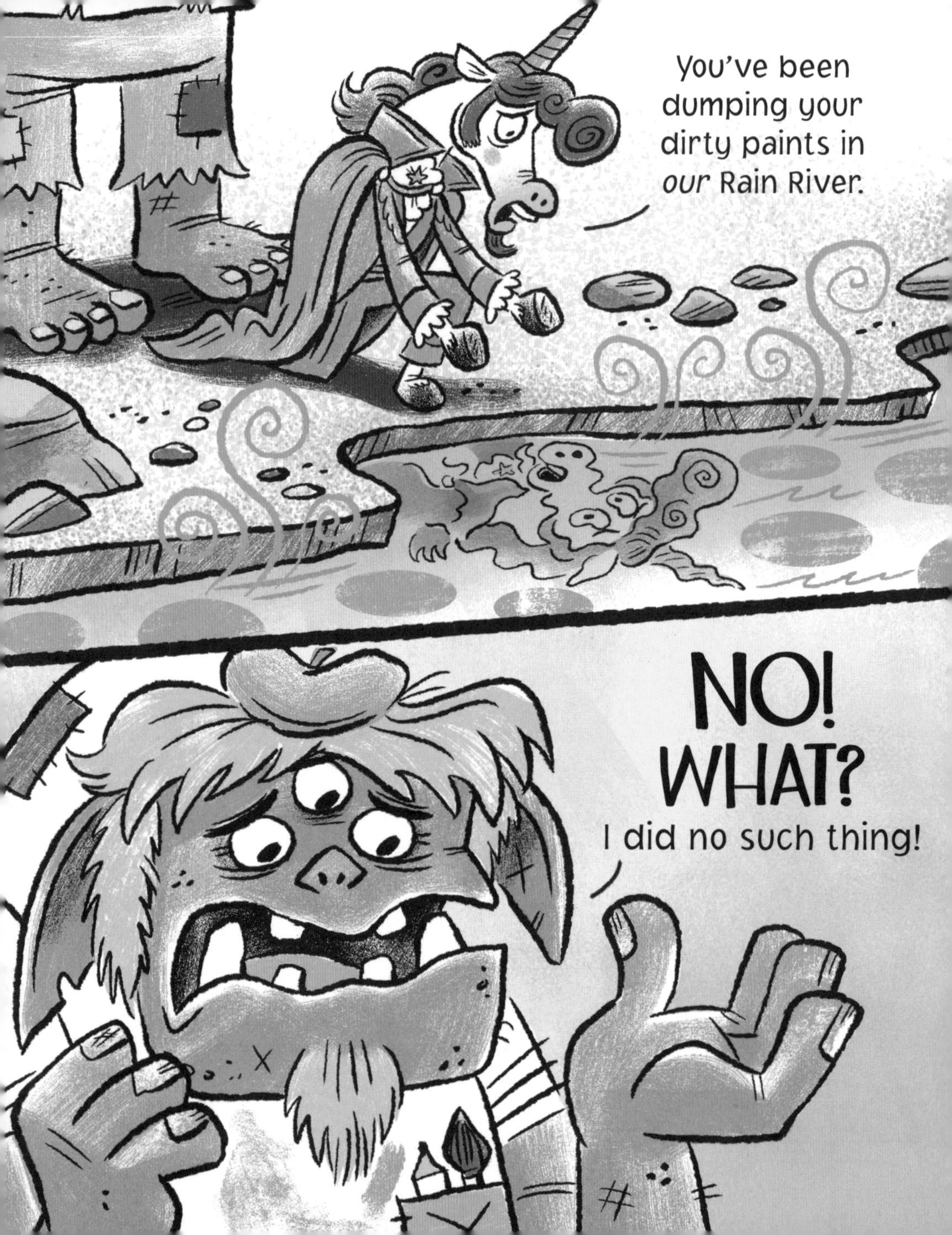
You've been dumping your dirty paints in *our* Rain River.
NO! WHAT?
I did no such thing!

We all know how

DIRTY

and

MESSY

trolls are—

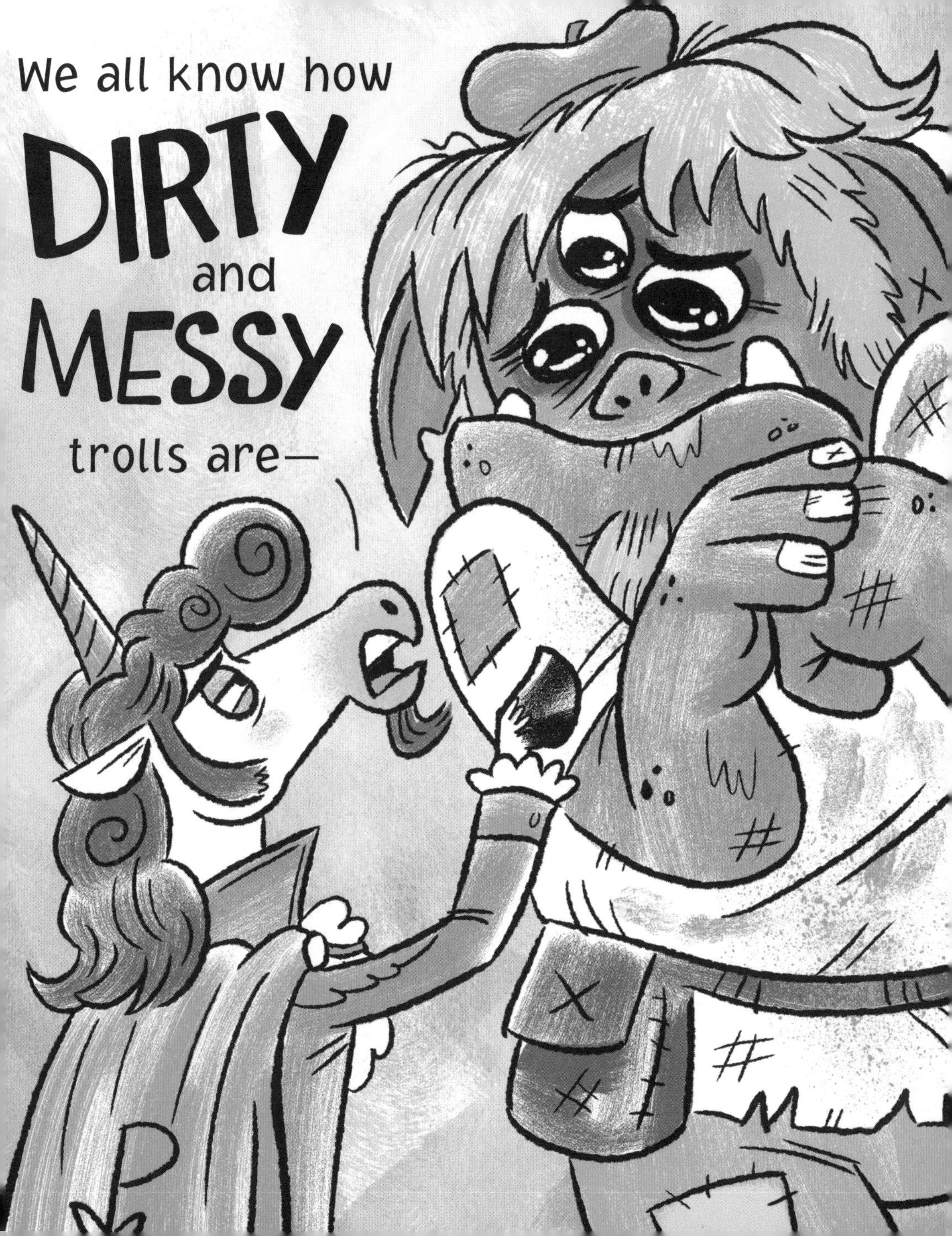

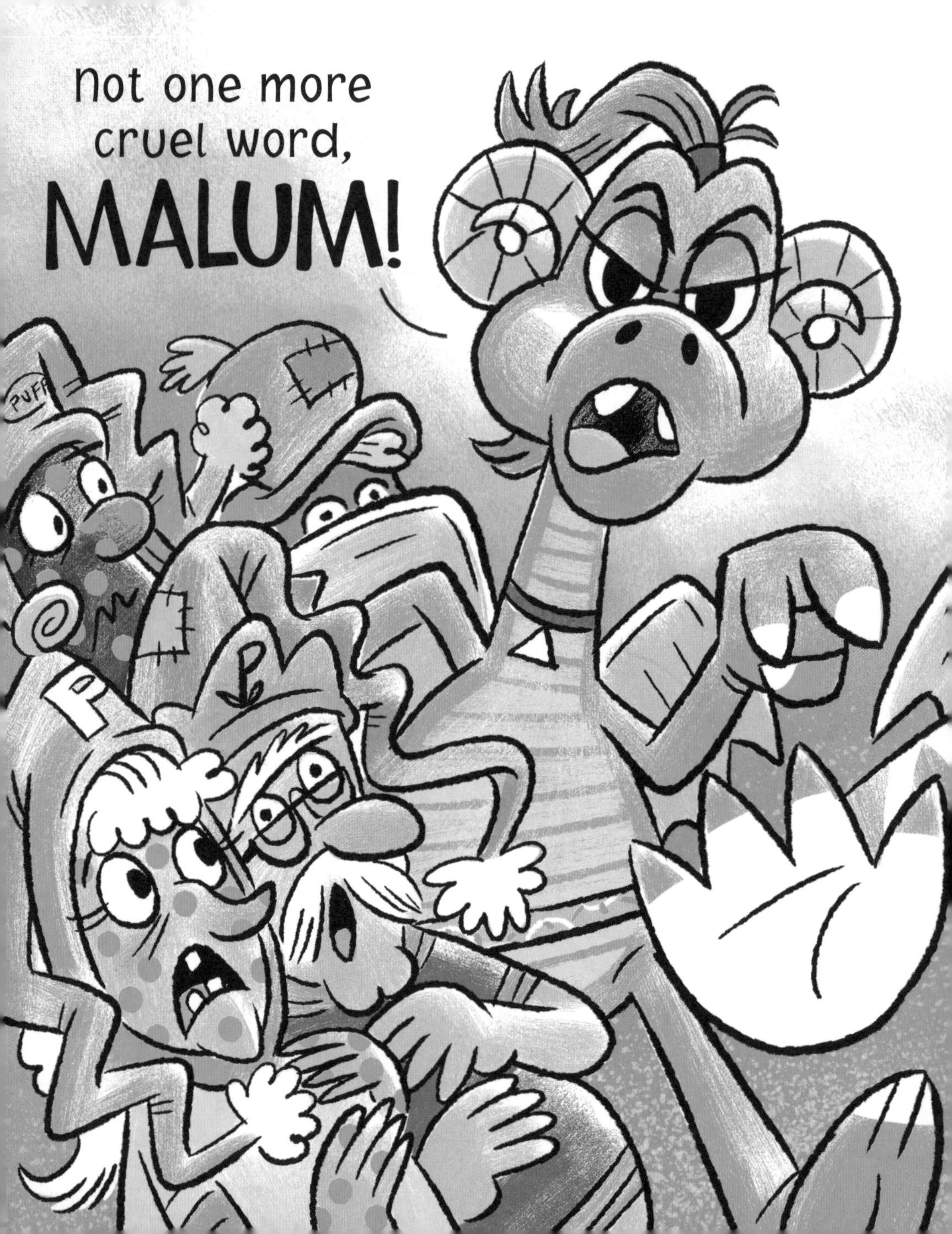
not one more cruel word, MALUM!
PUFF

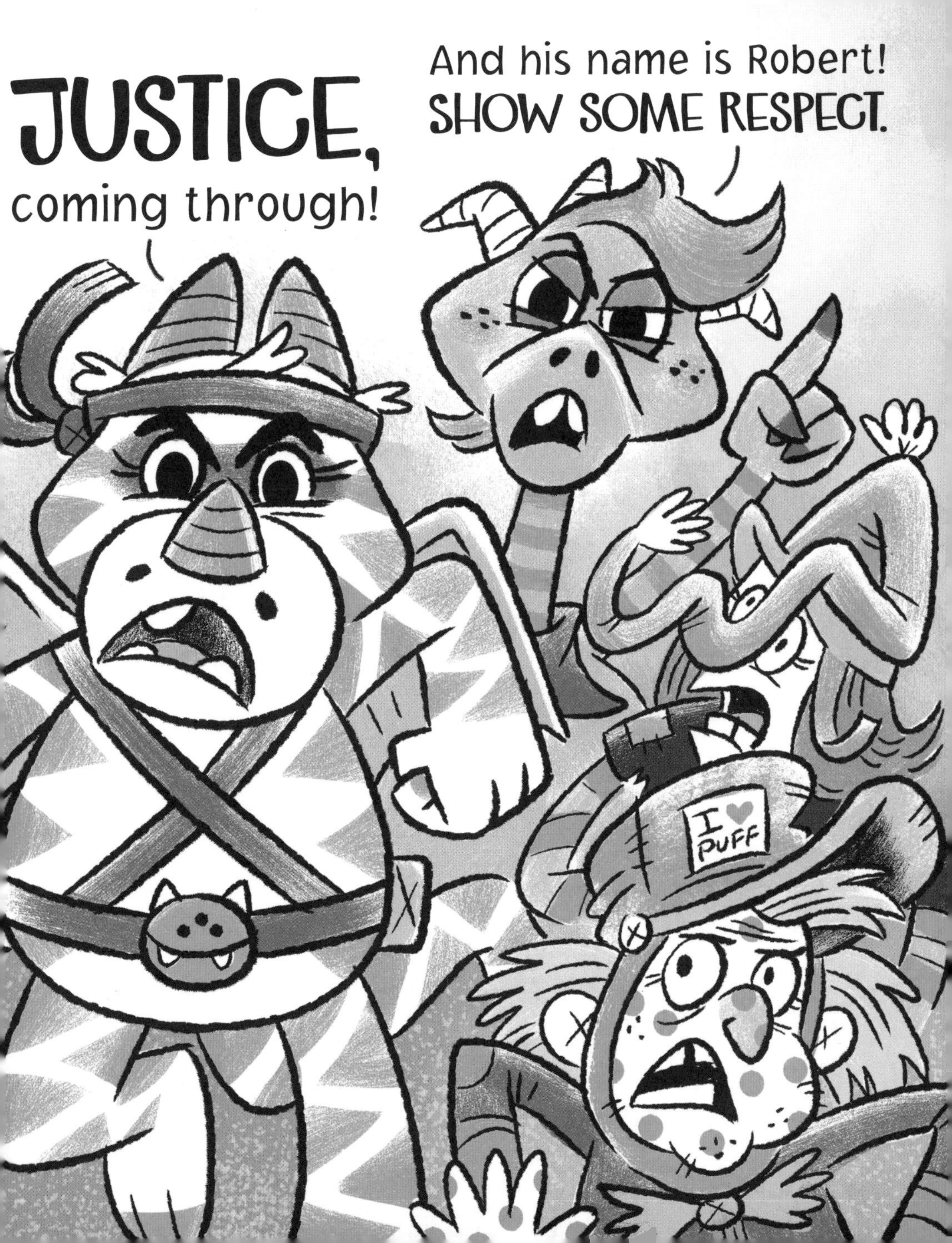
JUSTICE, coming through!
And his name is Robert! SHOW SOME RESPECT.
I ♥ PUFF

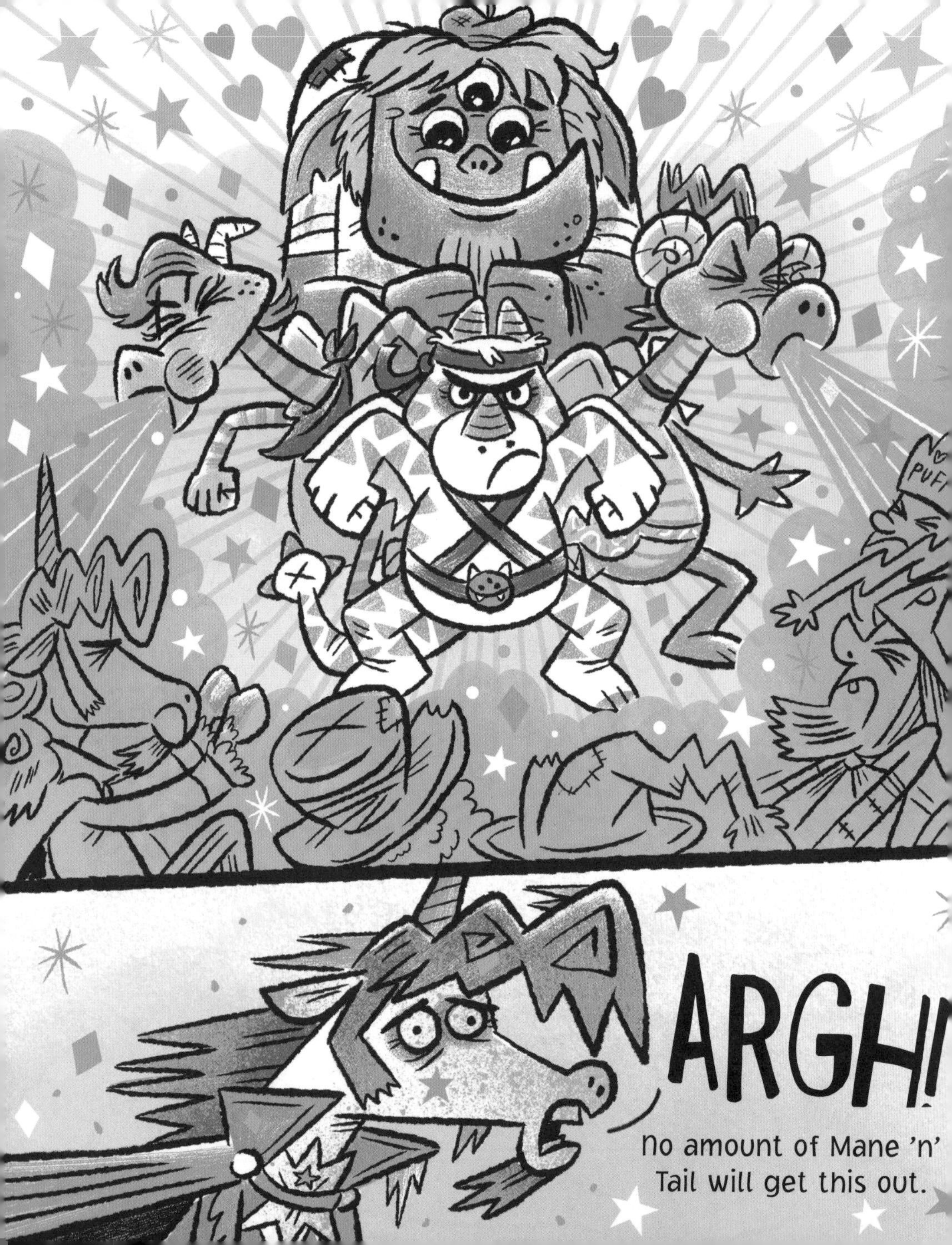
ARGH!
No amount of Mane 'n' Tail will get this out.

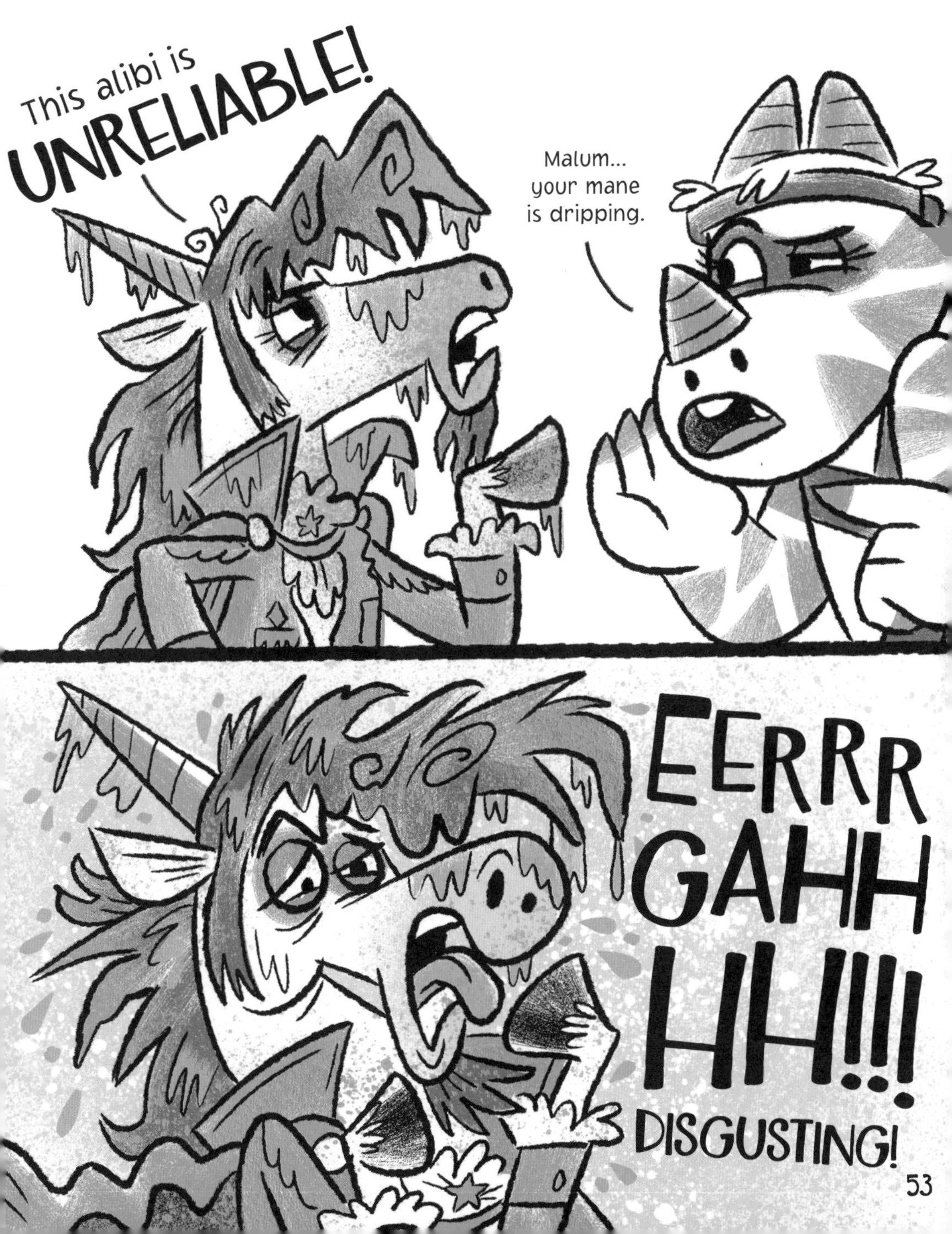
This alibi is UNRELIABLE!
Malum... your mane is dripping.
EERRRR GAHH HH!!!
DISGUSTING!

CHAPTER FOUR
THE PROOF'S IN THE SMOOTHIE

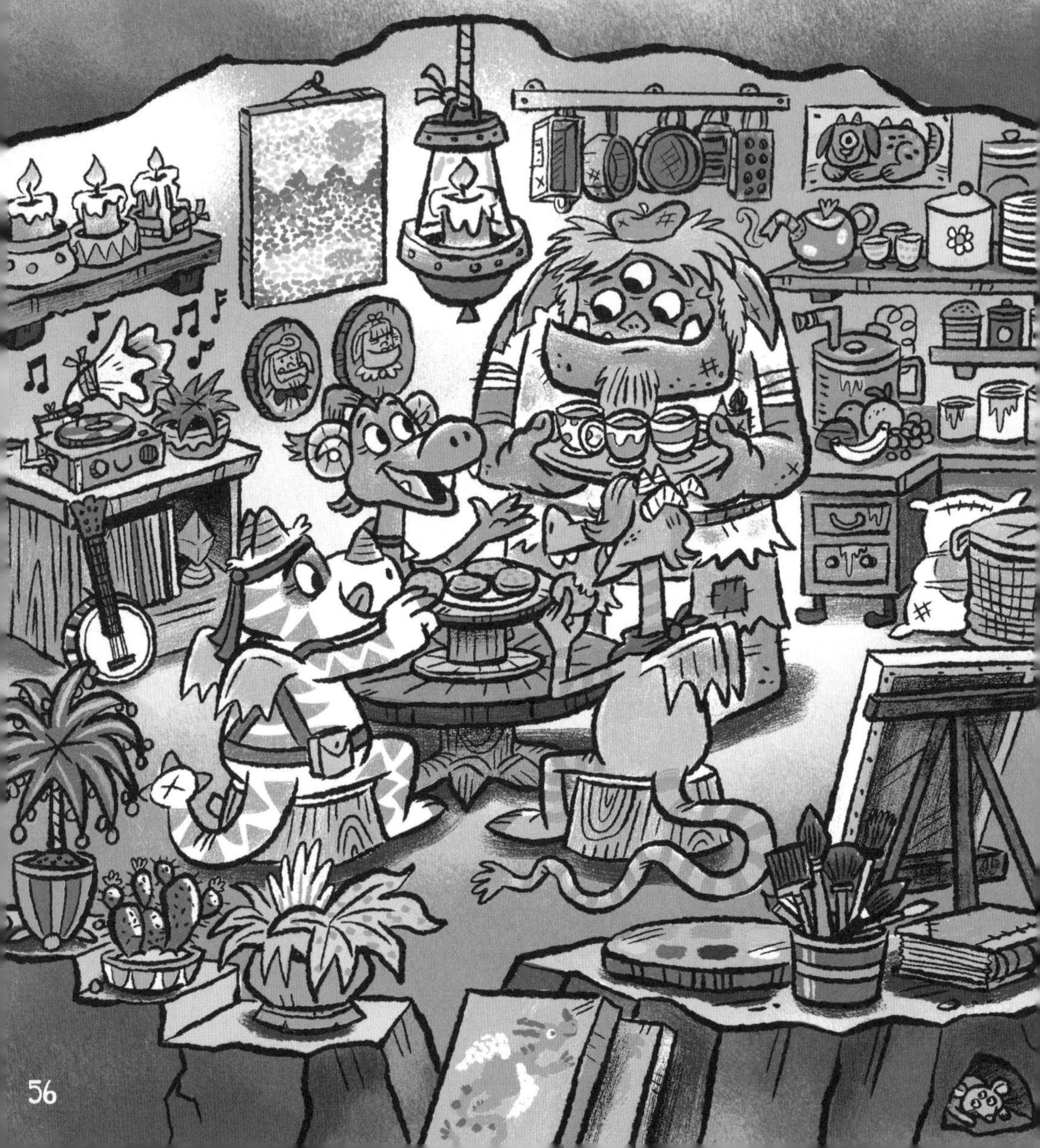

57

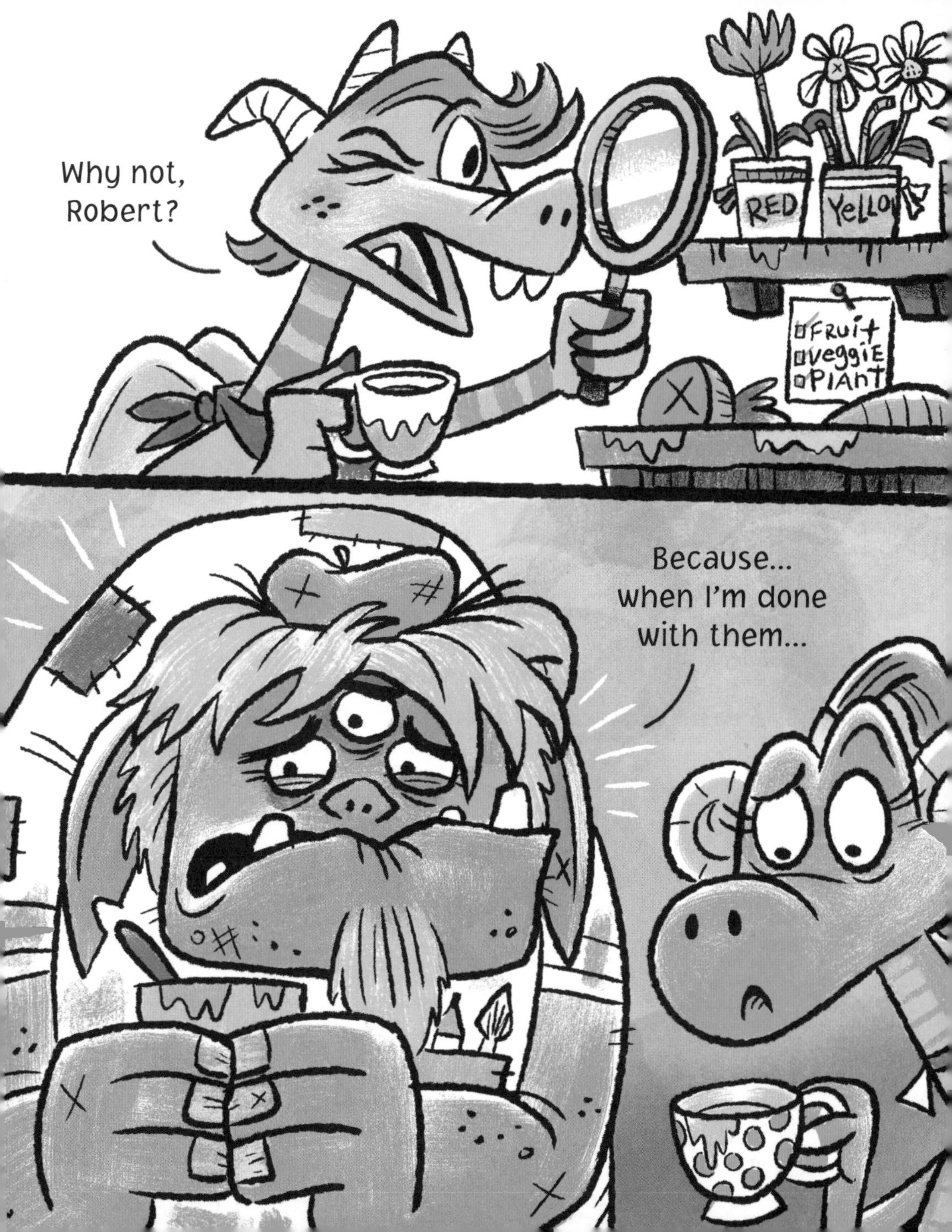
Why not, Robert?
RED
YeLLO
FRuit
veggiE
PlAnt
Because... when I'm done with them...

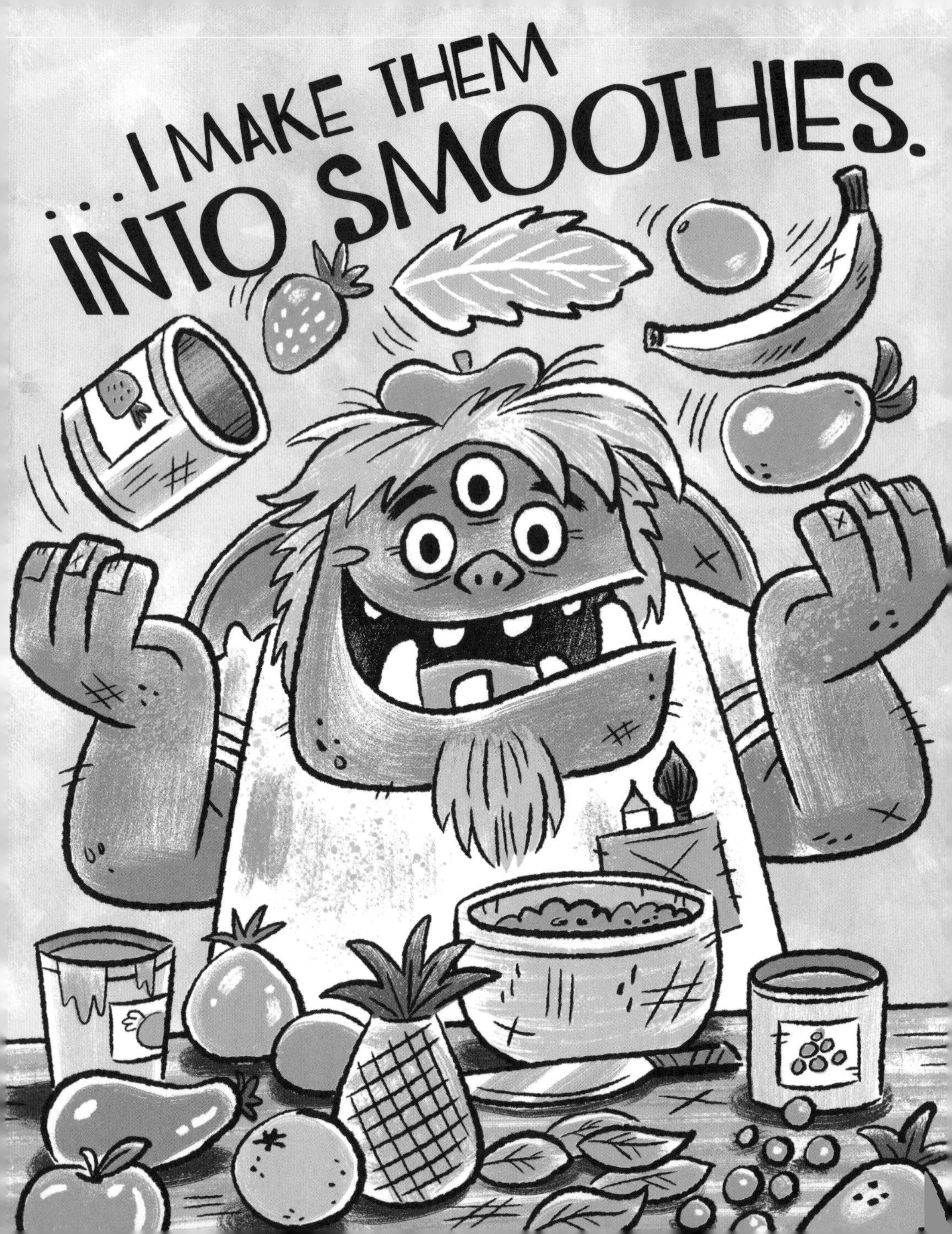
. . . I MAKE THEM
INTO SMOOTHIES.

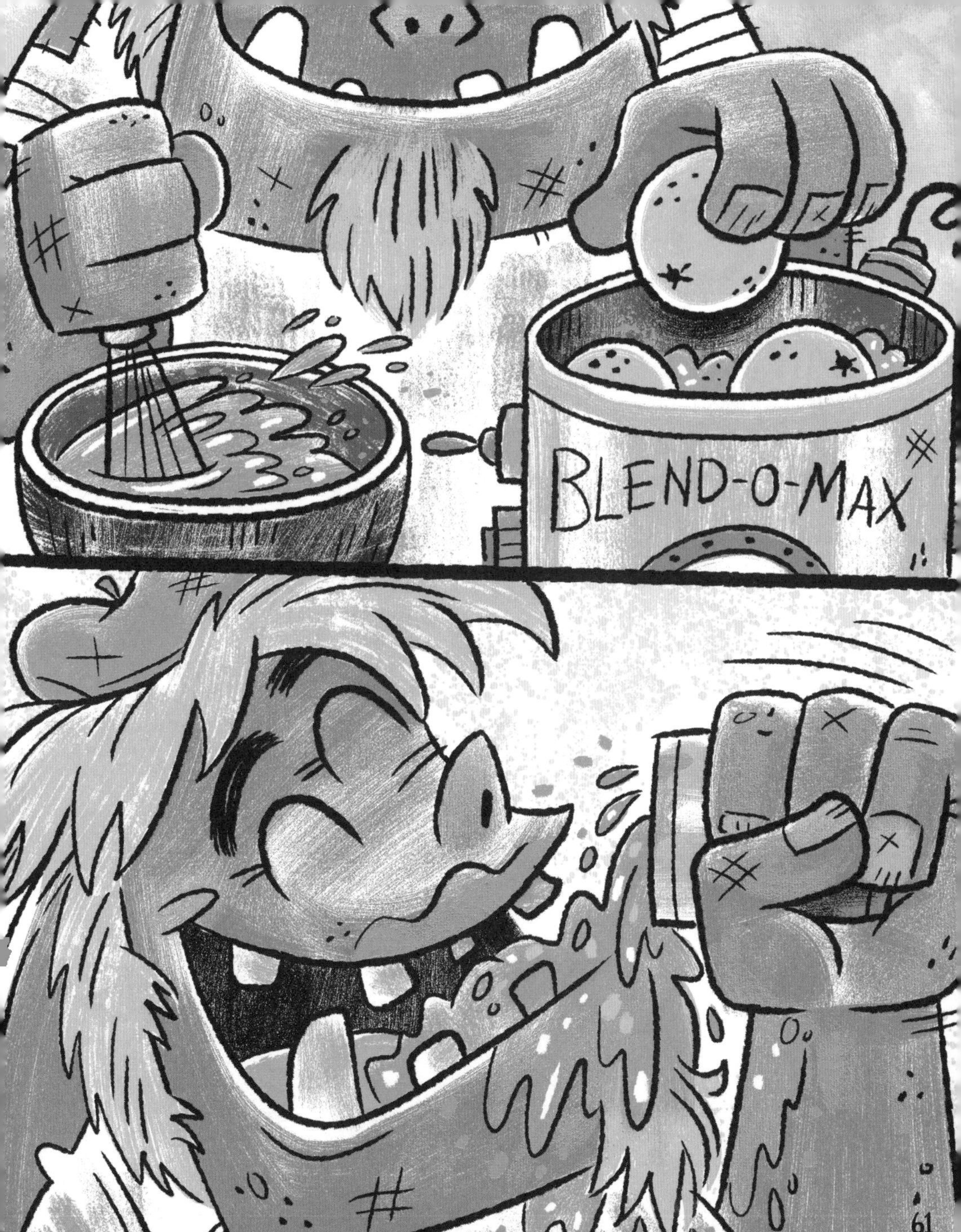
BLEND-O-MAX

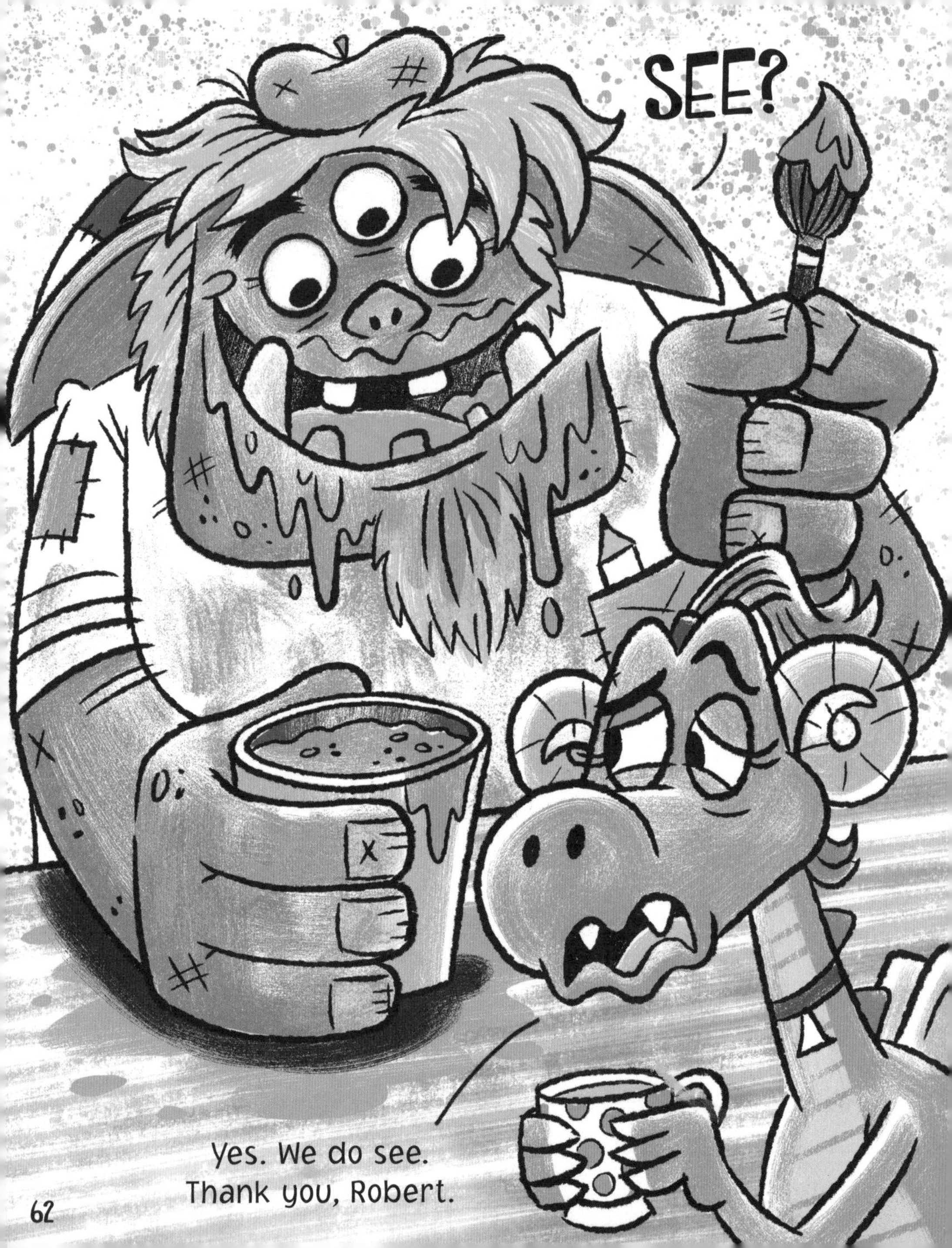
SEE?

Yes. We do see.
Thank you, Robert.

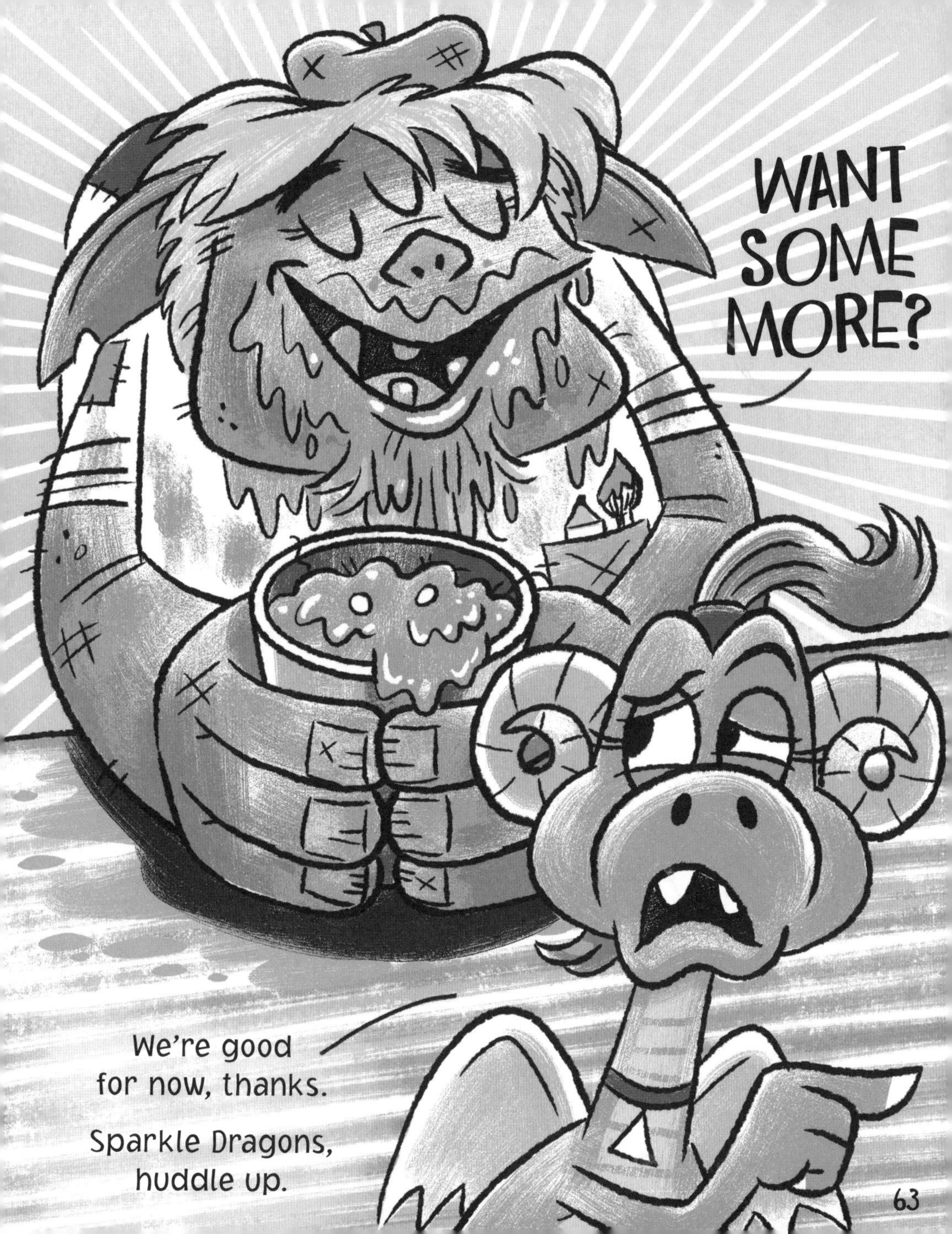
WANT SOME MORE?
We're good for now, thanks.
Sparkle Dragons, huddle up.

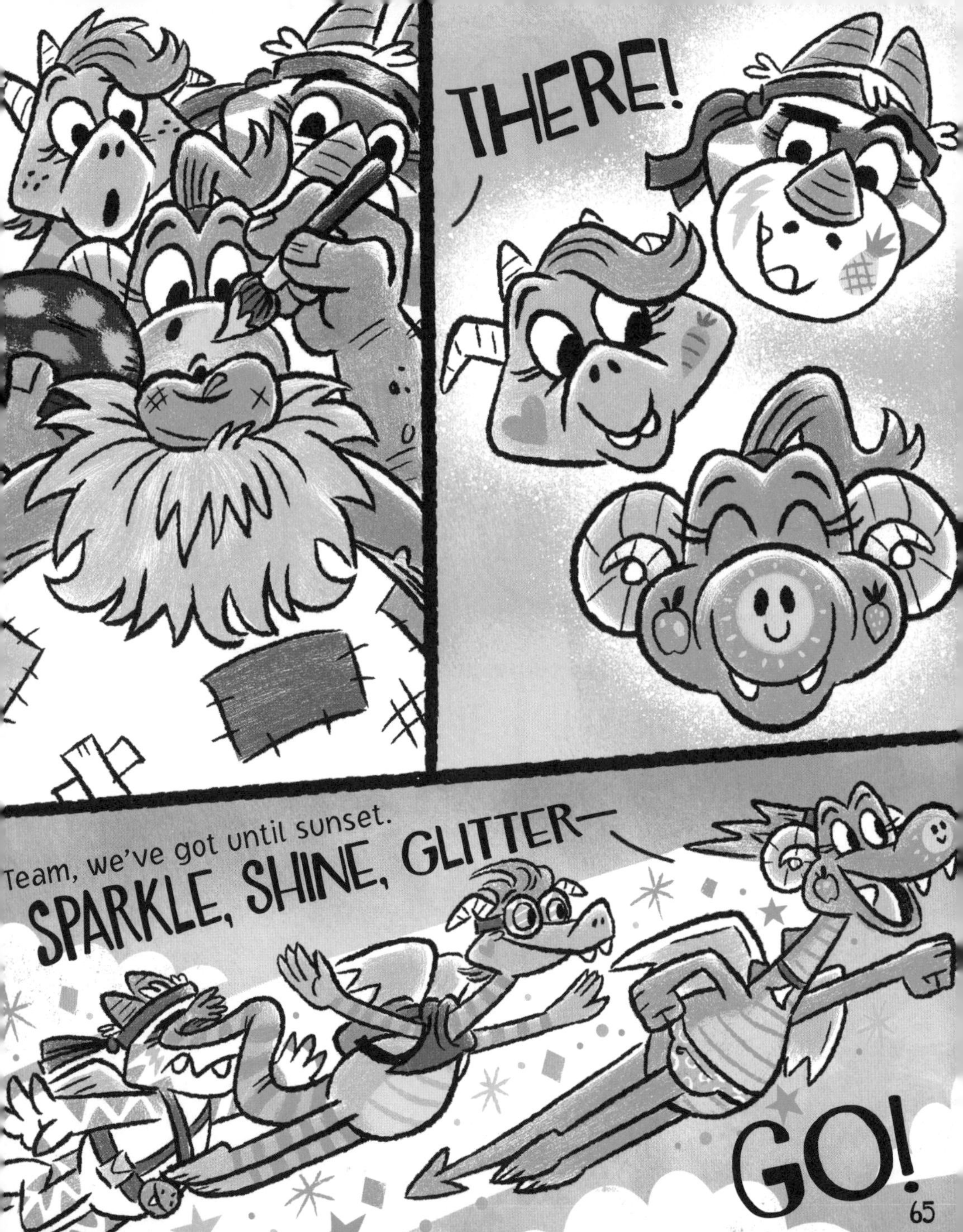
THERE!
Team, we've got until sunset.
SPARKLE, SHINE, GLITTER—
GO!

CHAPTER FIVE
CAVE SWEET CAVE

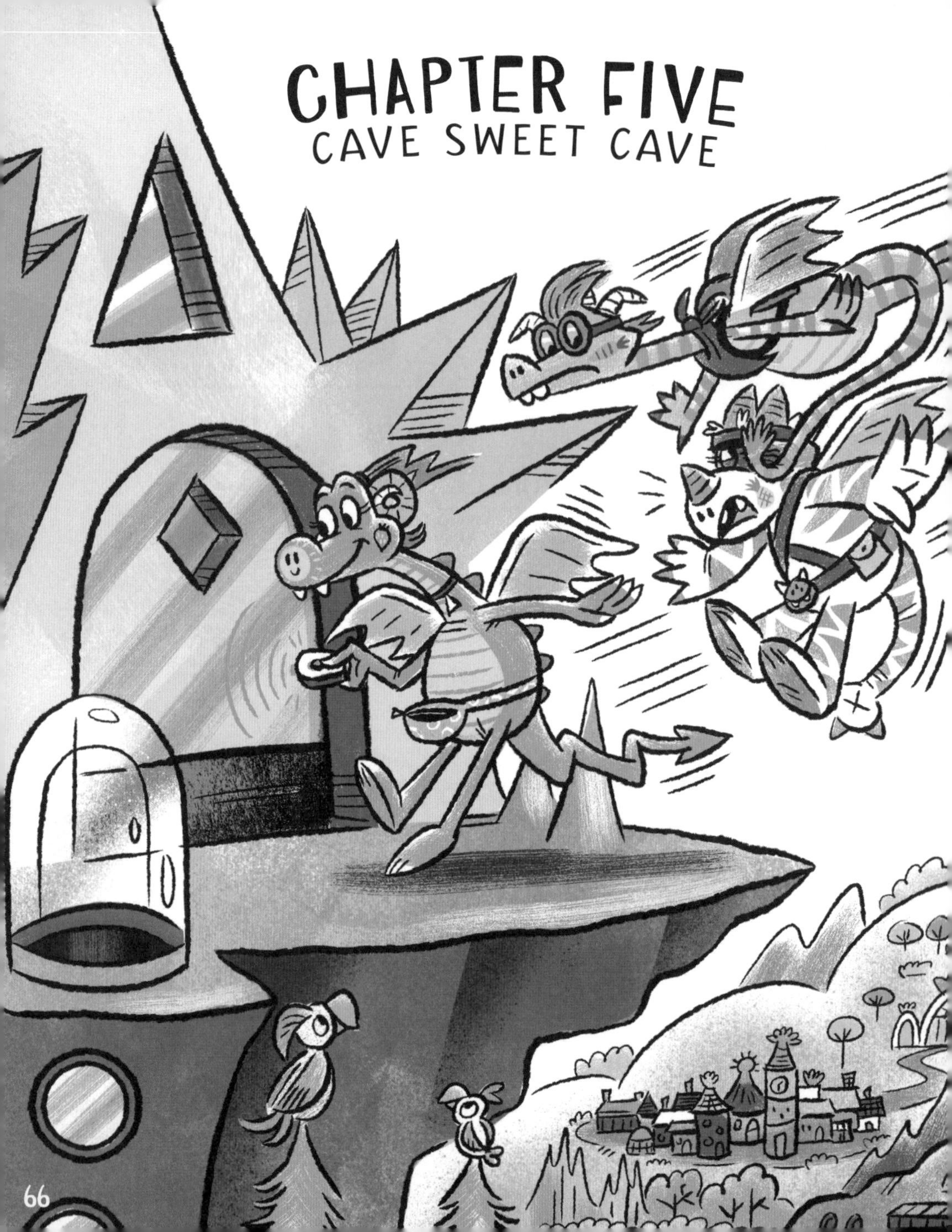

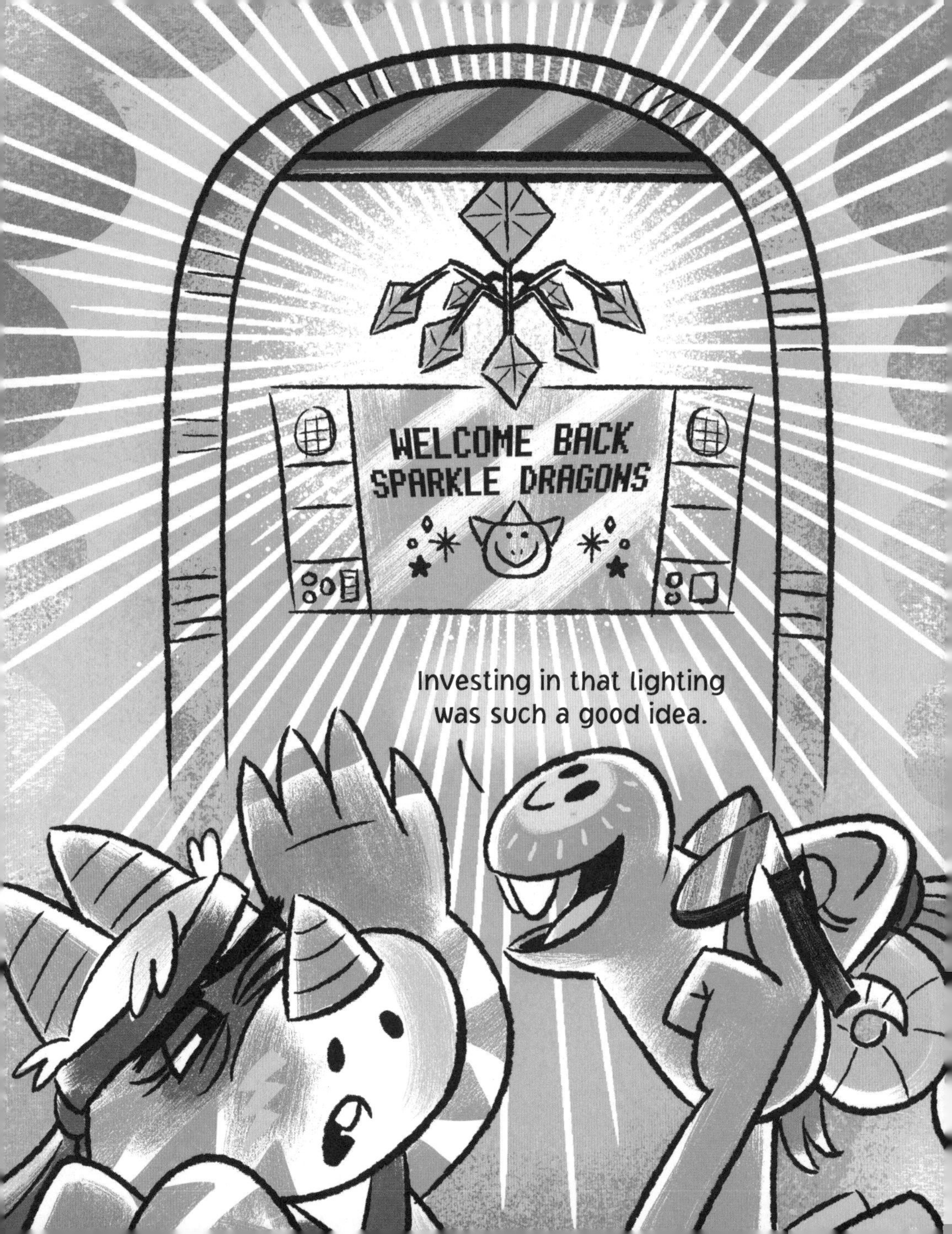
WELCOME BACK
SPARKLE DRAGONS
Investing in that lighting was such a good idea.

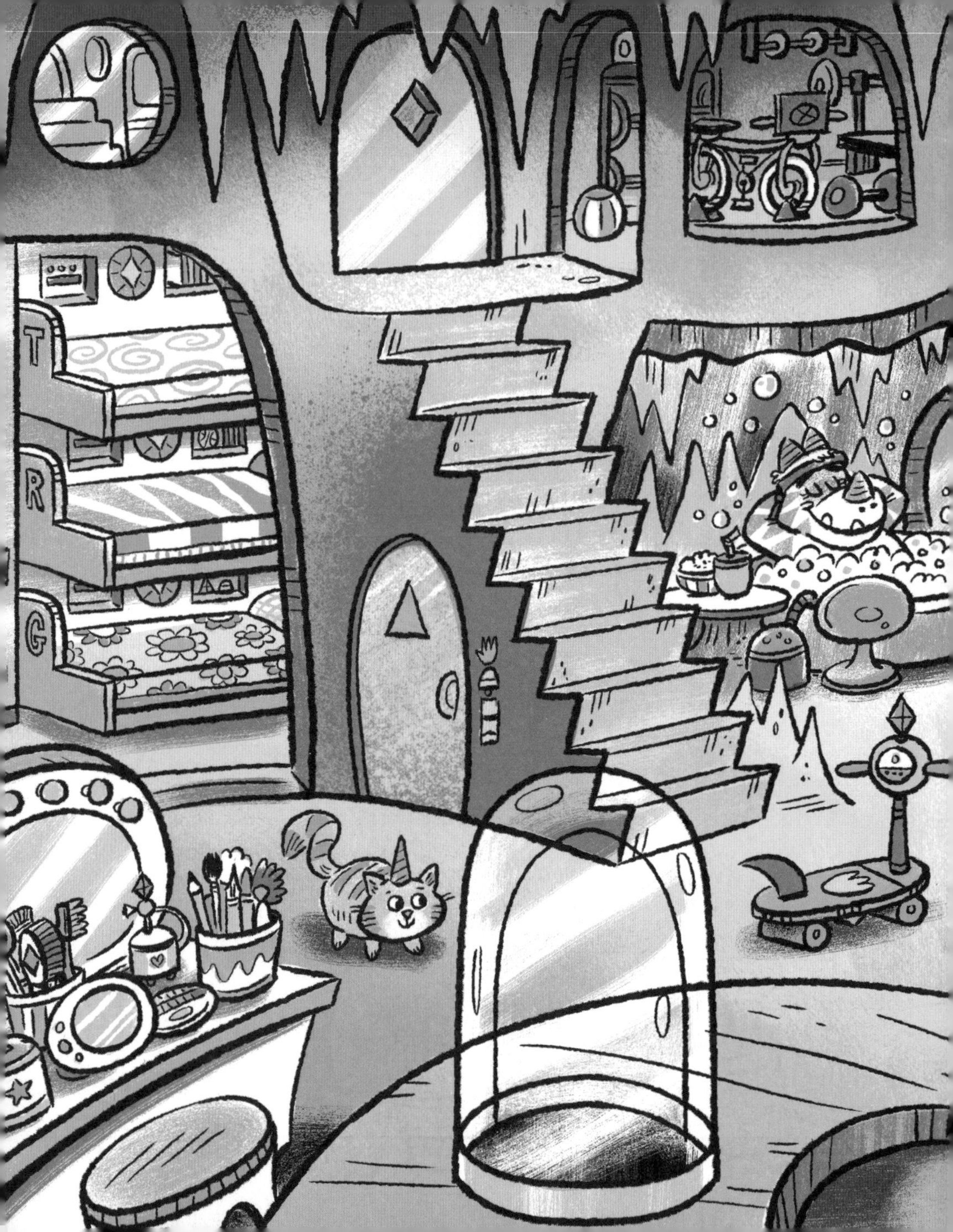
T
R
G

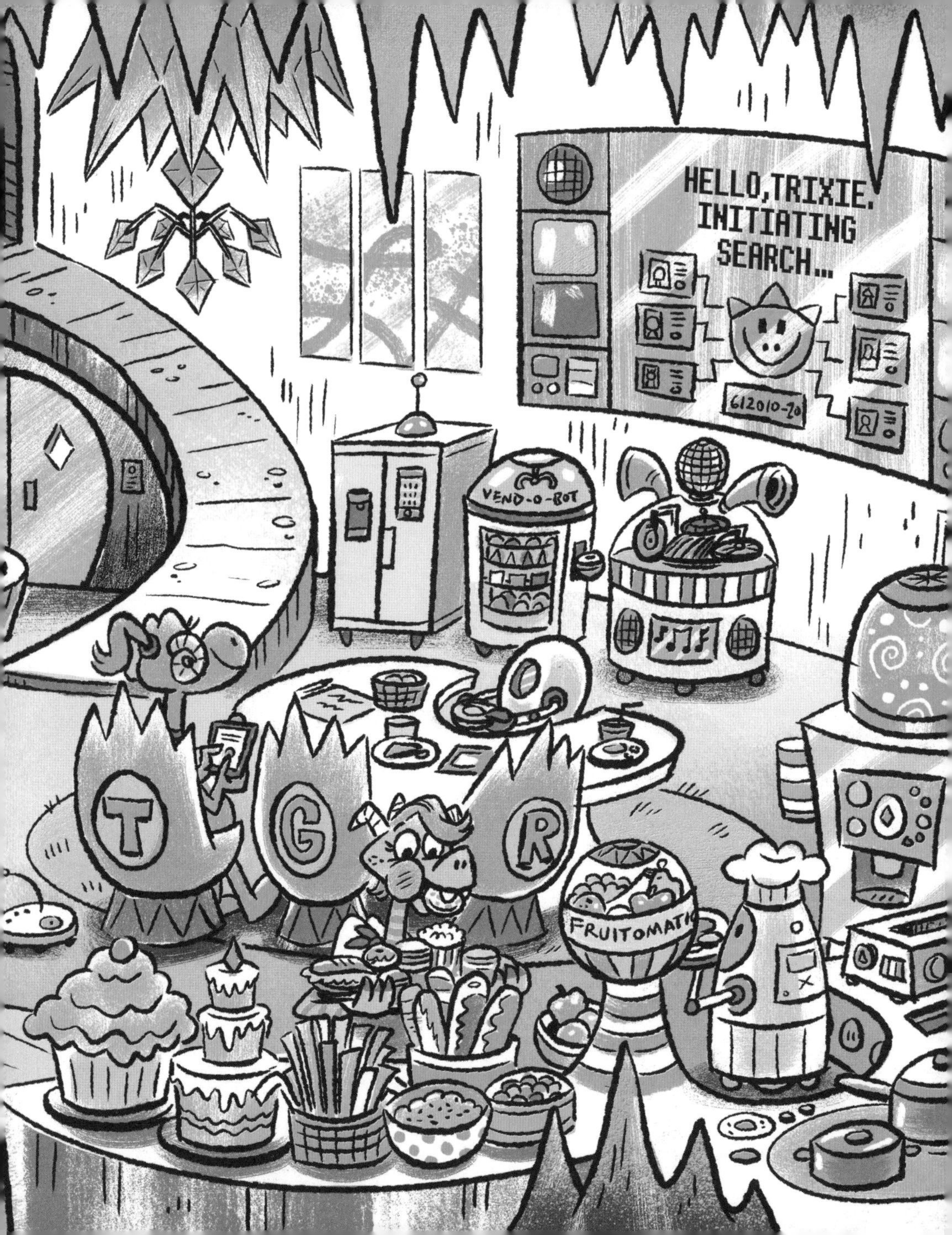
HELLO, TRIXIE.
INITIATING
SEARCH...
612010-20
VEND-O-BOT
T
G
R
FRUITOMATIC

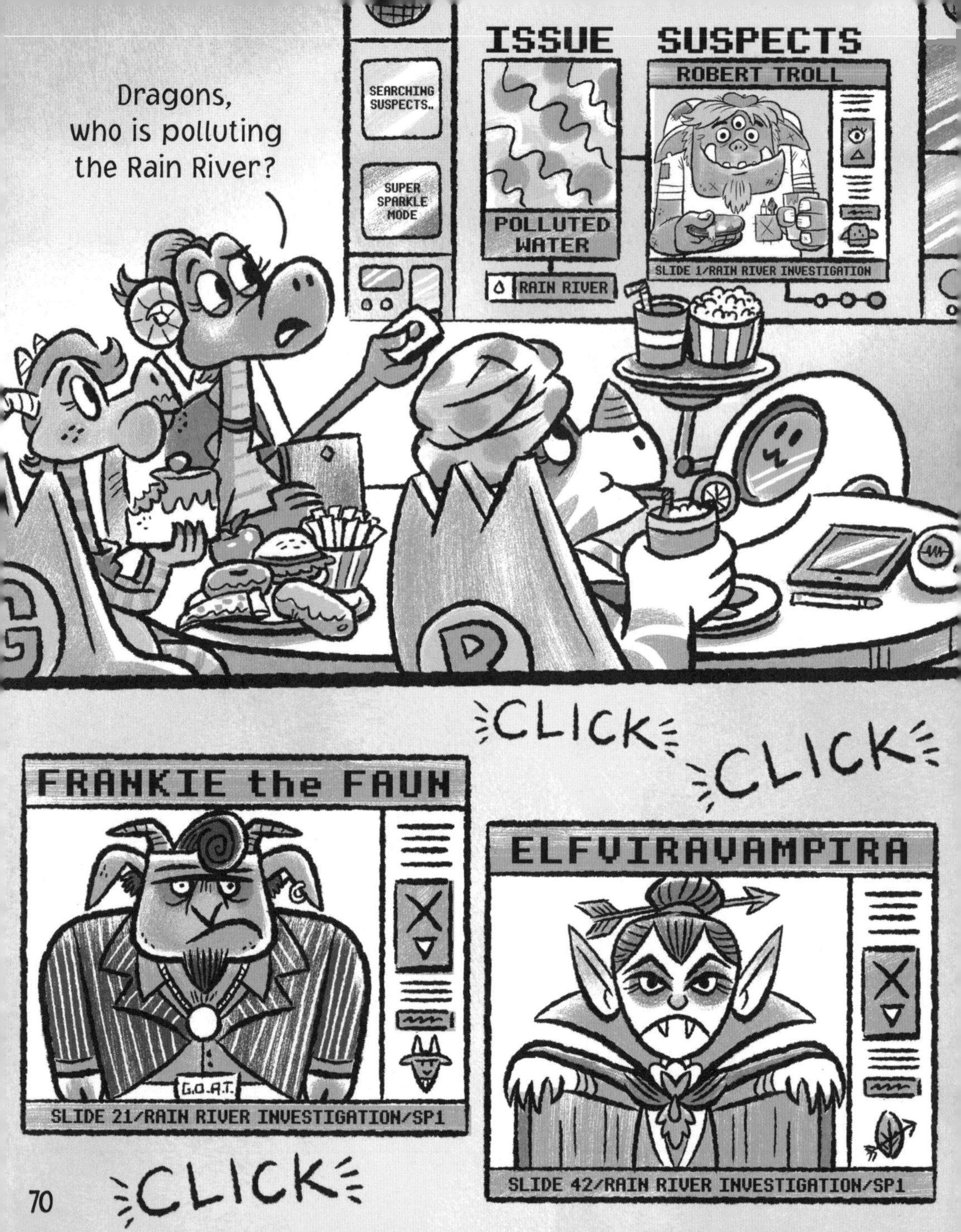
Dragons,
who is polluting
the Rain River?
ISSUE
SUSPECTS
SEARCHING SUSPECTS..
SUPER SPARKLE MODE
POLLUTED WATER
RAIN RIVER
ROBERT TROLL
SLIDE 1/RAIN RIVER INVESTIGATION
CLICK
CLICK
FRANKIE the FAUN
G.O.A.T.
SLIDE 21/RAIN RIVER INVESTIGATION/SP1
ELFVIRAVAMPIRA
SLIDE 42/RAIN RIVER INVESTIGATION/SP1
CLICK

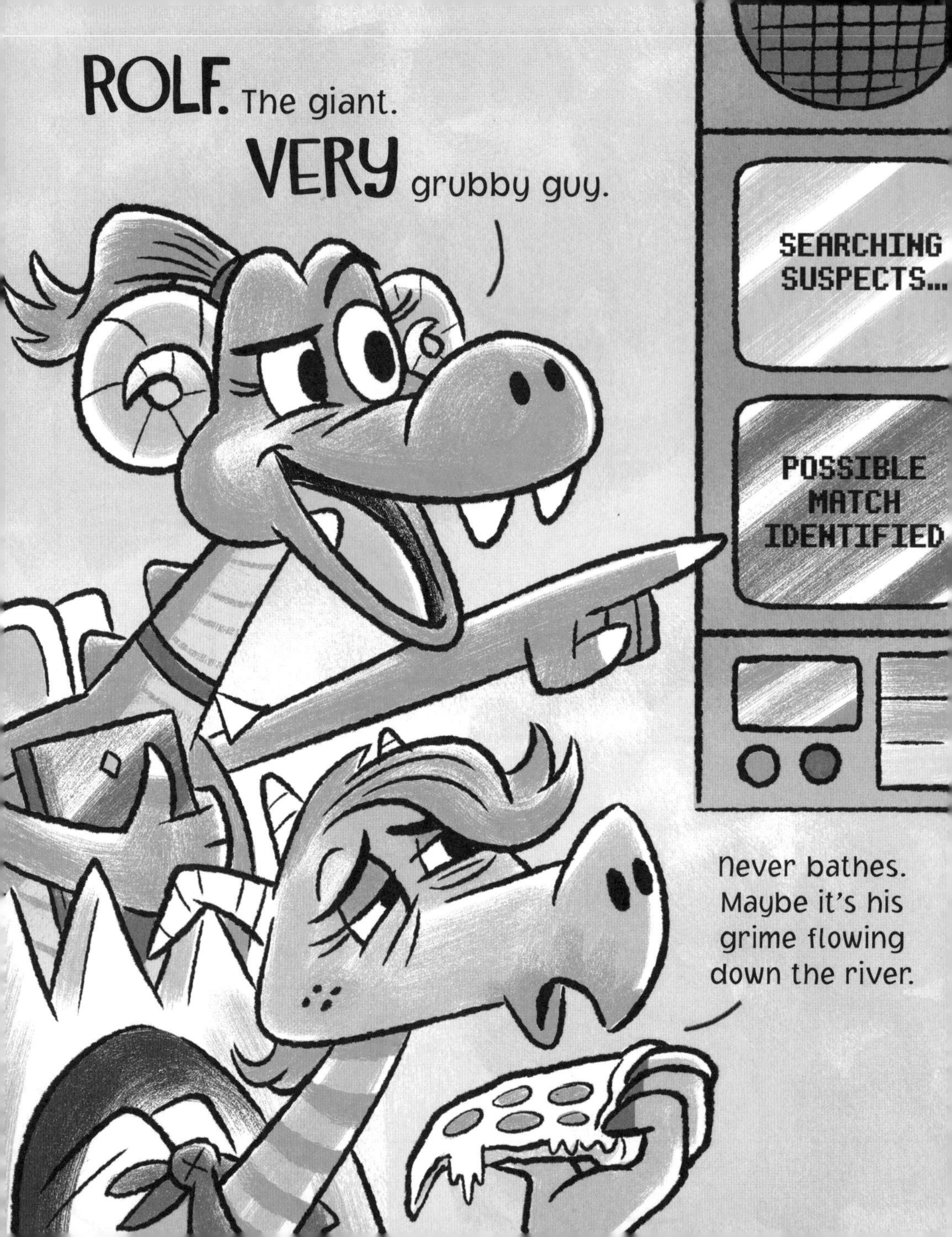
ROLF. The giant.
VERY grubby guy.
SEARCHING SUSPECTS...
POSSIBLE MATCH IDENTIFIED
Never bathes. Maybe it's his grime flowing down the river.

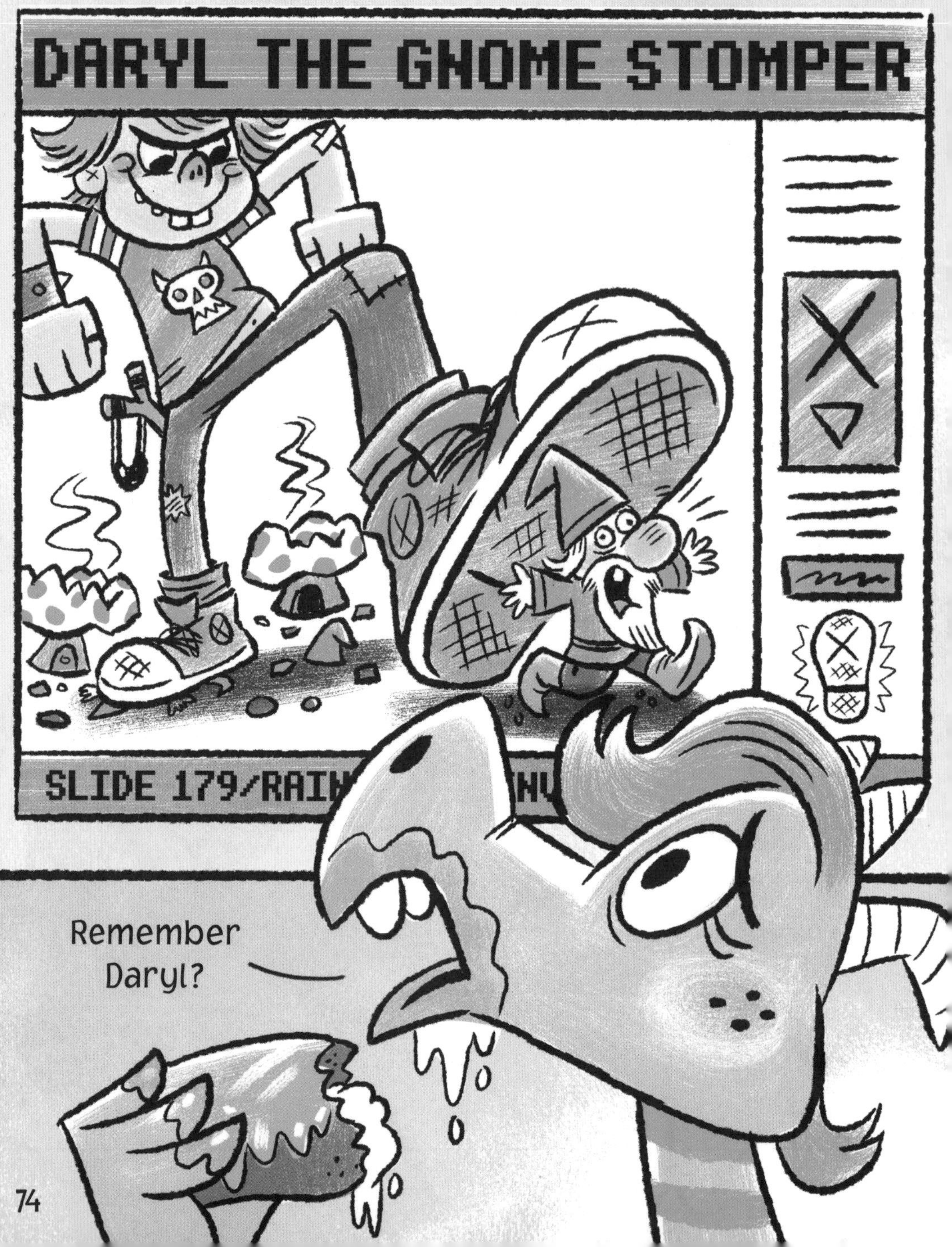
DARYL THE GNOME STOMPER
SLIDE 179/RAI
Remember Daryl?

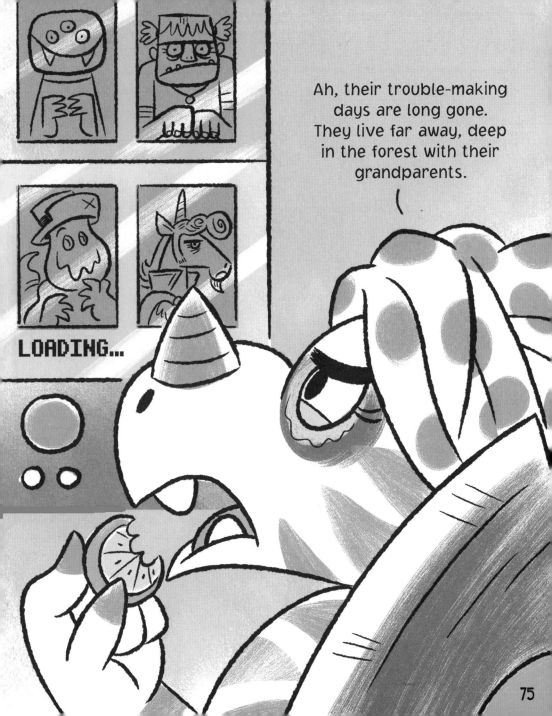

Ah, their trouble-making days are long gone. They live far away, deep in the forest with their grandparents.

LOADING...

CHAPTER SIX
GLITTERY GUMSHOES INVESTIGATE

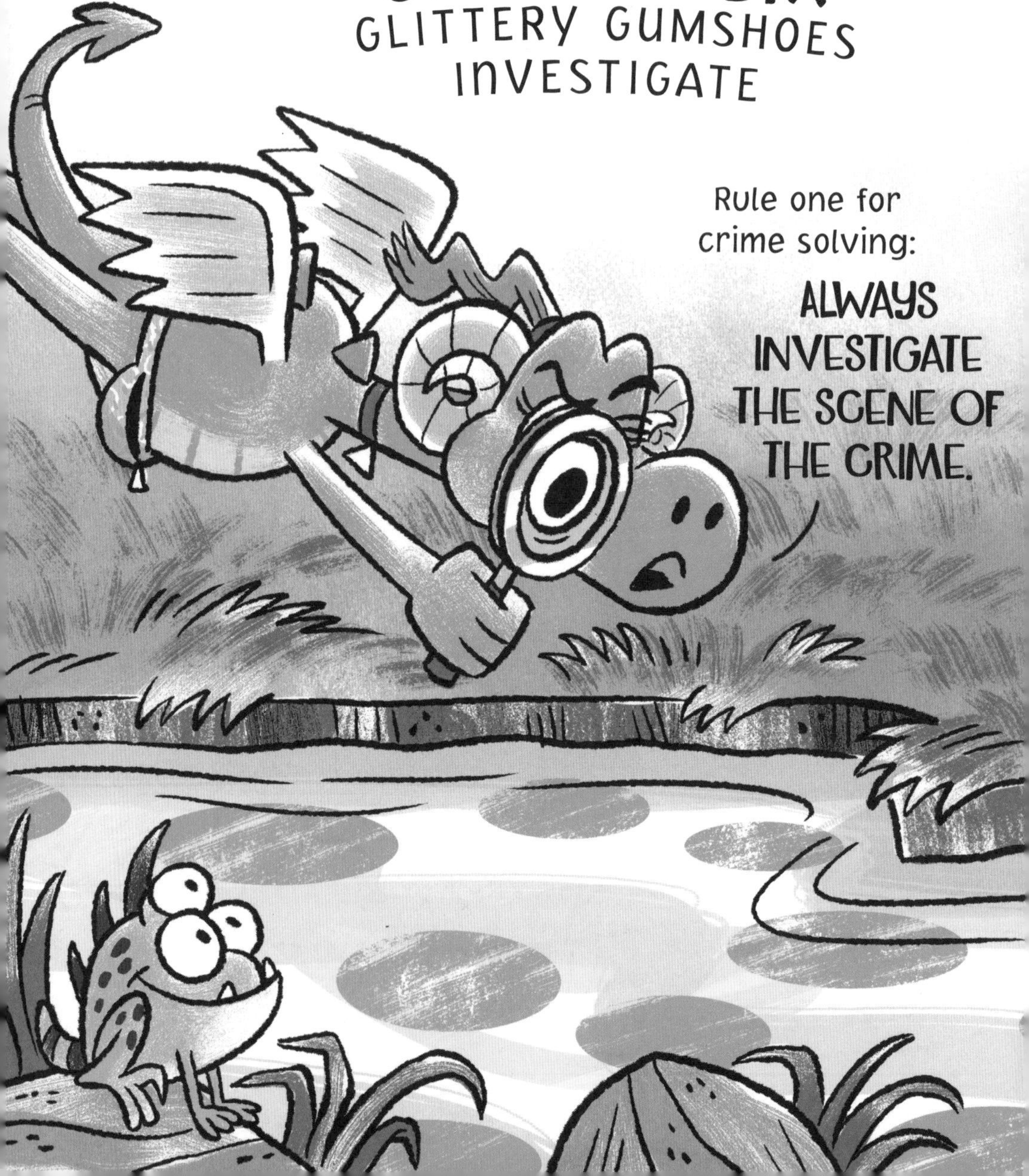
Rule one for crime solving:
ALWAYS INVESTIGATE THE SCENE OF THE CRIME.

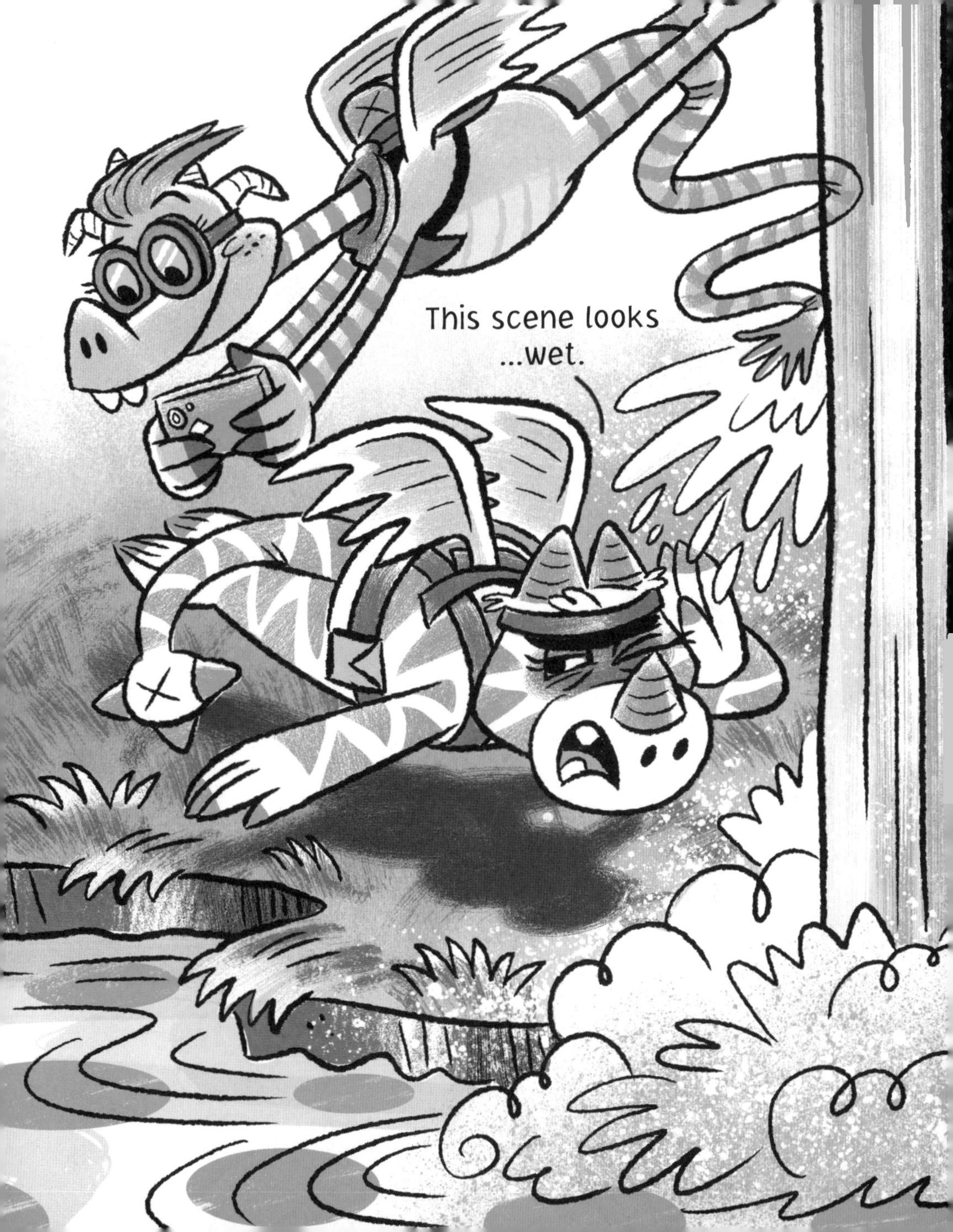
This scene looks ...wet.

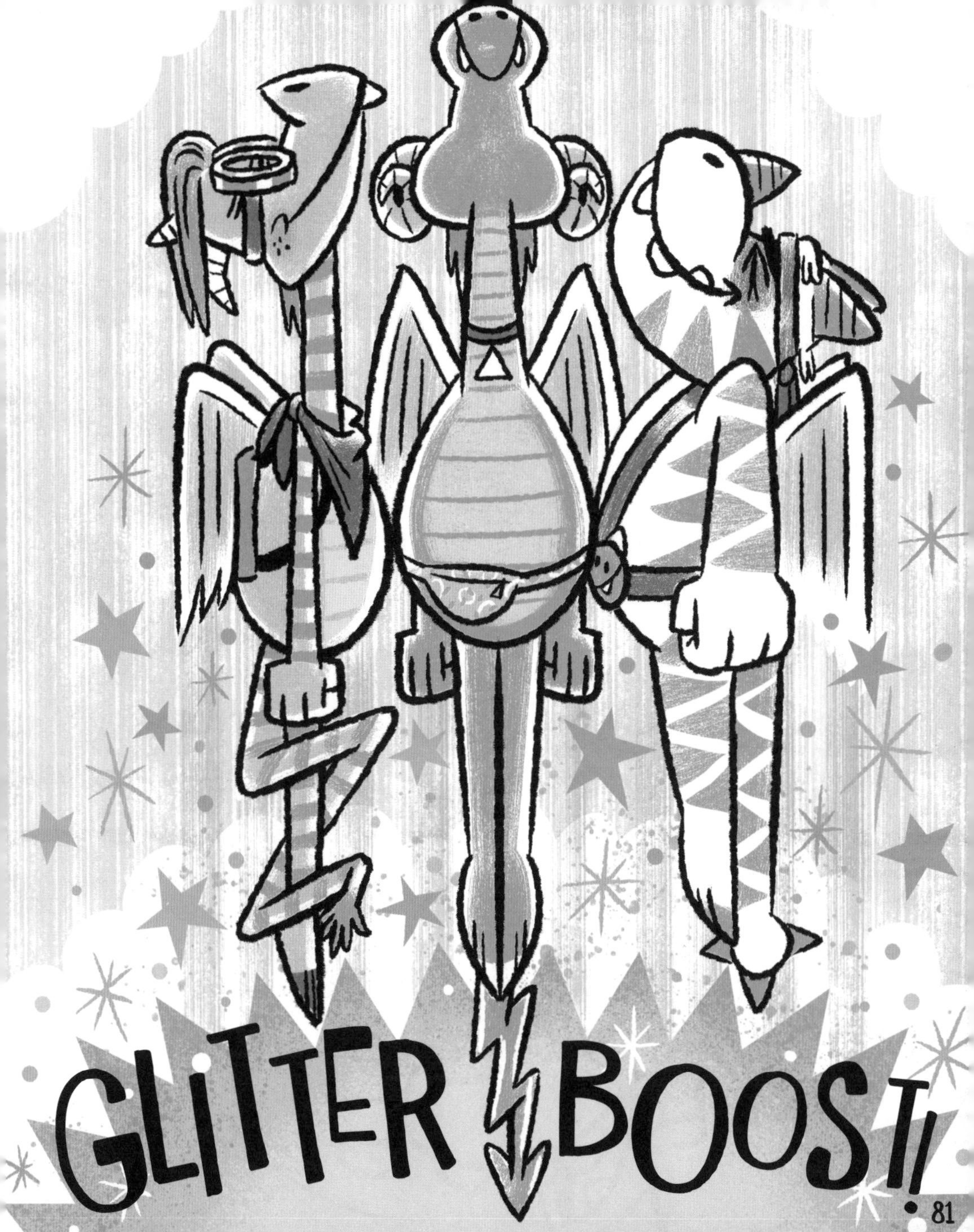
GLITTER BOOST!!

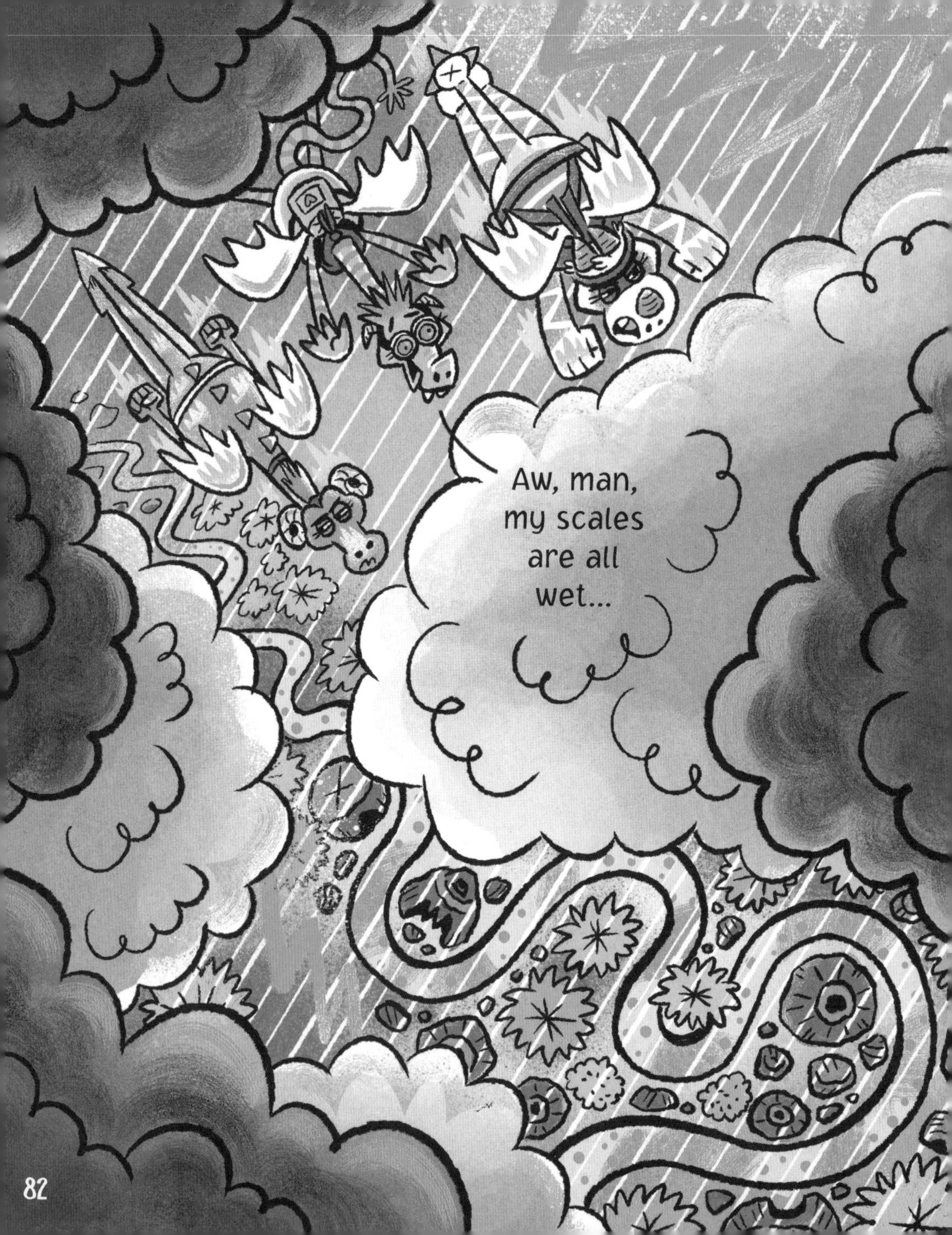
Aw, man, my scales are all wet...

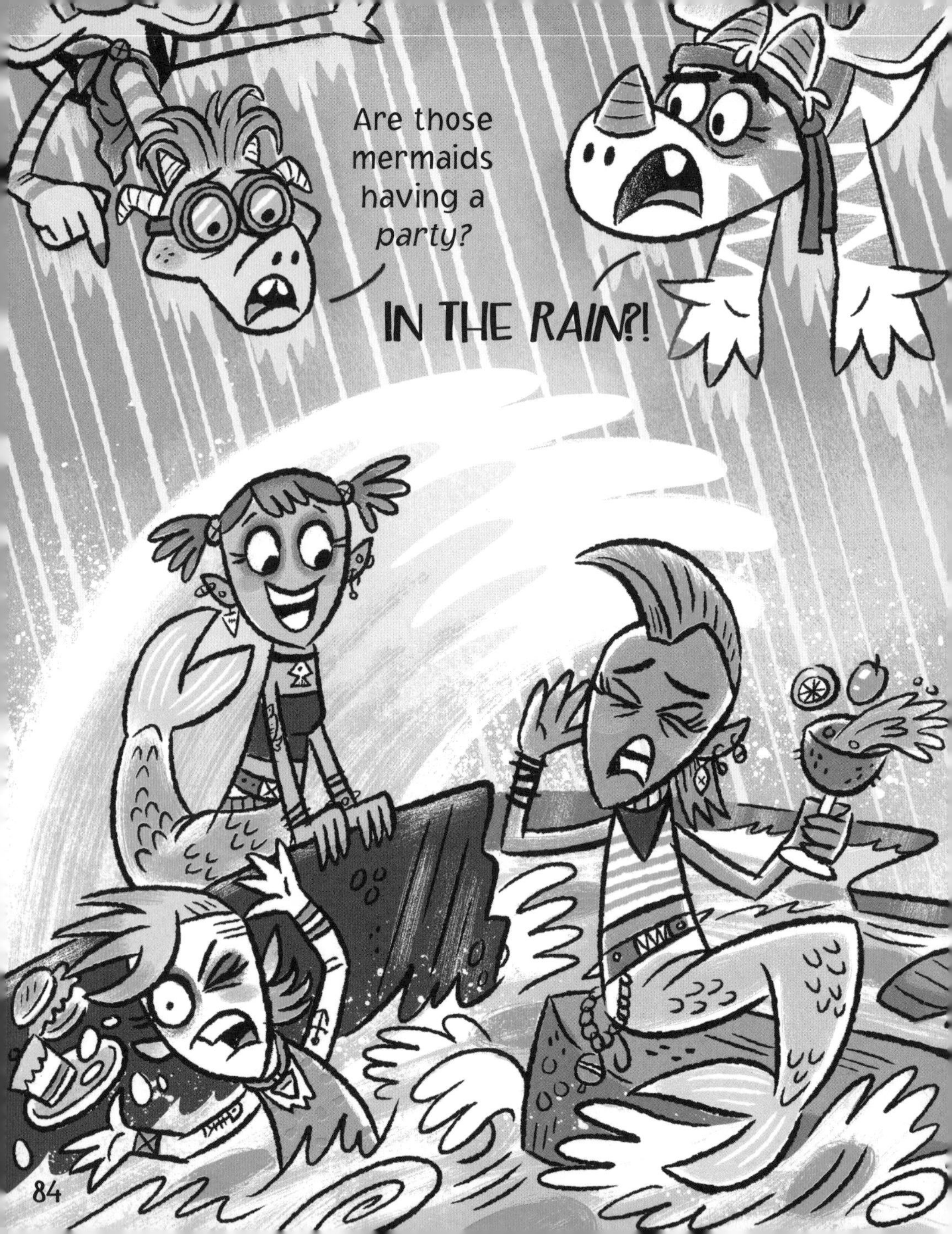
Are those mermaids having a *party?*
IN THE RAIN?!

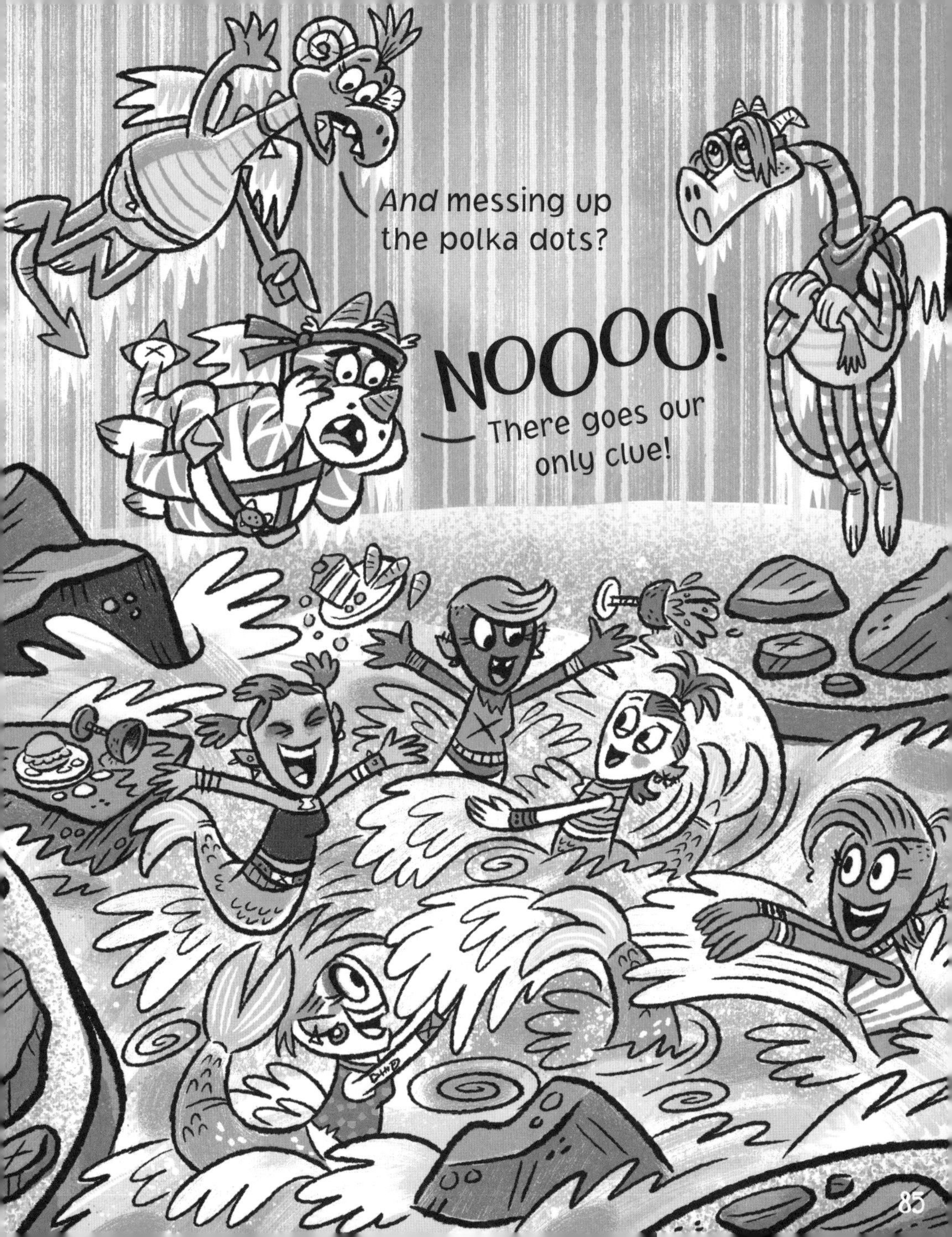
And messing up the polka dots?
NOOOO!
There goes our only clue!

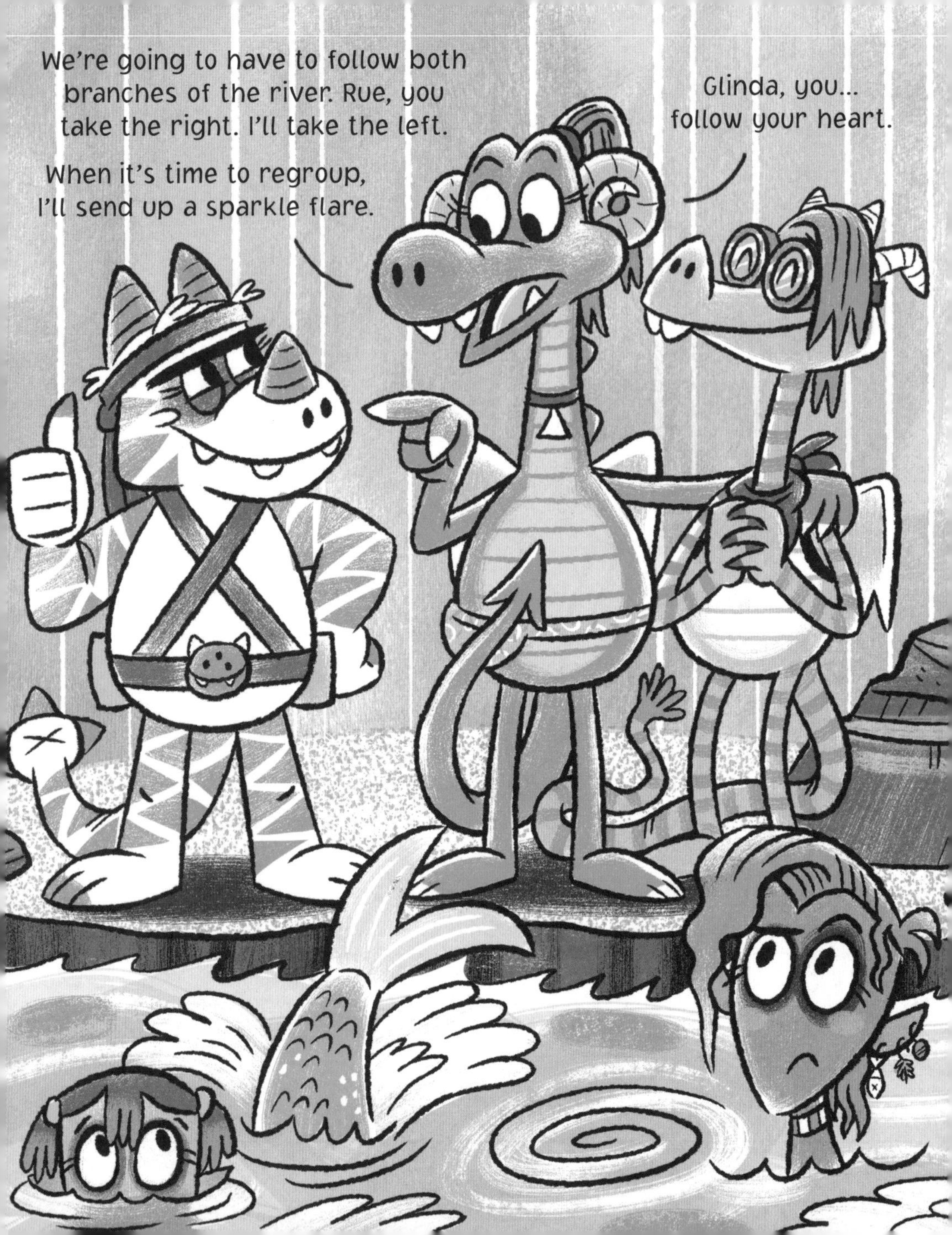

We're going to have to follow both branches of the river. Rue, you take the right. I'll take the left.
When it's time to regroup, I'll send up a sparkle flare.
Glinda, you... follow your heart.

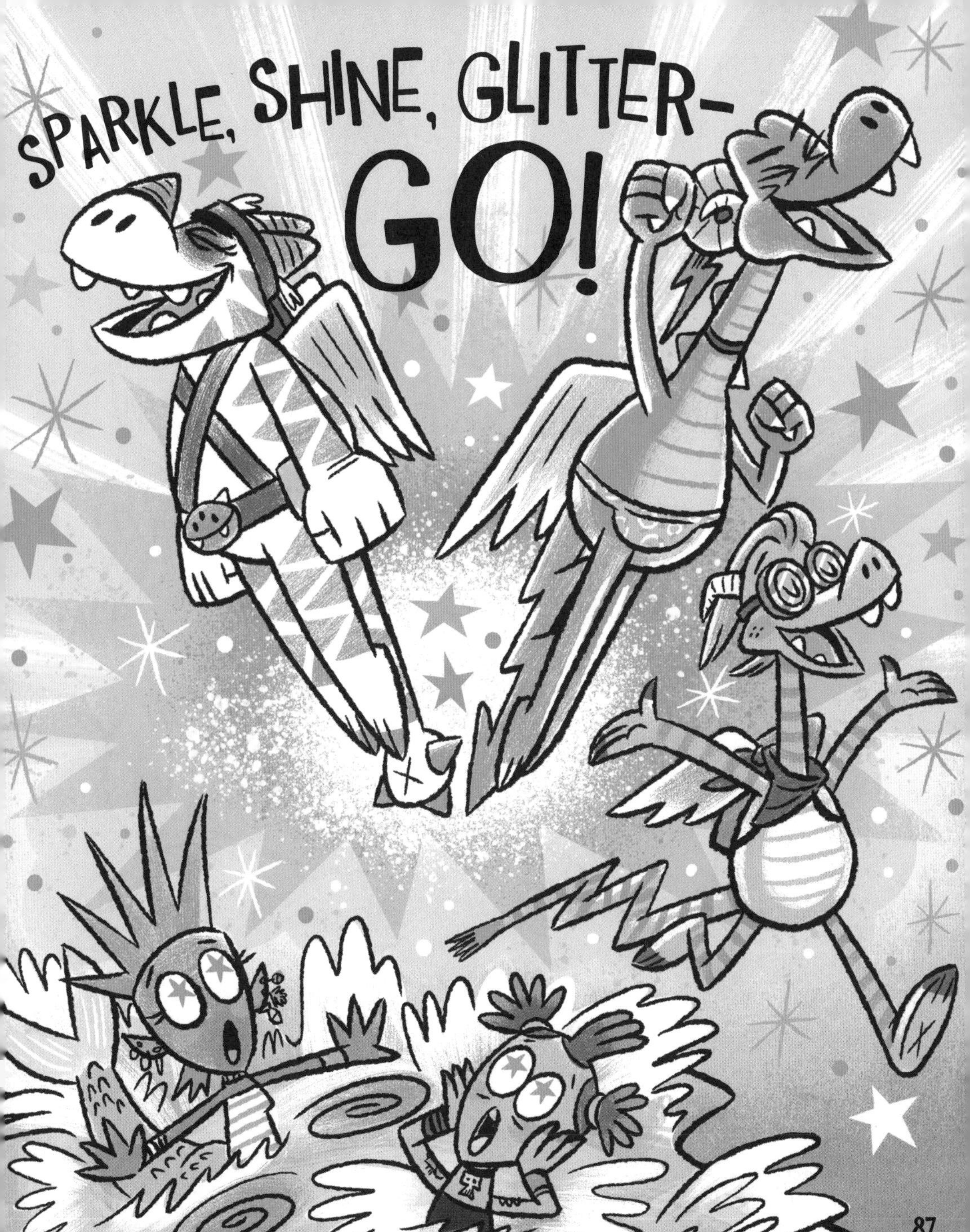
SPARKLE, SHINE, GLITTER—
GO!

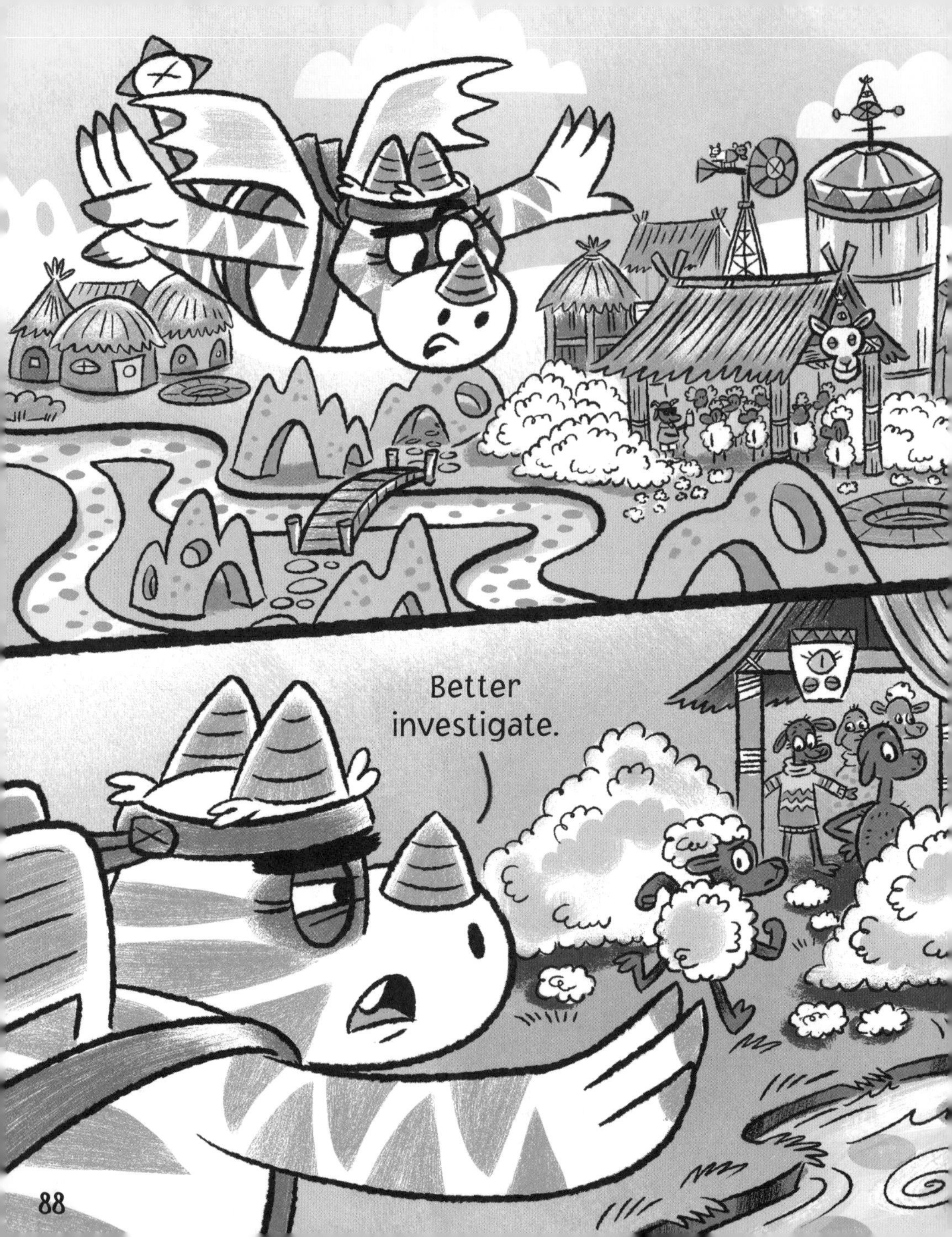
Better investigate.

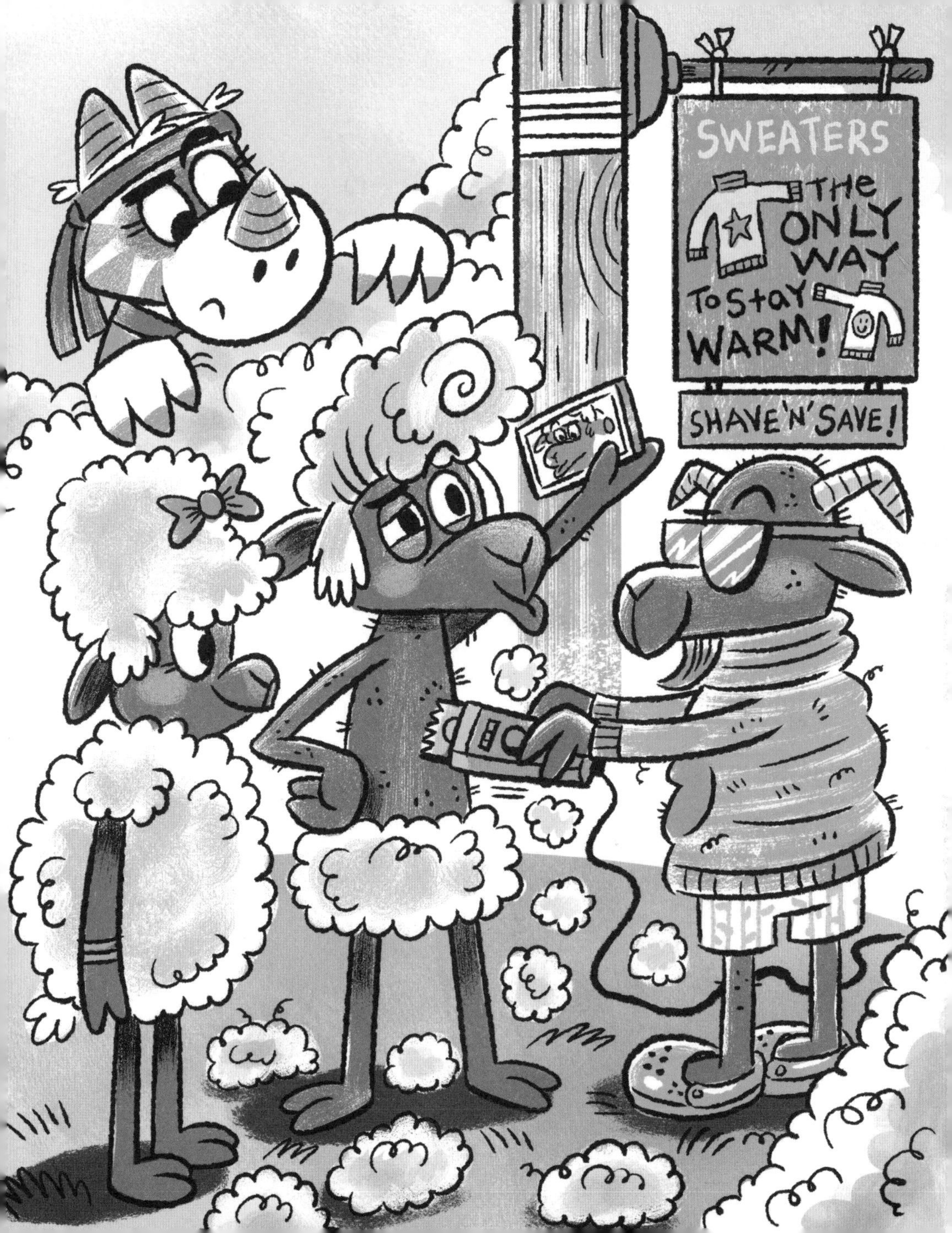
SWEATERS
THE ONLY WAY To Stay WARM!
SHAVE 'N' SAVE!

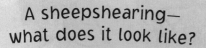

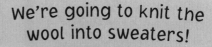

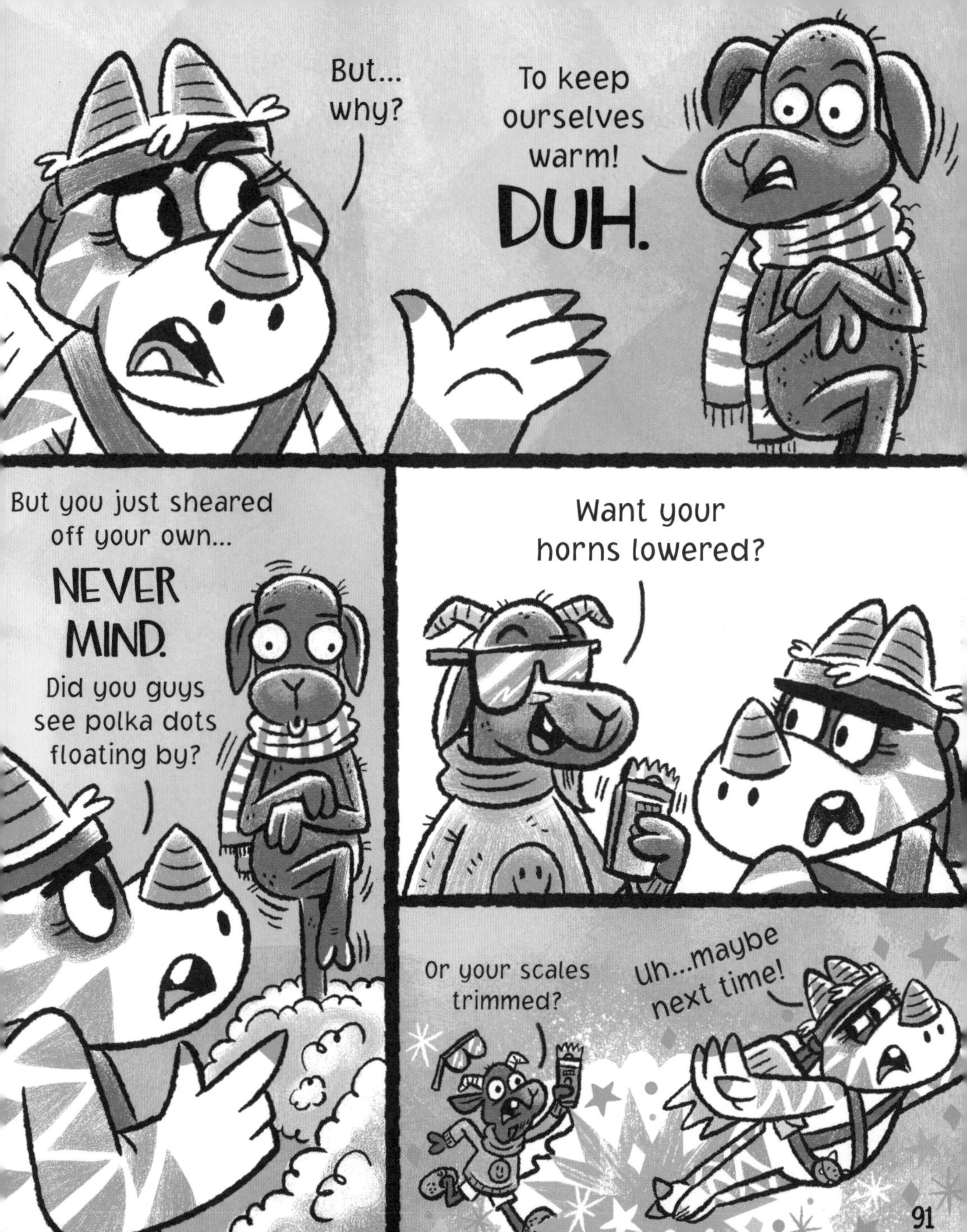
But... why?
To keep ourselves warm!
DUH.
But you just sheared off your own...
NEVER MIND.
Did you guys see polka dots floating by?
Want your horns lowered?
Or your scales trimmed?
Uh...maybe next time!

FOLLOW MY HEART! FOLLOW MY HEART! FOLLOW MY HEART! FOLLOW MY HEART! FOLLOW MY HEART!
FOLLOW MY HEART,
FOLLOW... MY...

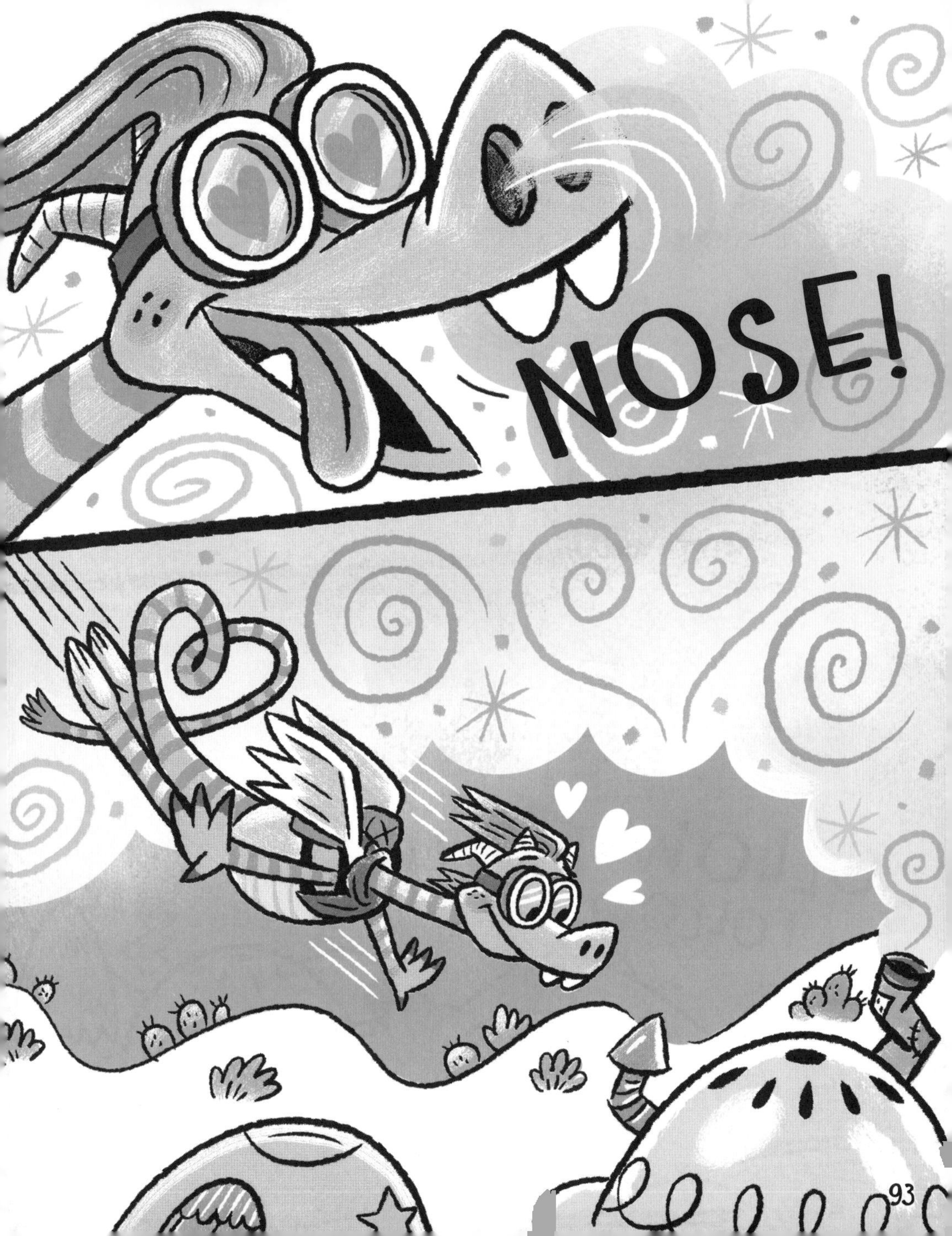
NOSE!

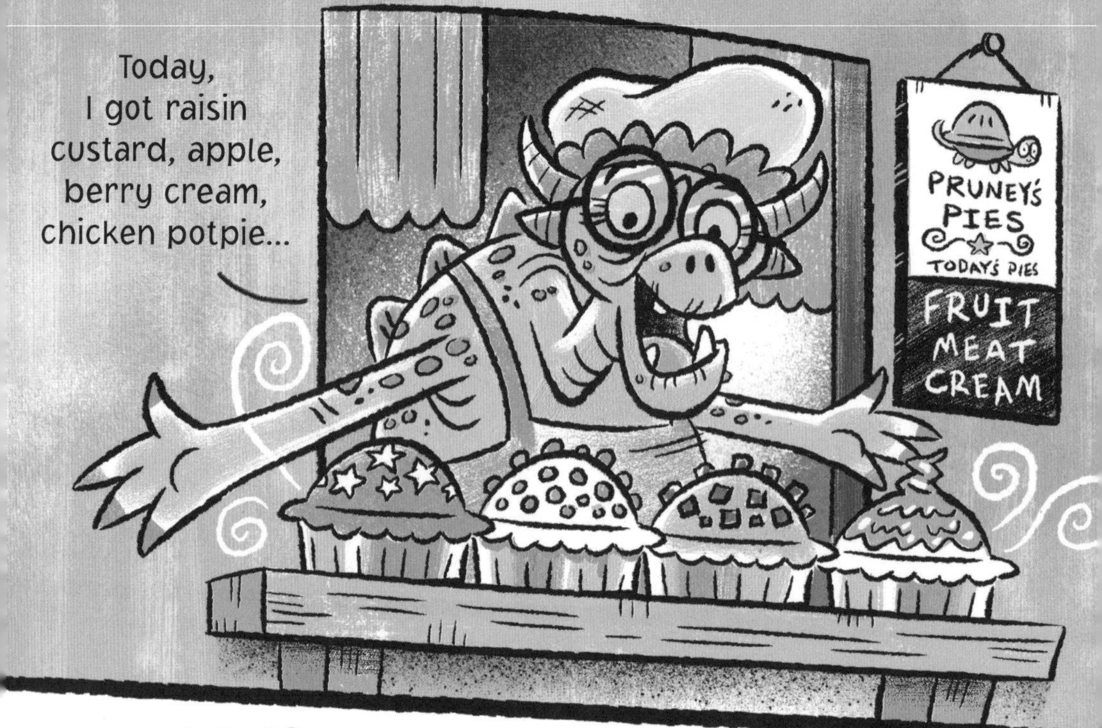
Today, I got raisin custard, apple, berry cream, chicken potpie...
PRUNEY'S PIES
TODAY'S PIES
FRUIT
MEAT
CREAM

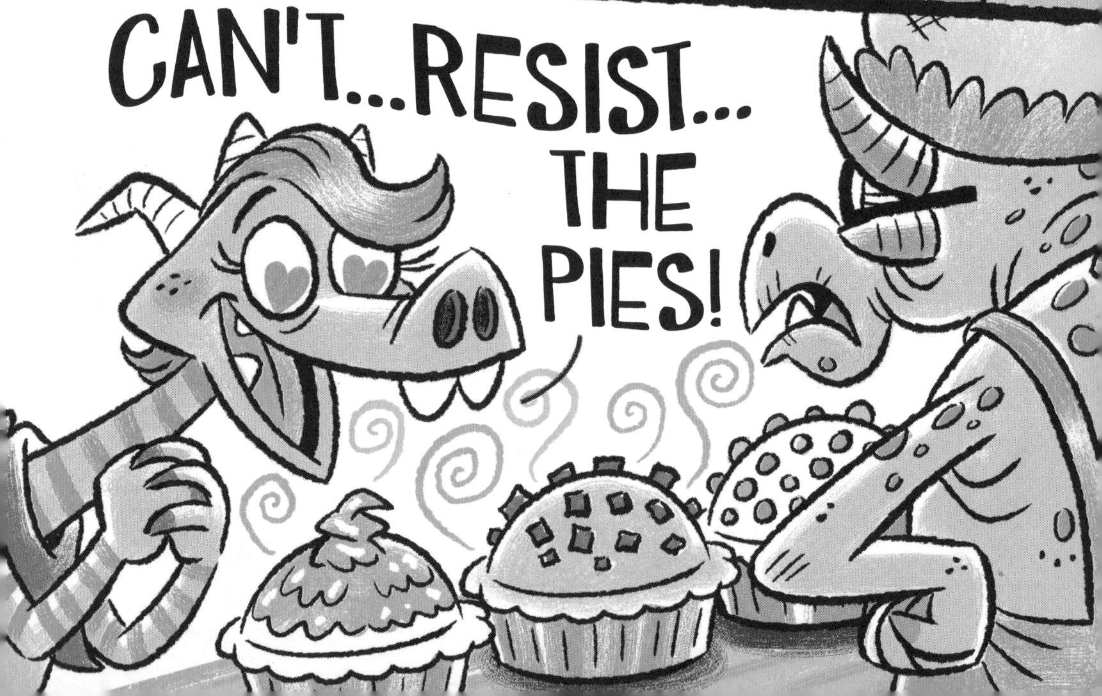
CAN'T...RESIST... THE PIES!

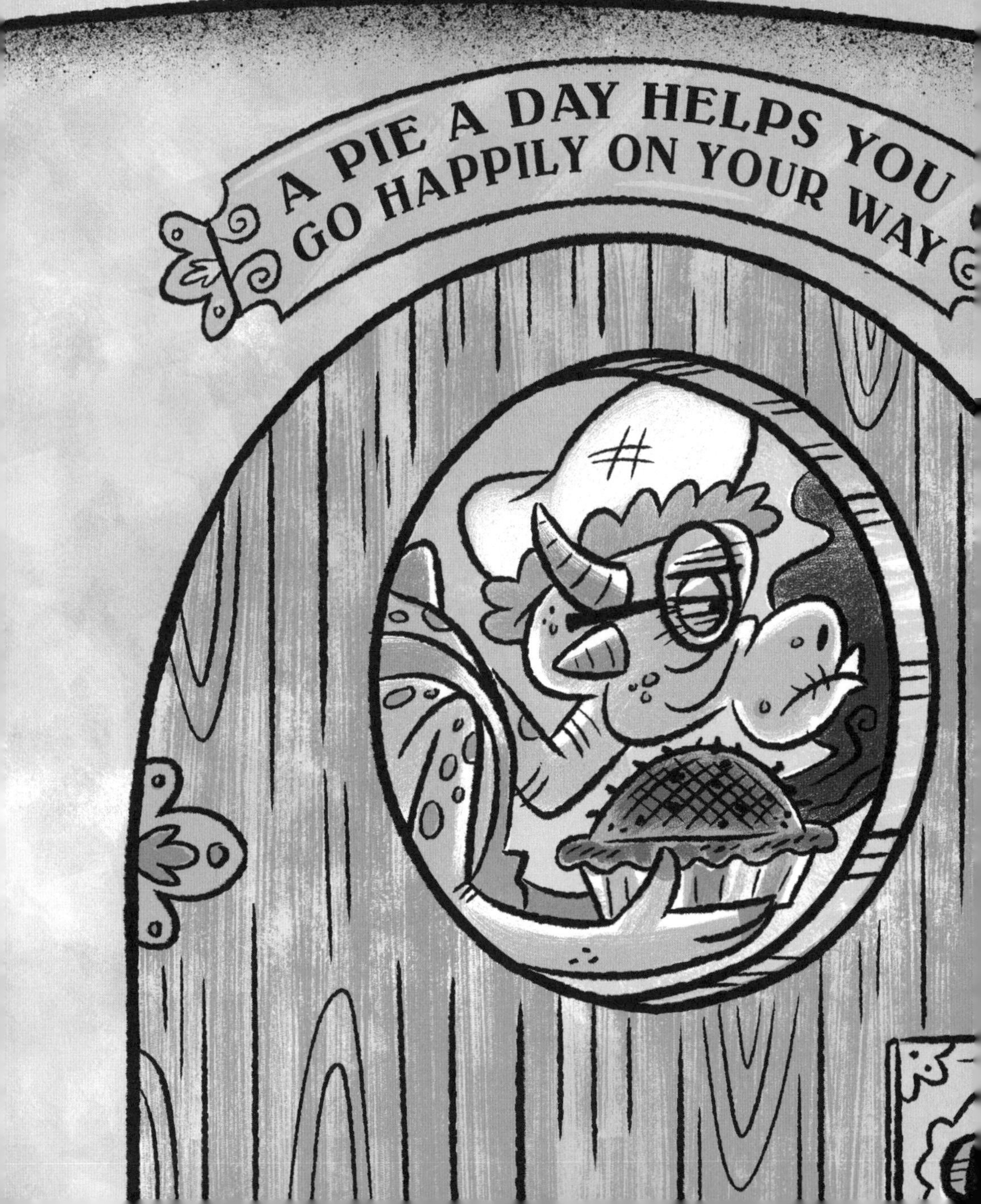
A PIE A DAY HELPS YOU
GO HAPPILY ON YOUR WAY

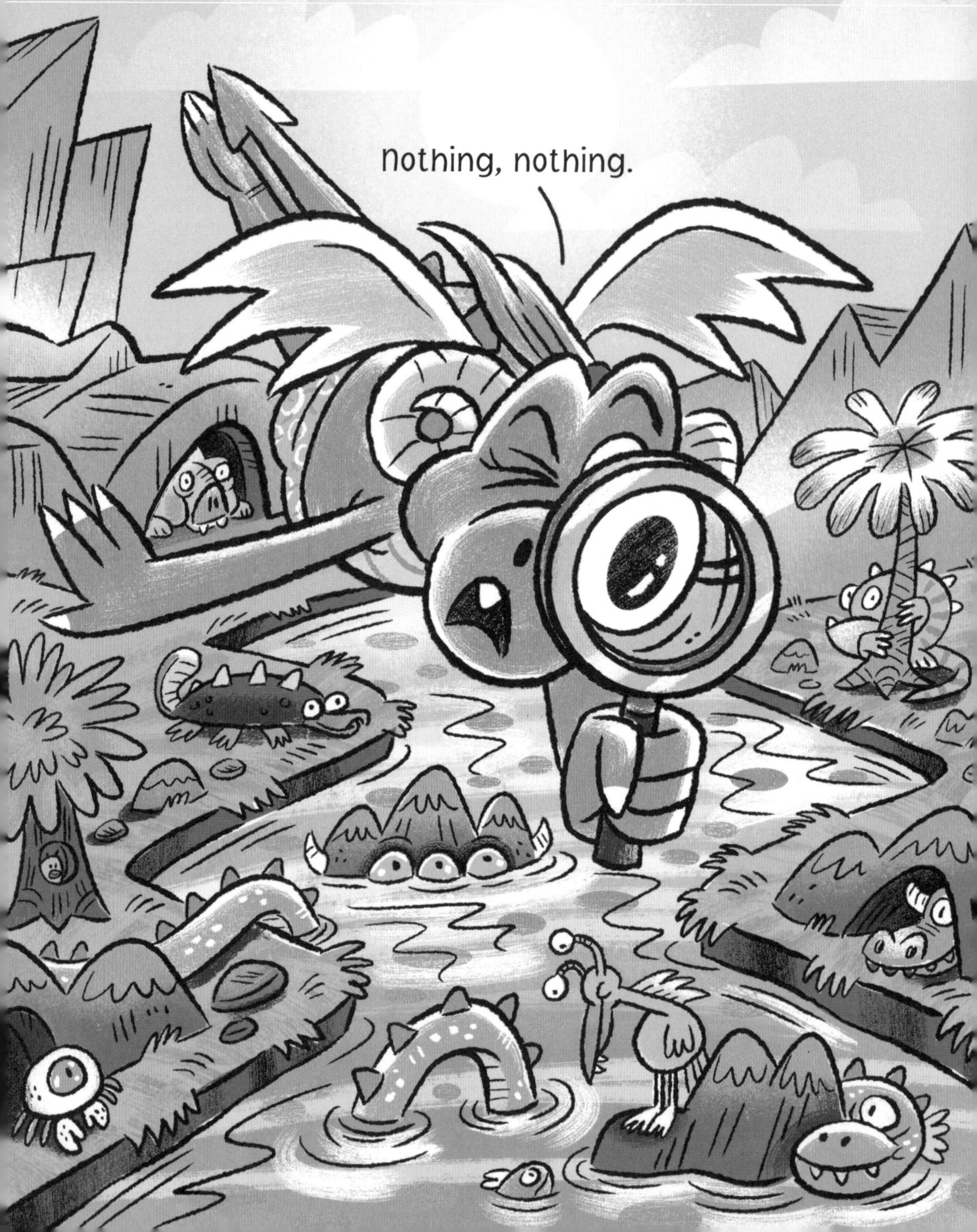
nothing, nothing.

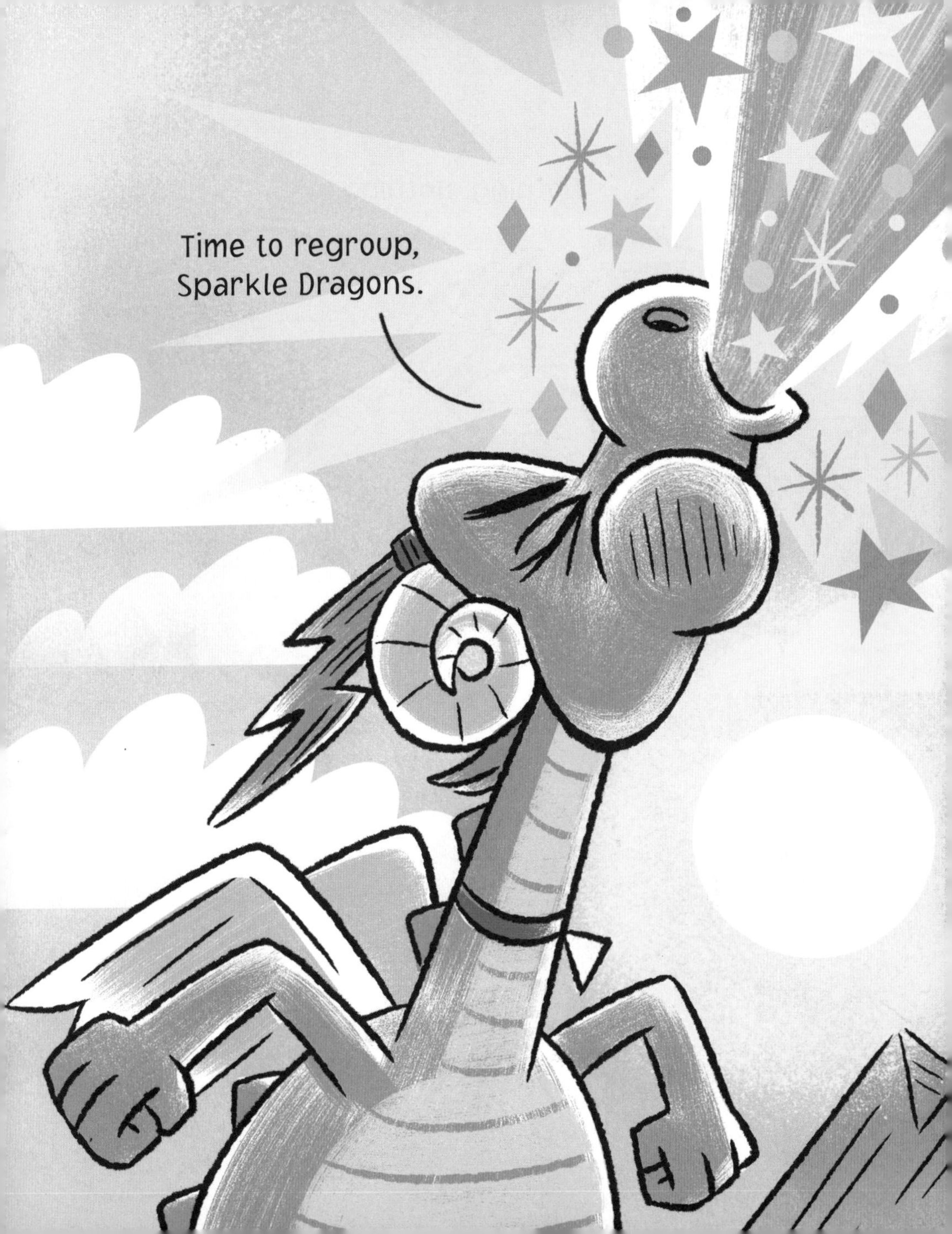
Time to regroup,
Sparkle Dragons.

CHAPTER SEVEN
FOLLOW THAT RAINBOW

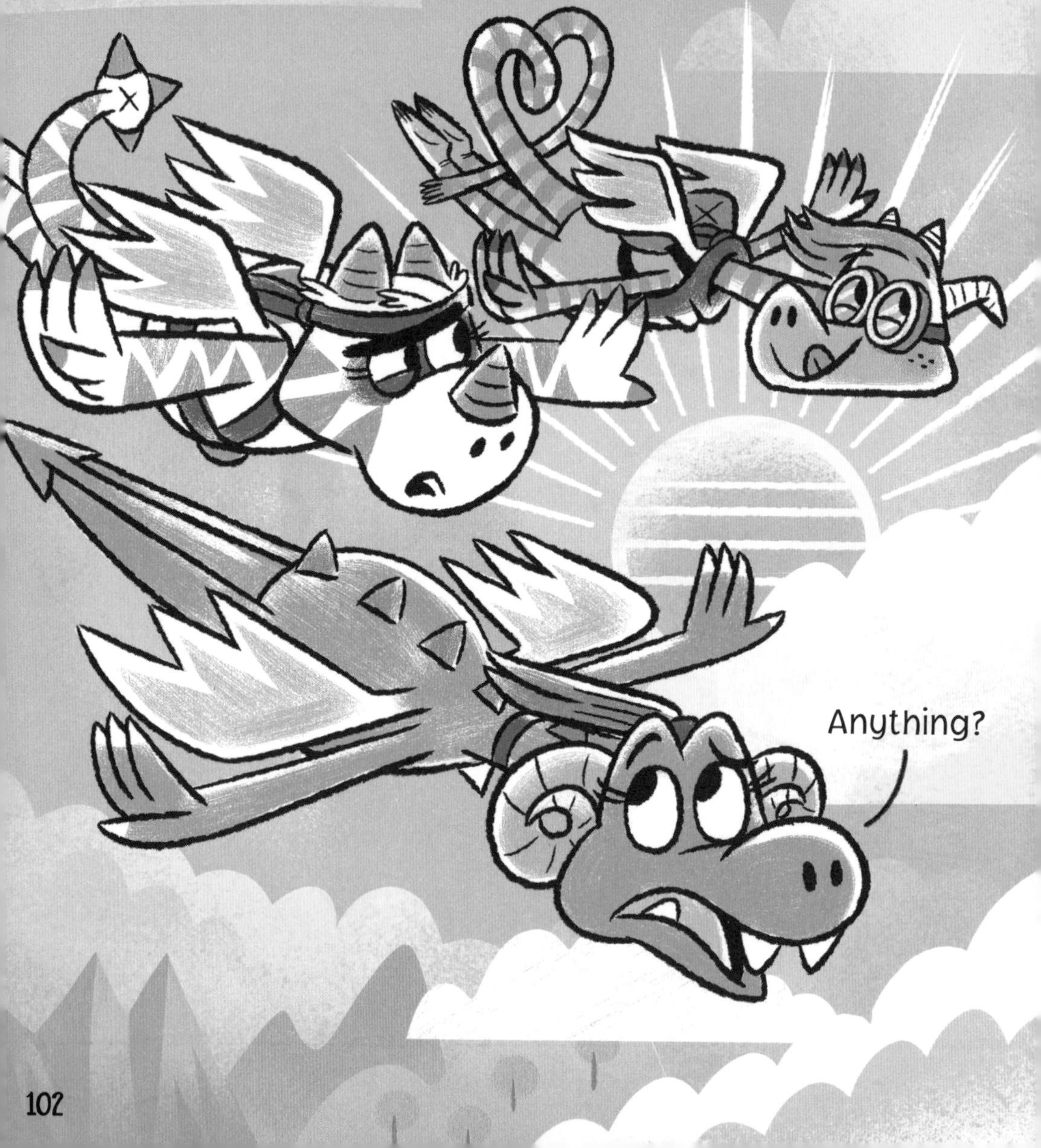
Anything?

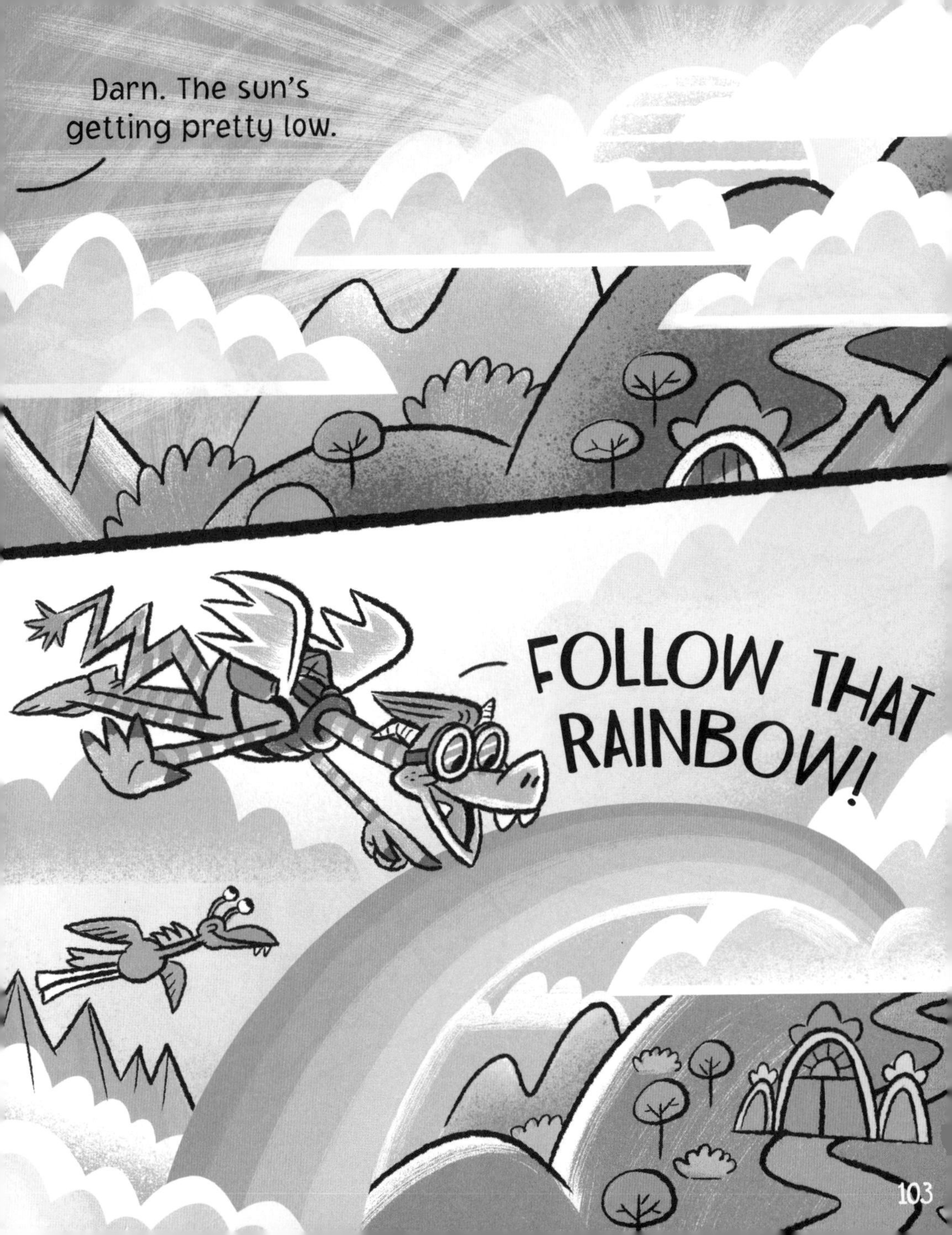
Darn. The sun's getting pretty low.
FOLLOW THAT RAINBOW!

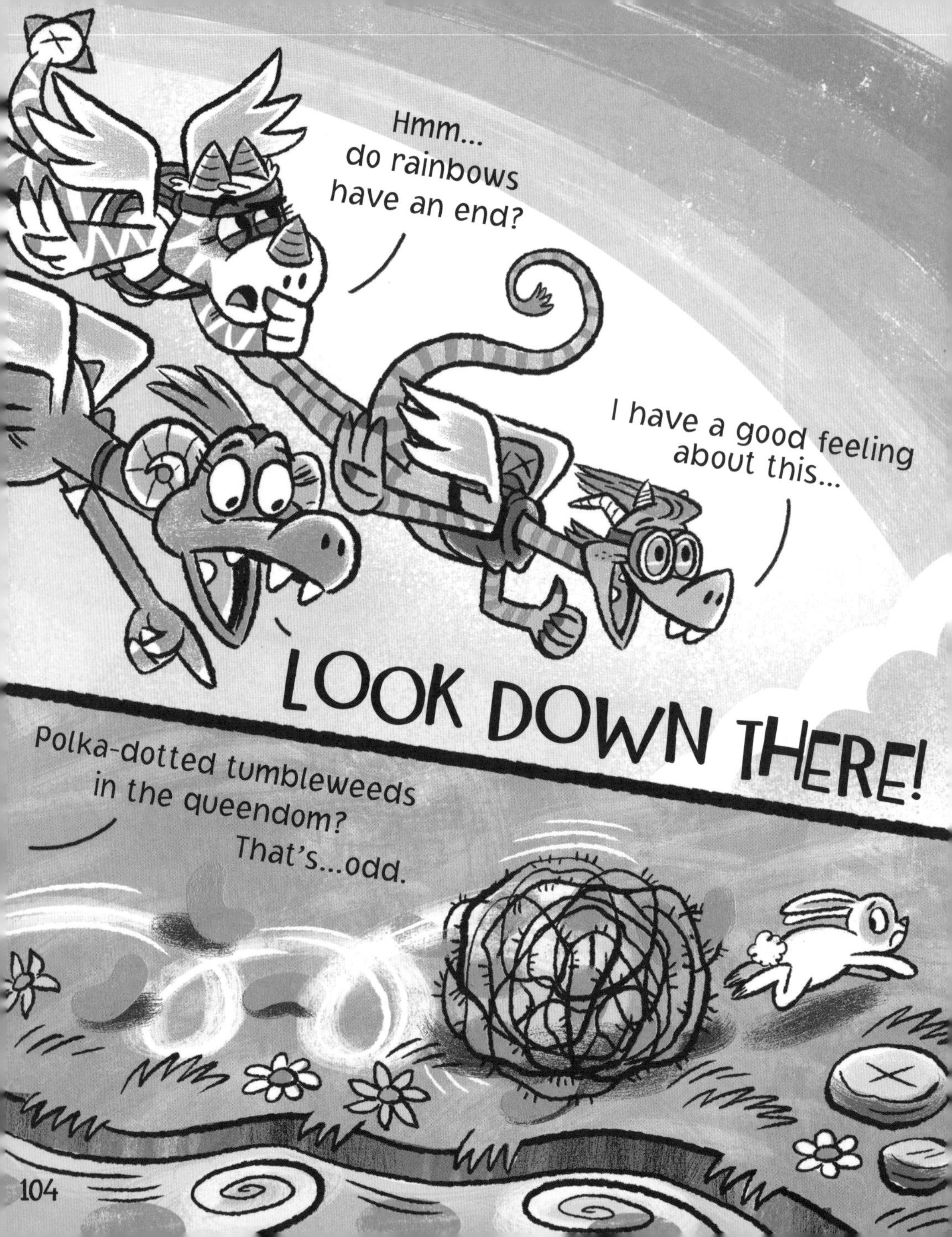
Hmm... do rainbows have an end?
I have a good feeling about this...
LOOK DOWN THERE!
Polka-dotted tumbleweeds in the queendom? That's...odd.

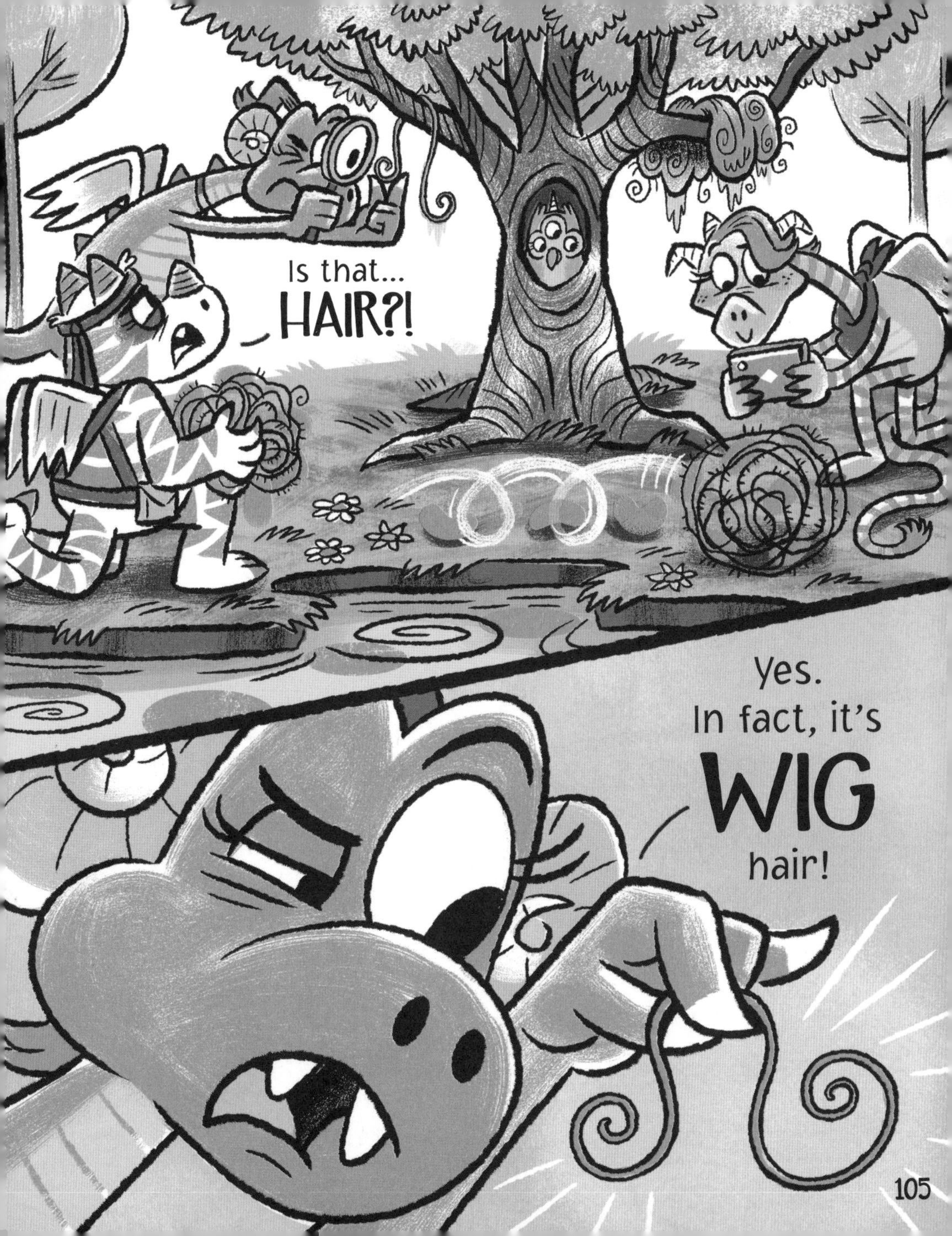
Is that...
HAIR?!
Yes.
In fact, it's
WIG
hair!

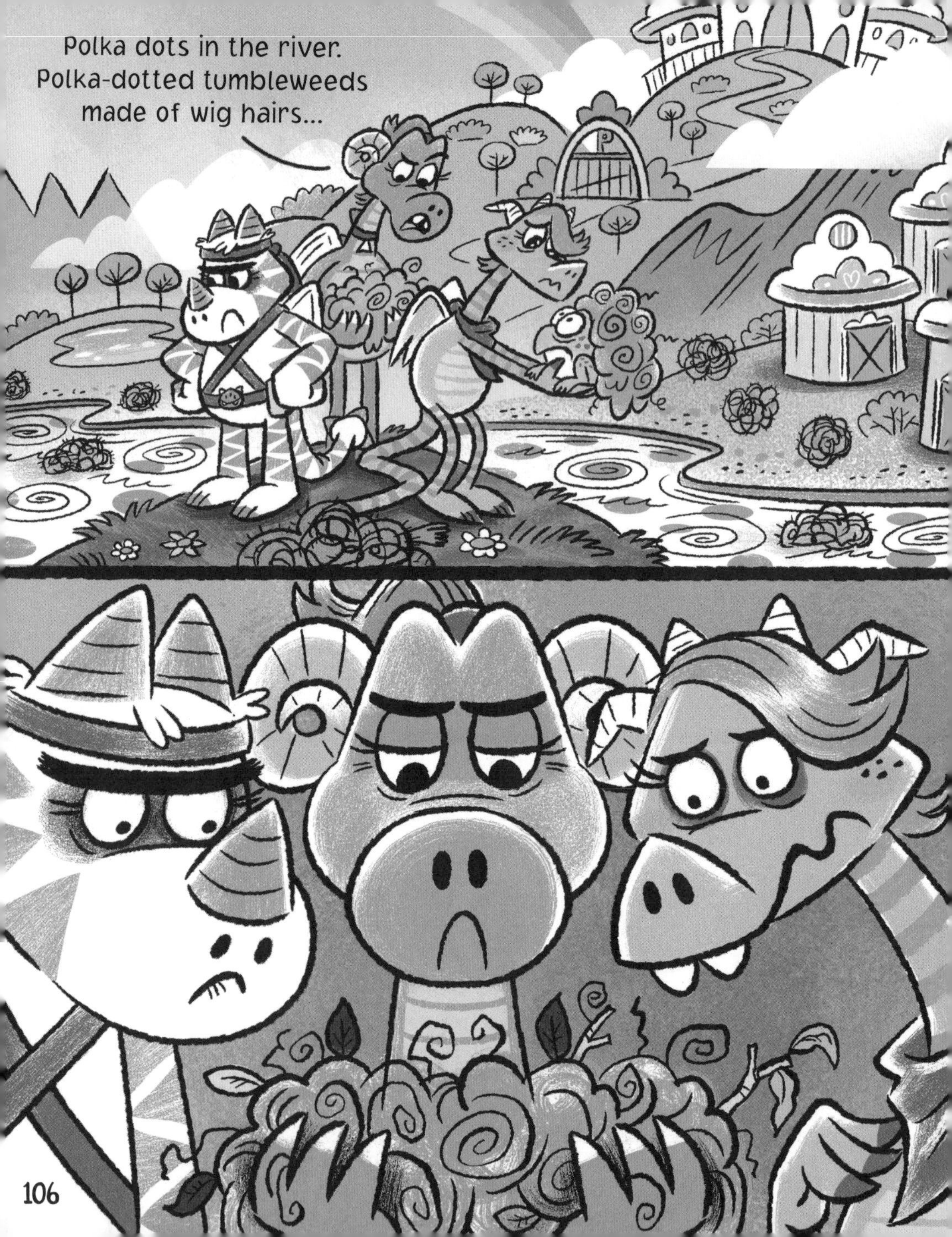
Polka dots in the river.
Polka-dotted tumbleweeds
made of wig hairs...

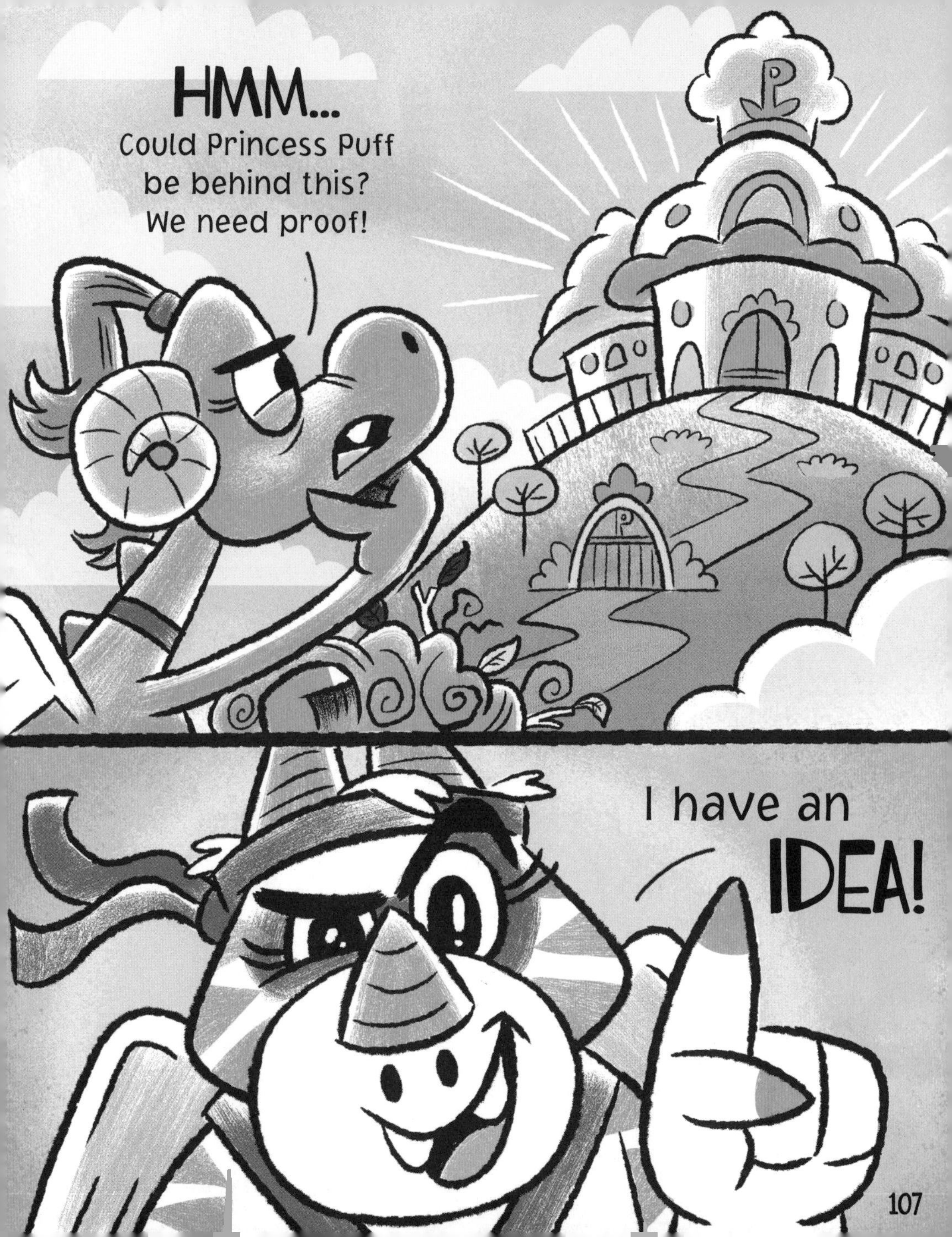
HMM...
Could Princess Puff be behind this? We need proof!
I have an IDEA!

CHAPTER EIGHT
THE UNINVITED GUEST

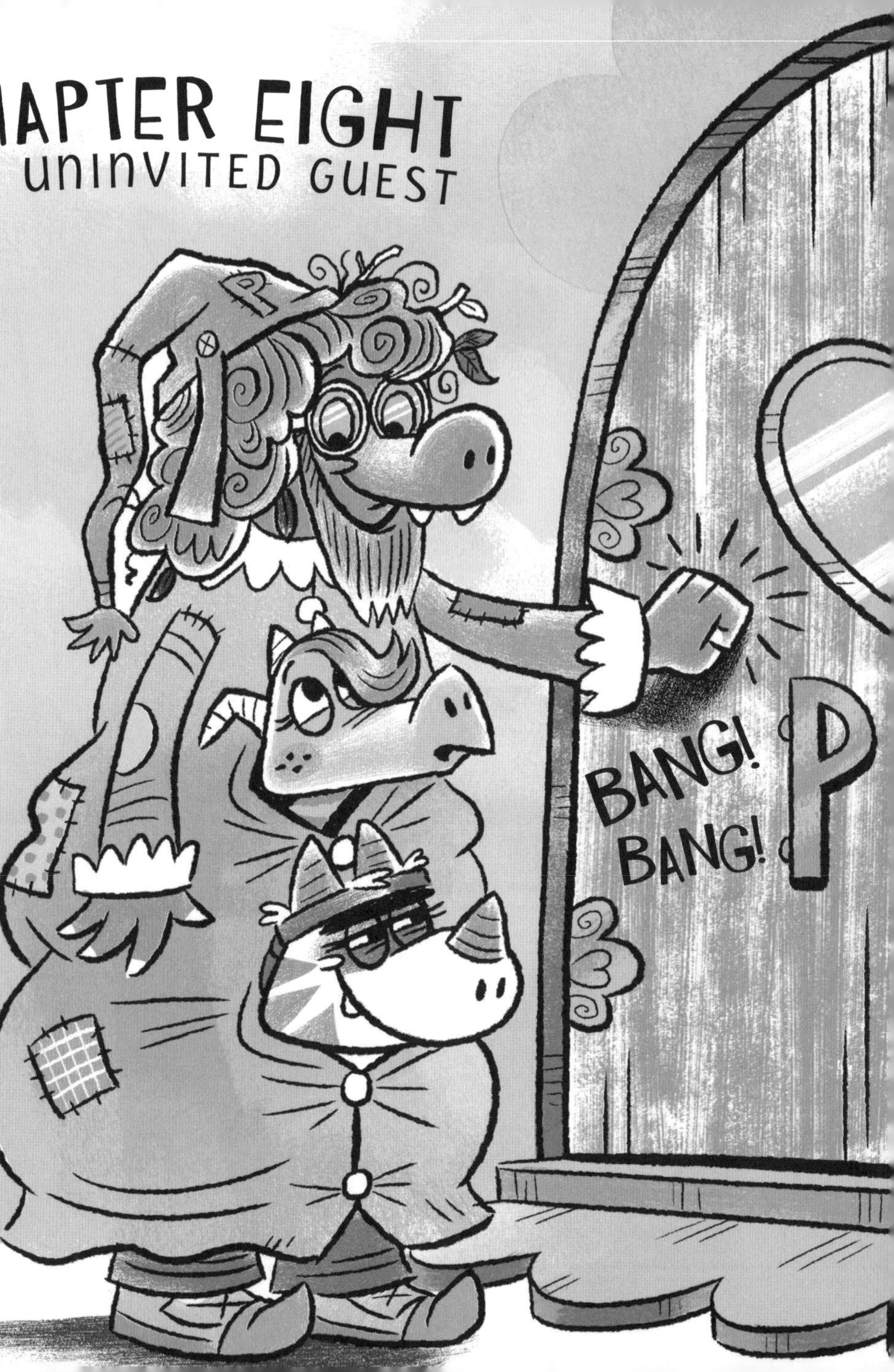
BANG!
BANG!

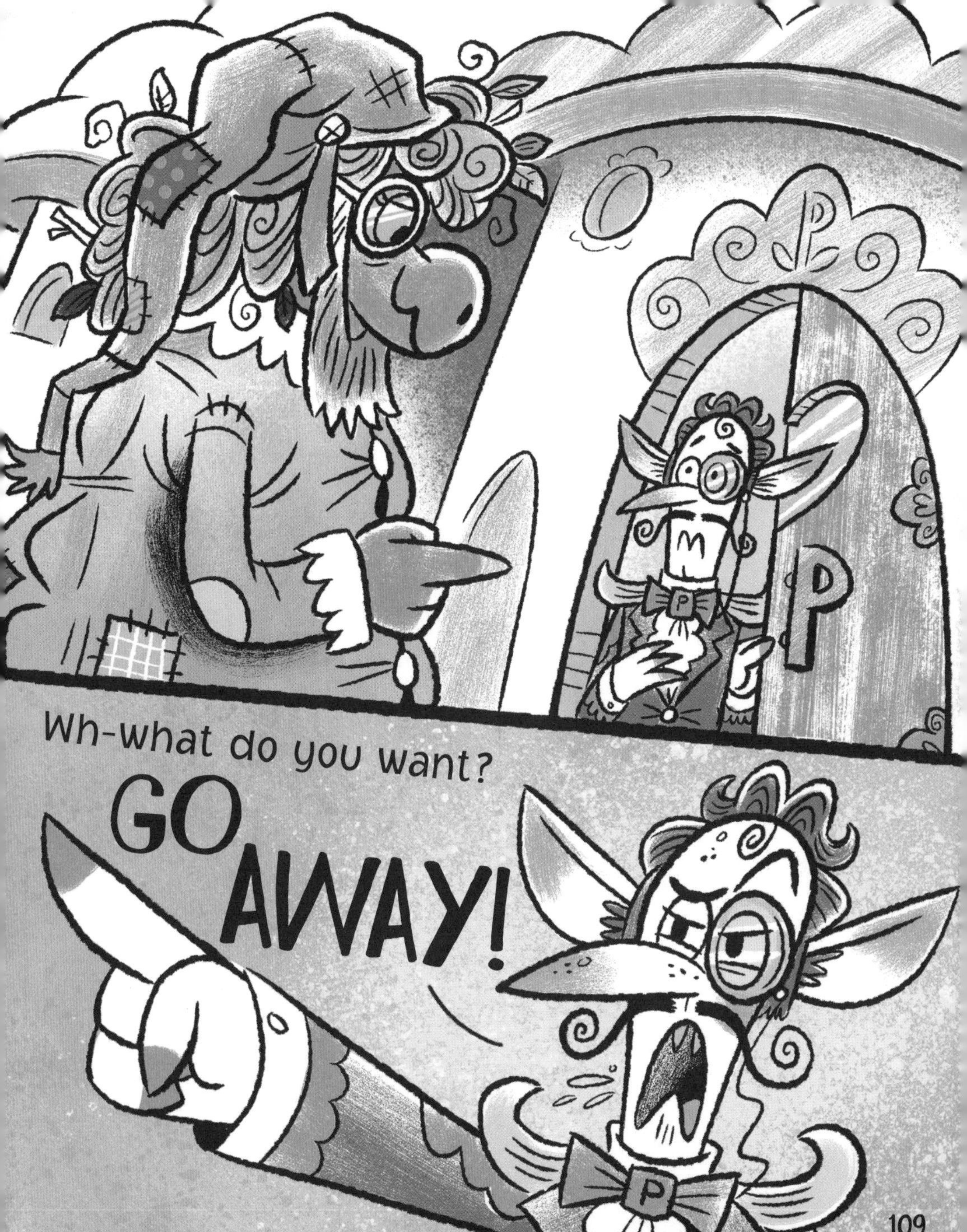

Wh-what do you want?
GO AWAY!

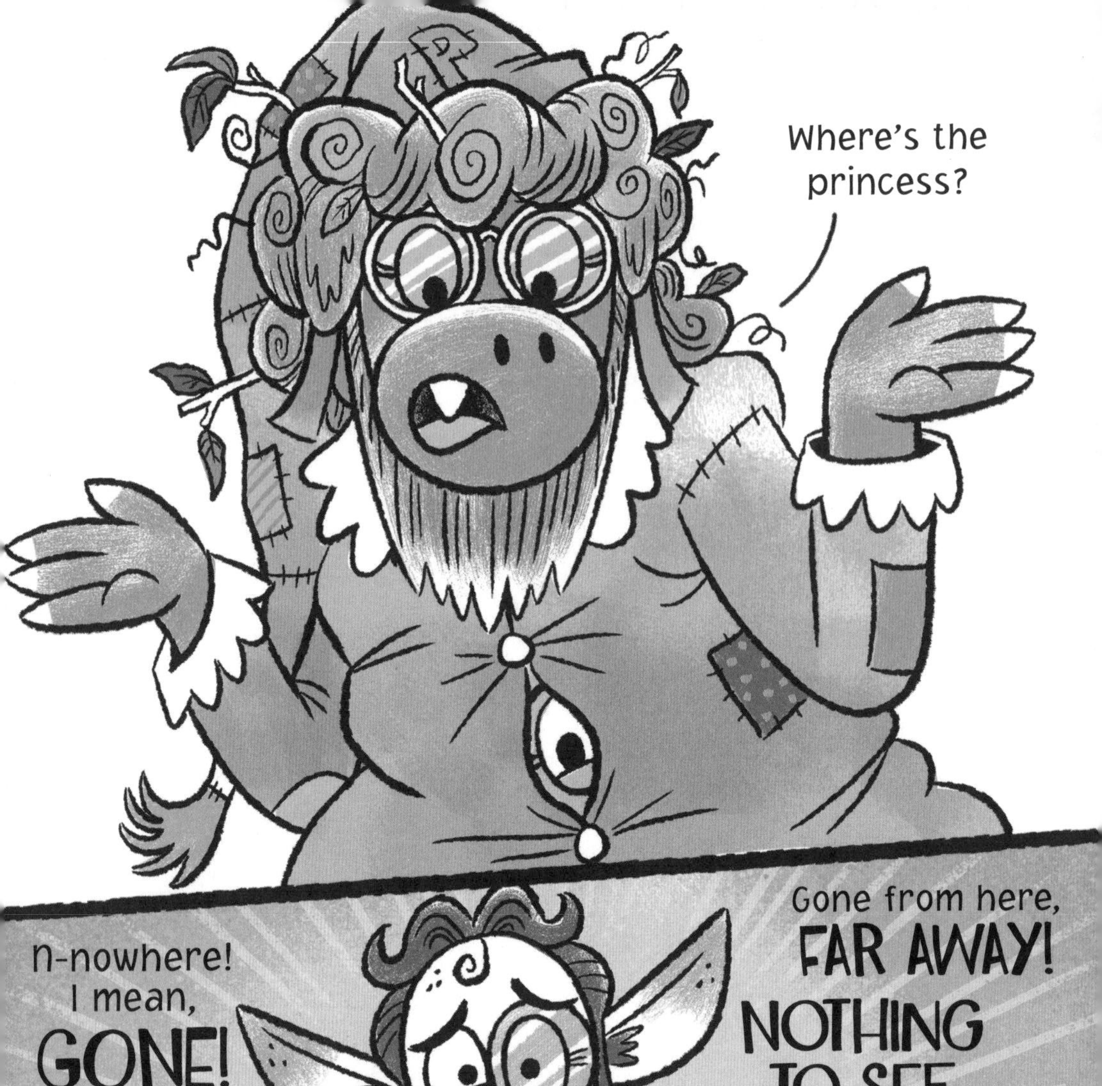
Where's the princess?

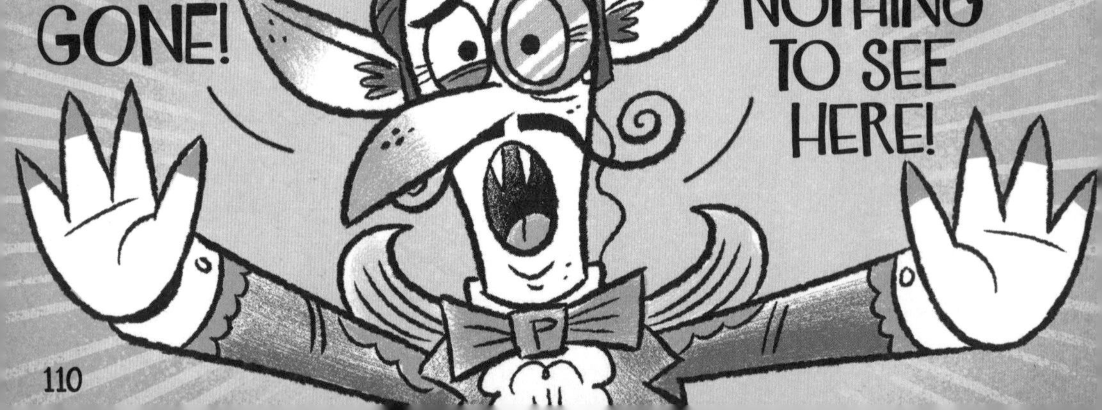
N-nowhere! I mean, GONE!
Gone from here, FAR AWAY!
NOTHING TO SEE HERE!

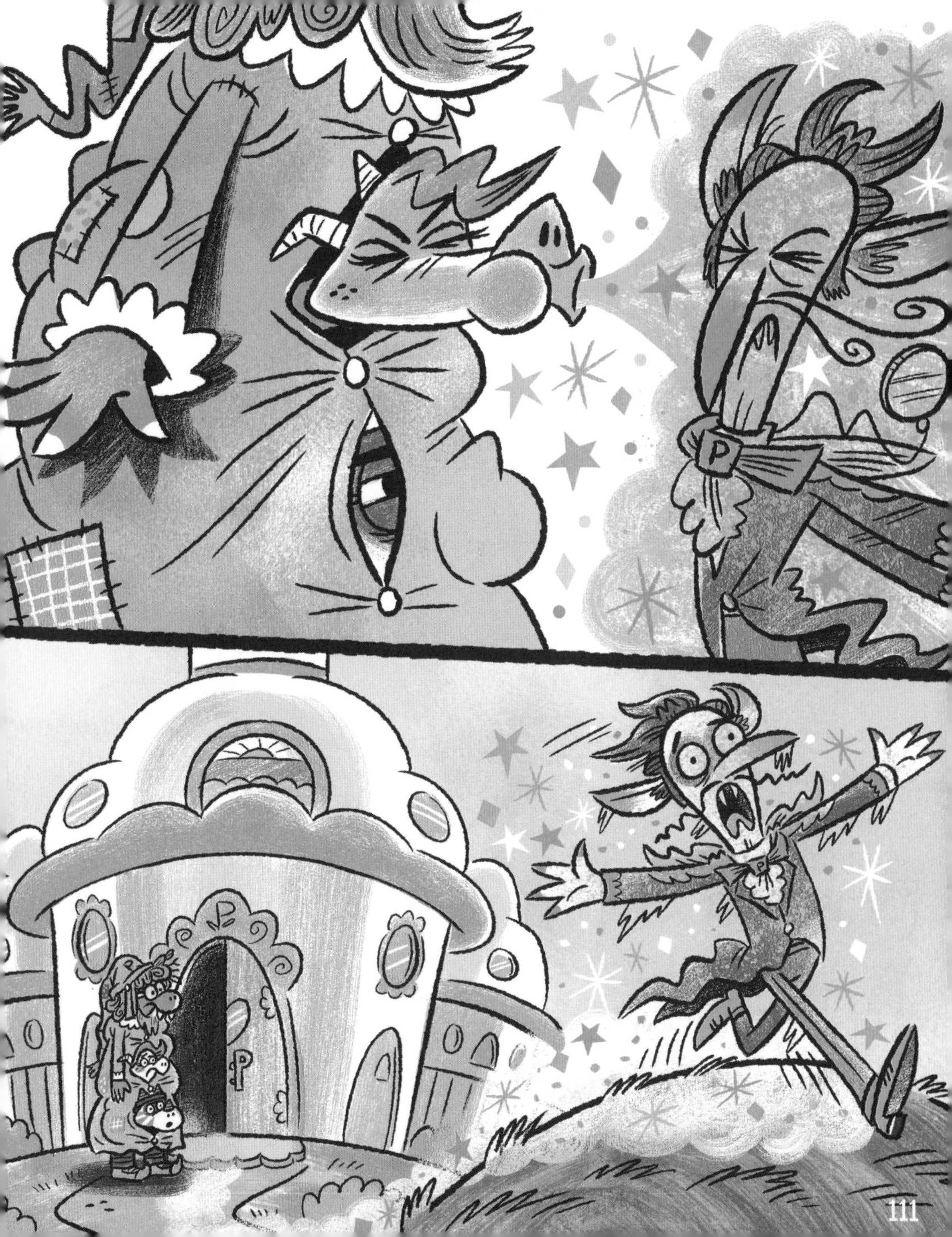

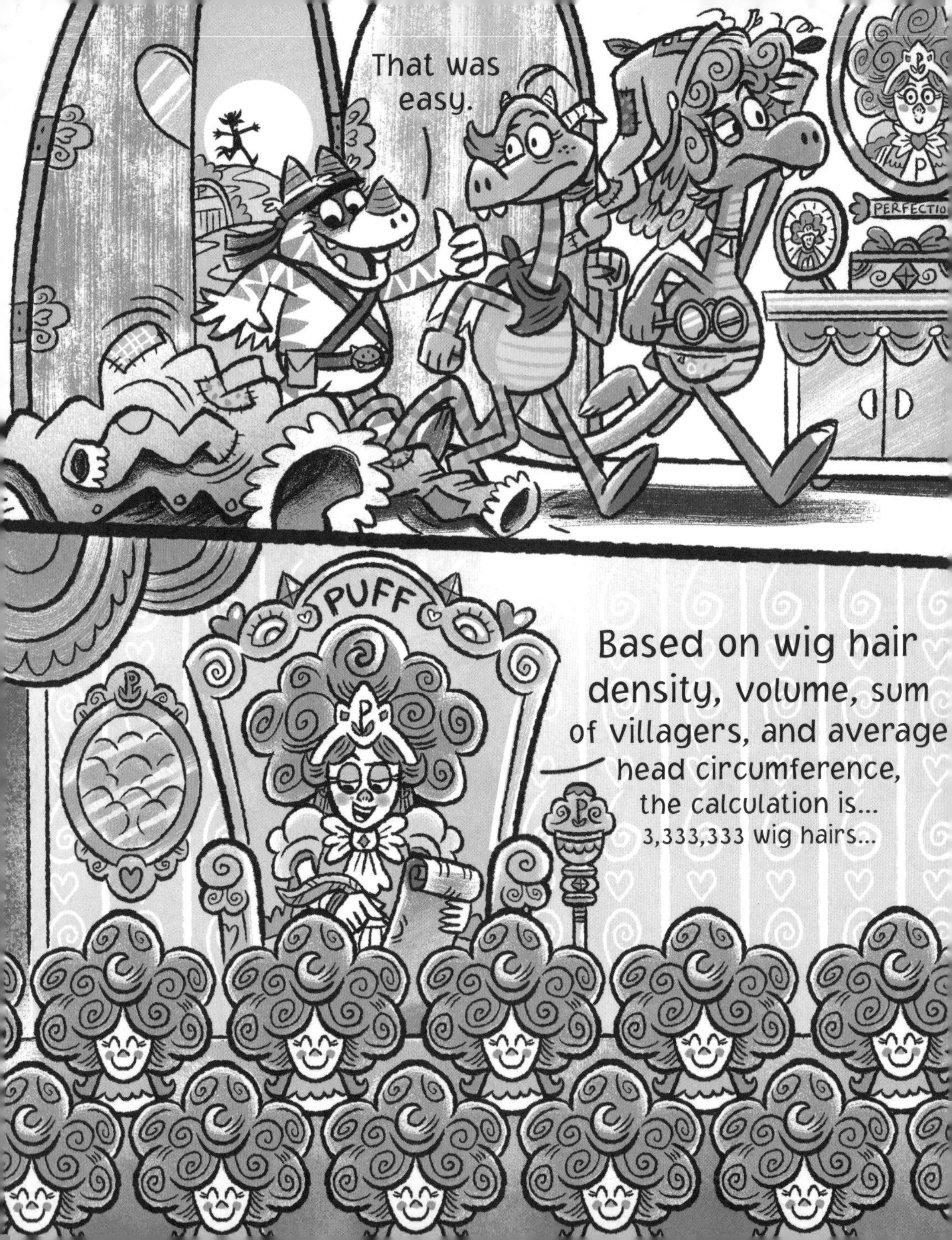
That was easy.
PERFECTION
PUFF
Based on wig hair density, volume, sum of villagers, and average head circumference, the calculation is... 3,333,333 wig hairs...

113

CHAPTER NINE
HER PUFFINESS IS...DEFLATED.

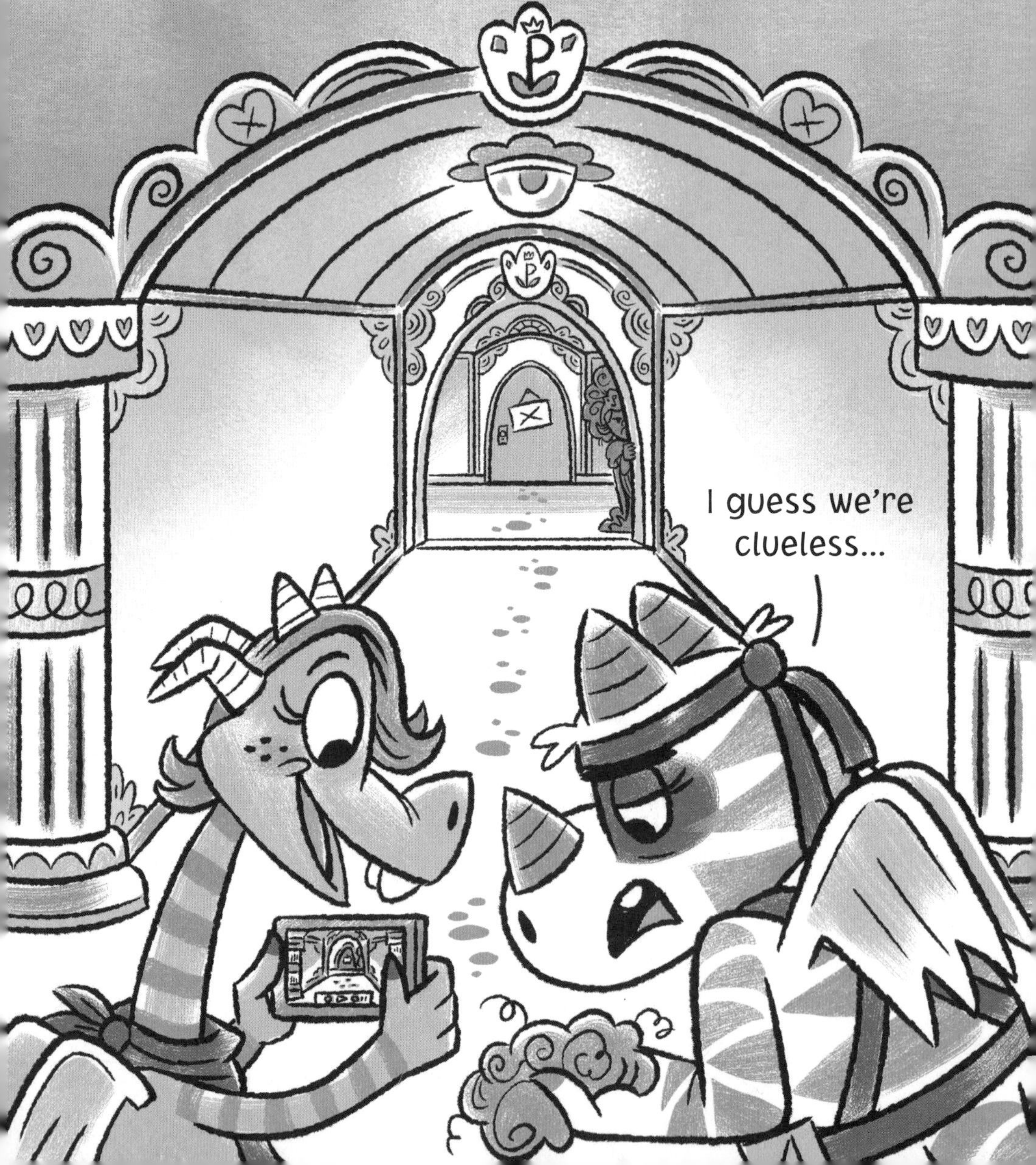
I guess we're clueless...

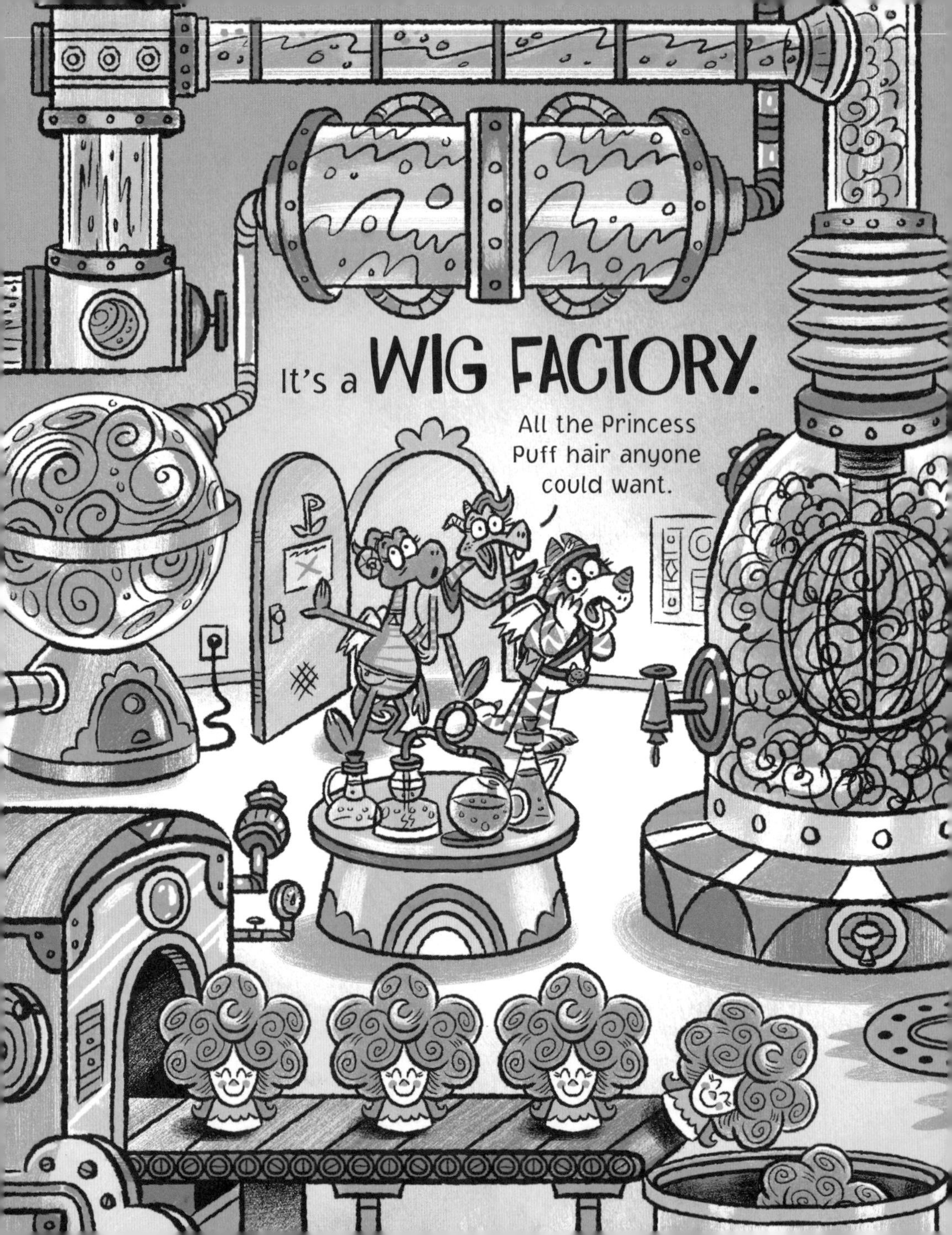
It's a WIG FACTORY.
All the Princess Puff hair anyone could want.

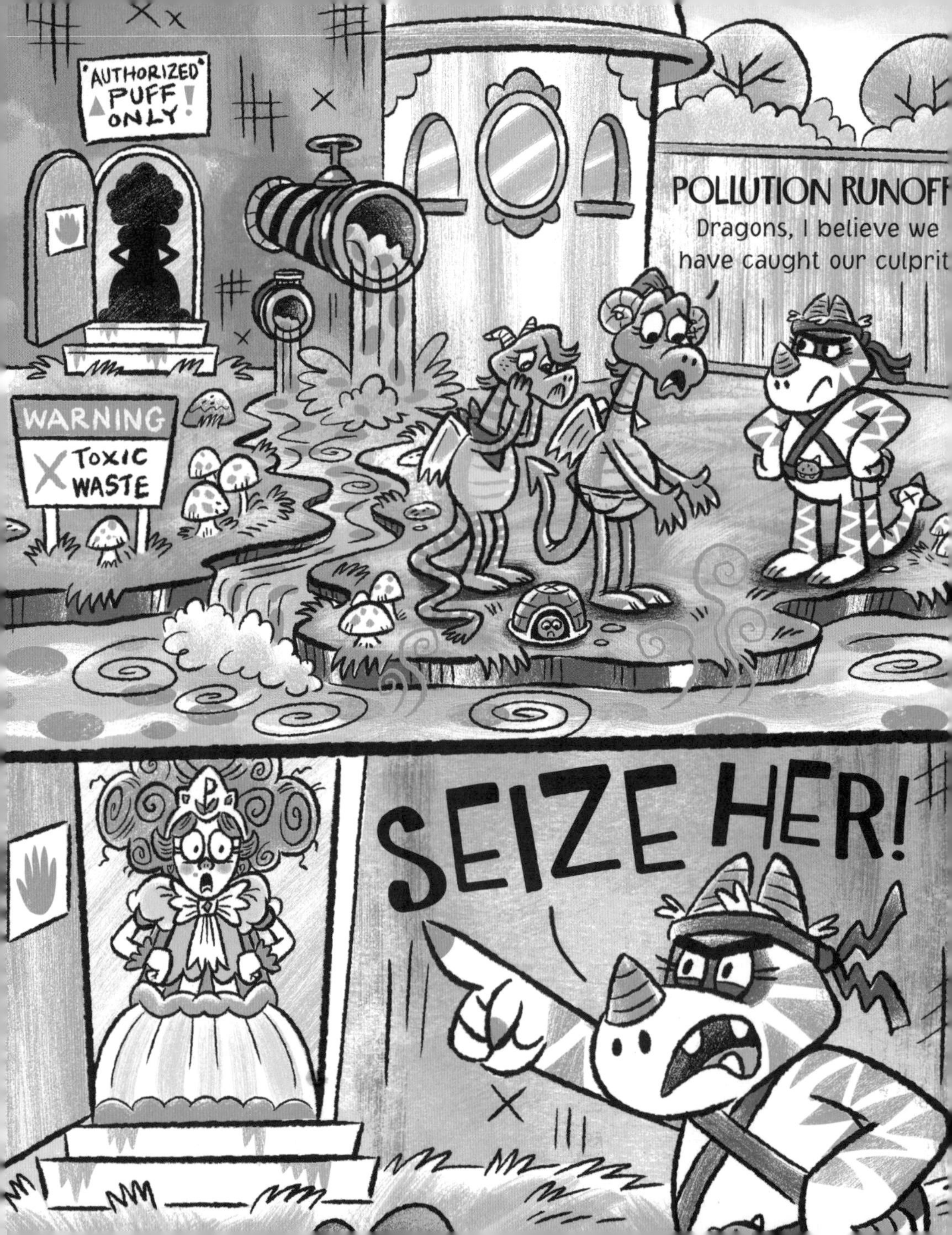

"AUTHORIZED"
PUFF
ONLY!
POLLUTION RUNOFF
WARNING
TOXIC
WASTE
Dragons, I believe we have caught our culprit
SEIZE HER!

You don't understand!

I'M INNOCENT!

The Sparkle Dragons promised to be back by sunset—

129

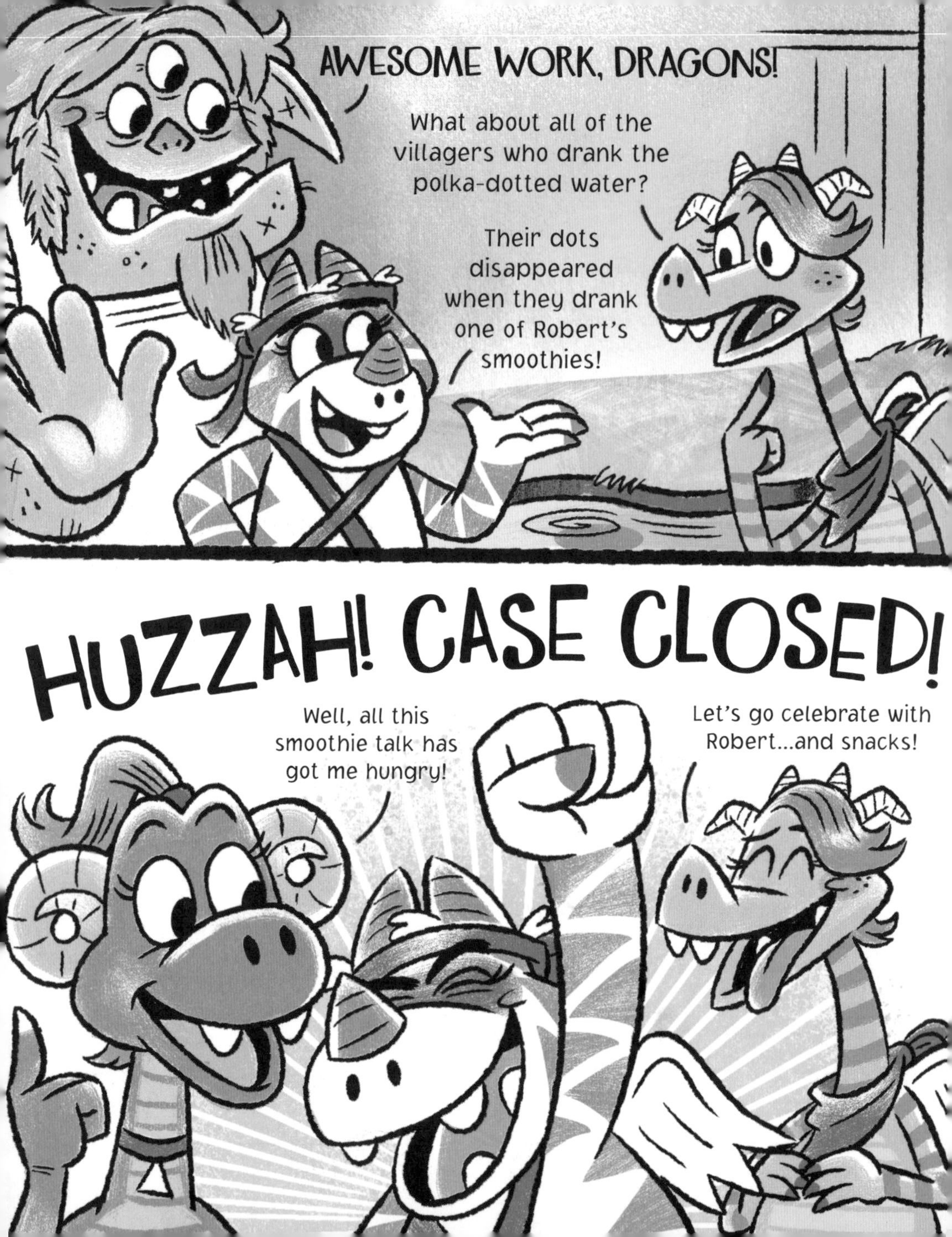
AWESOME WORK, DRAGONS!
What about all of the villagers who drank the polka-dotted water?
Their dots disappeared when they drank one of Robert's smoothies!
HUZZAH! CASE CLOSED!
Well, all this smoothie talk has got me hungry!
Let's go celebrate with Robert...and snacks!

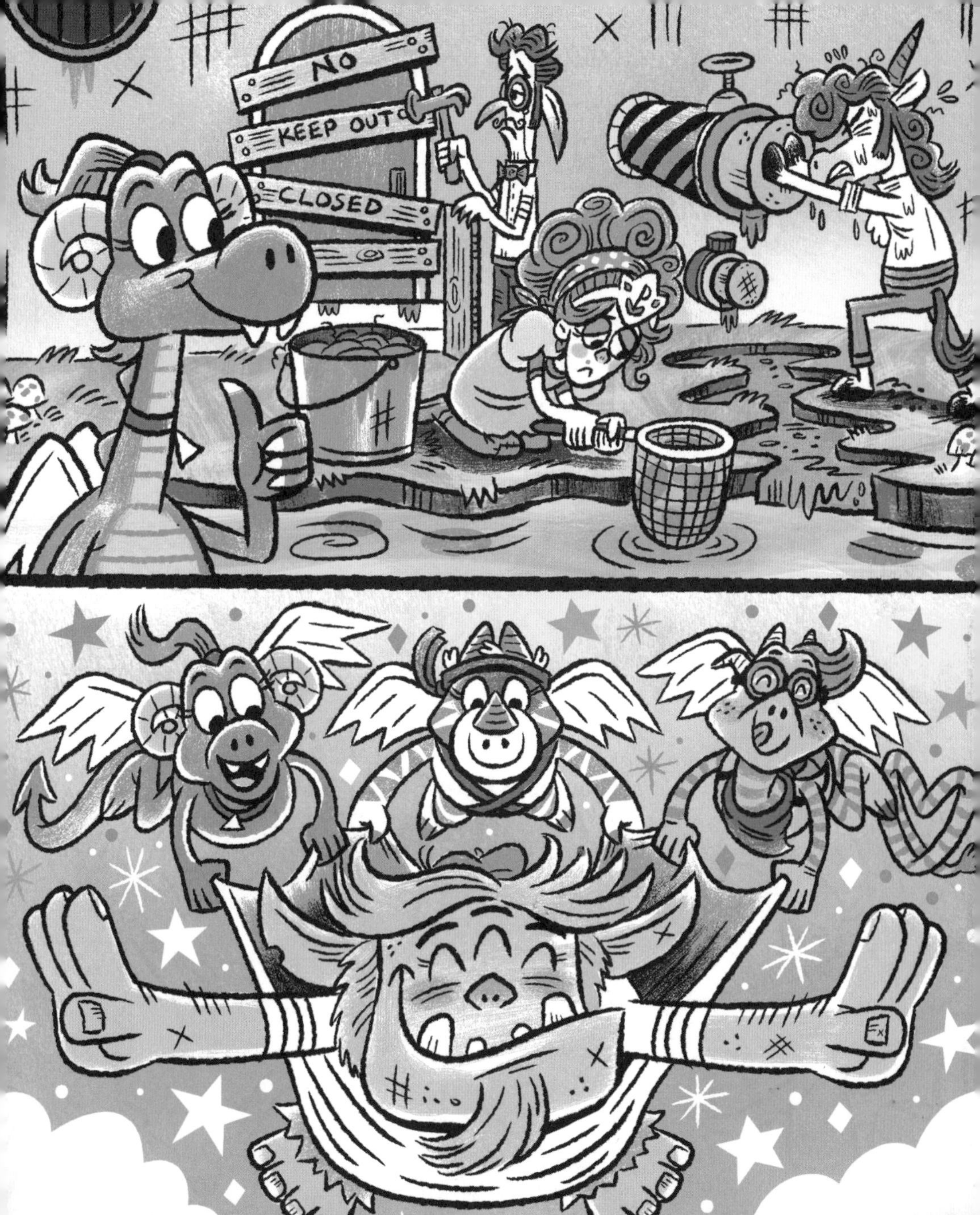
NO
KEEP OUT
CLOSED

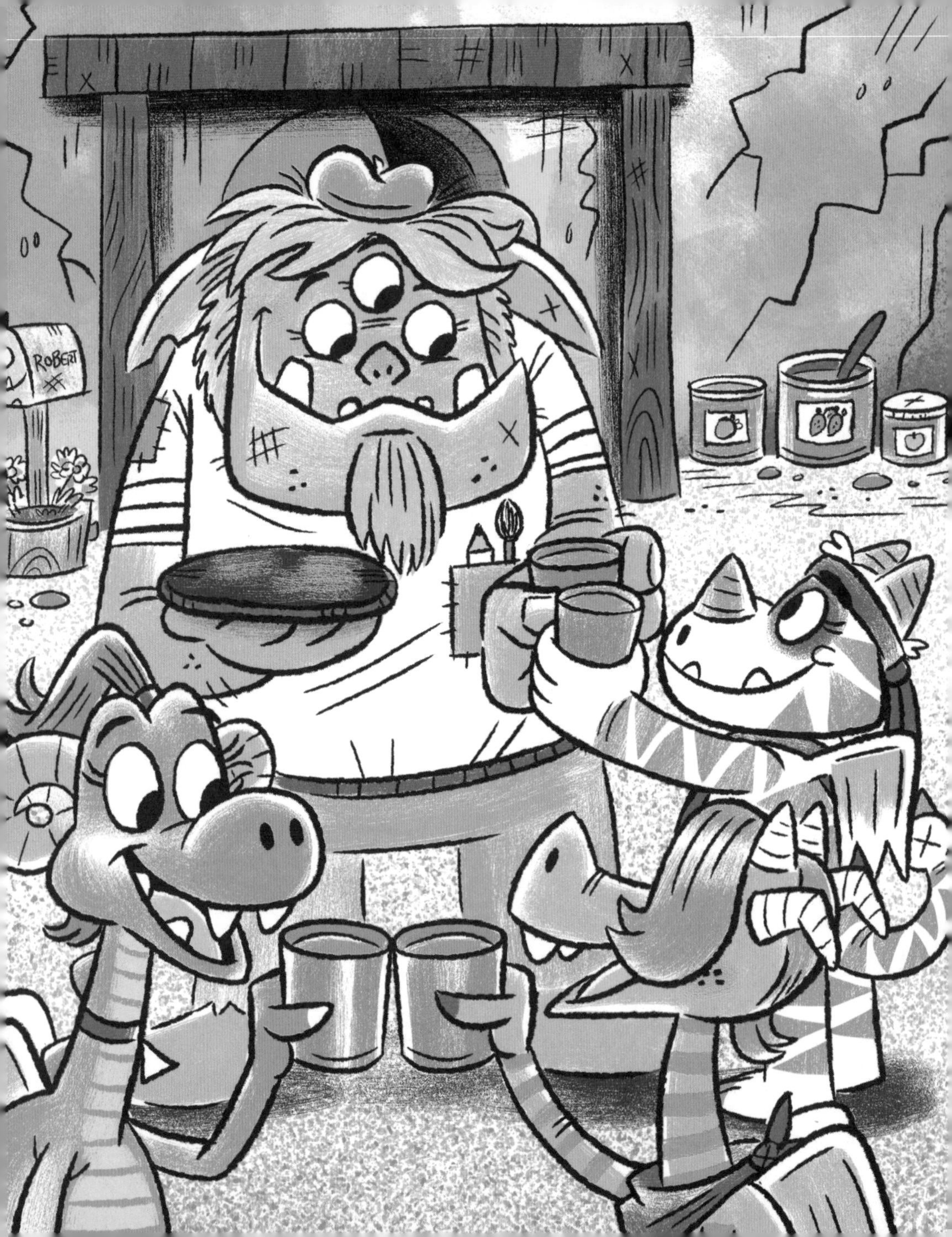
ROBERT

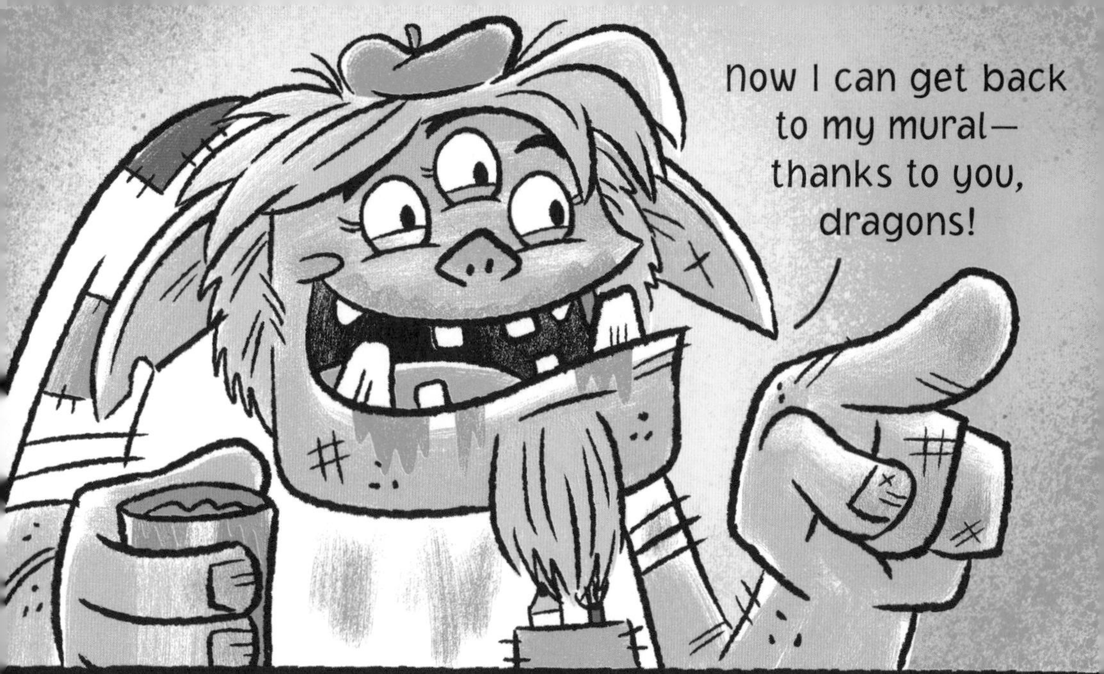
Now I can get back to my mural—thanks to you, dragons!

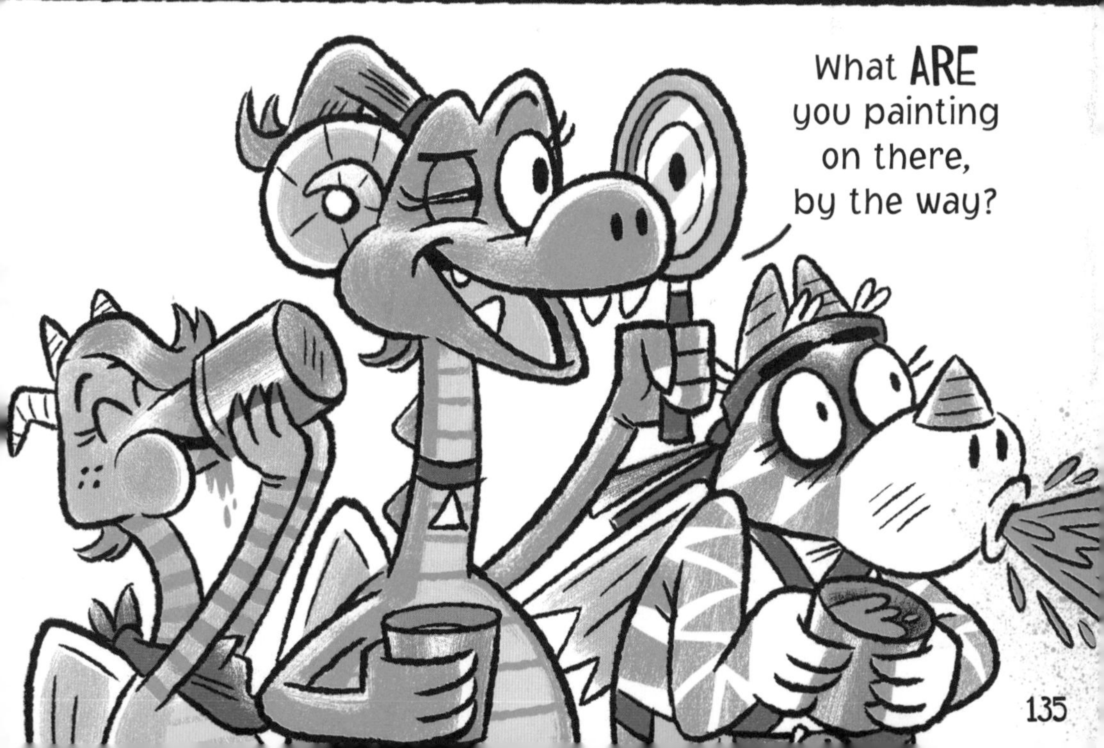
What ARE you painting on there, by the way?

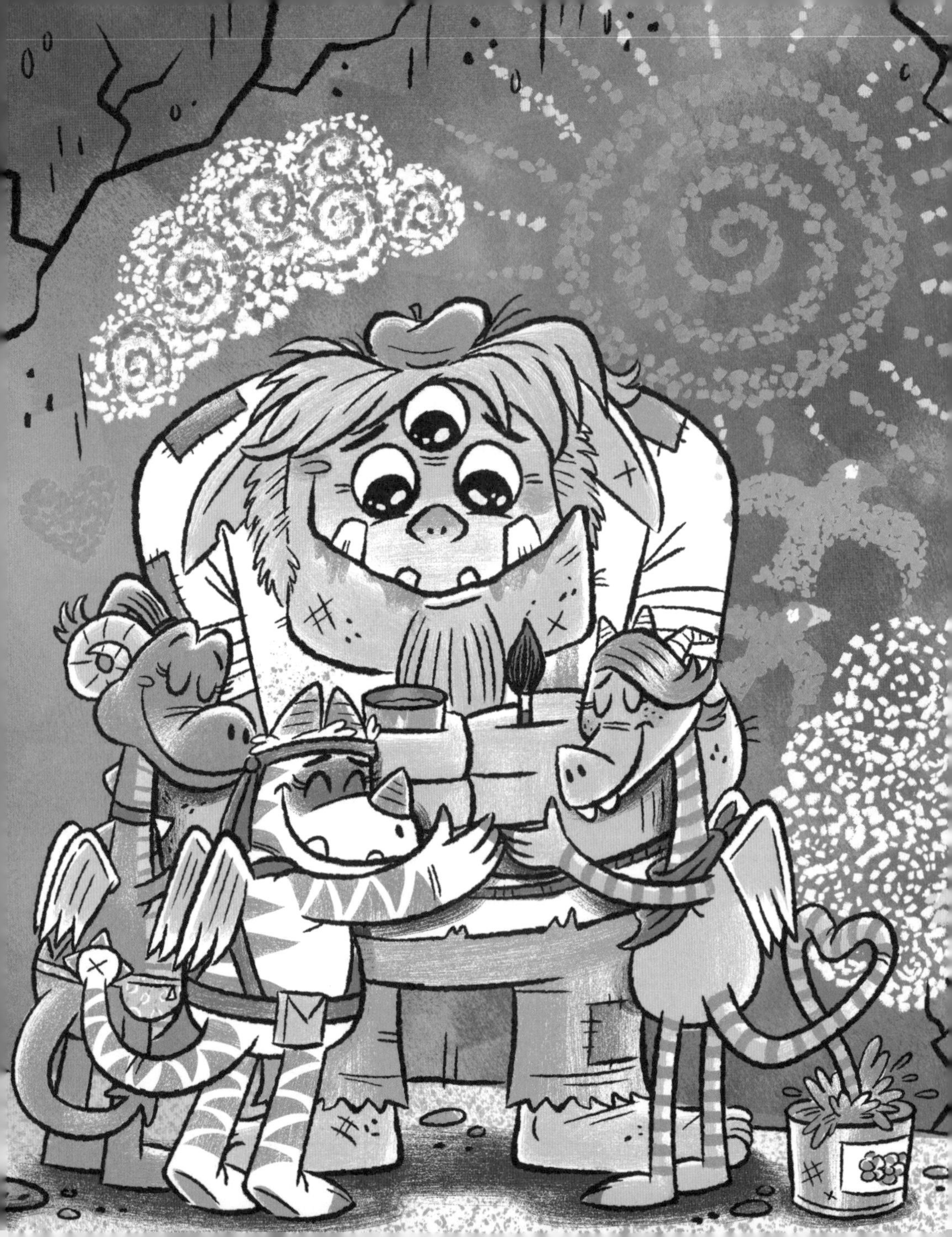

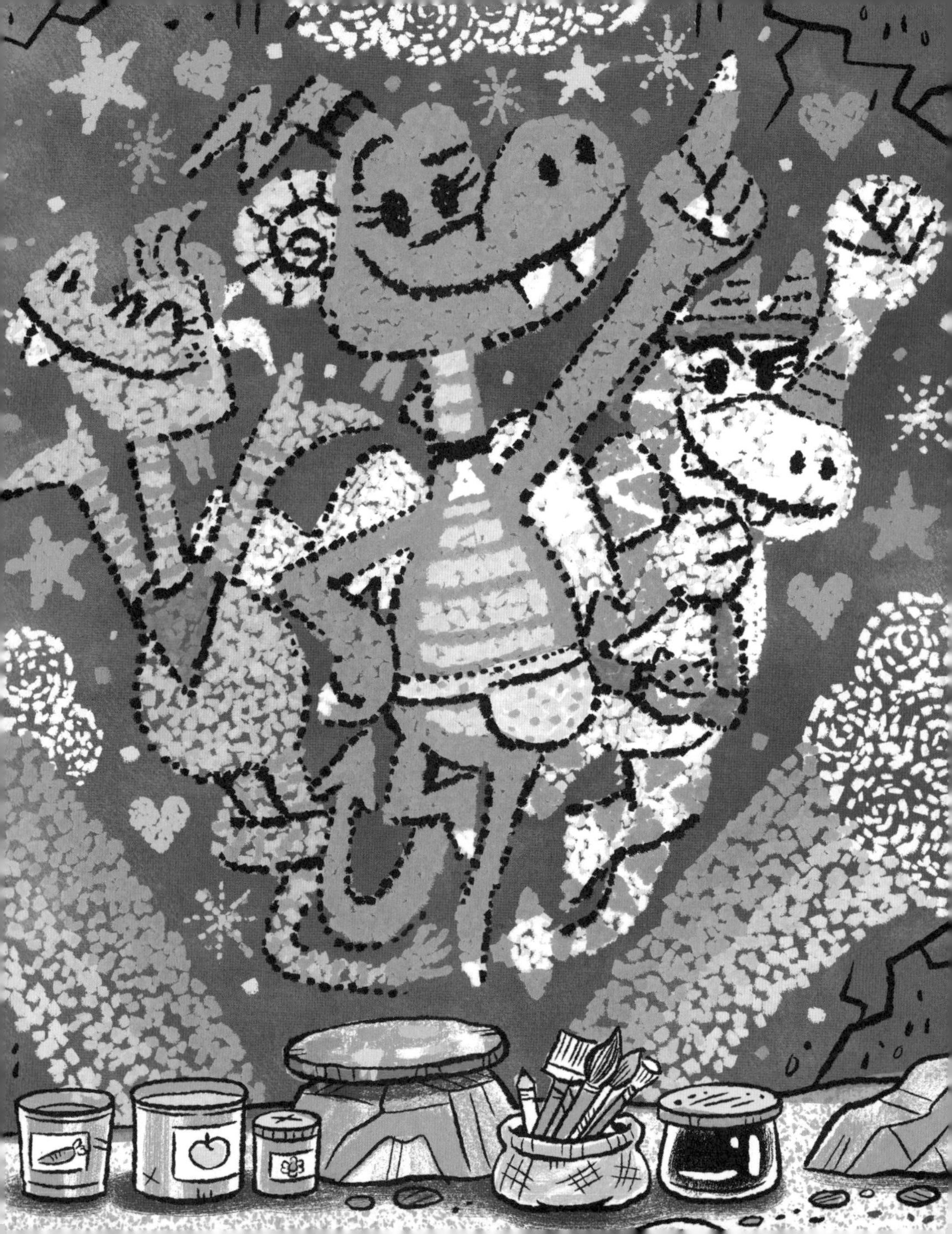

CHAPTER ELEVEN
RAIN RIVER RENEWED

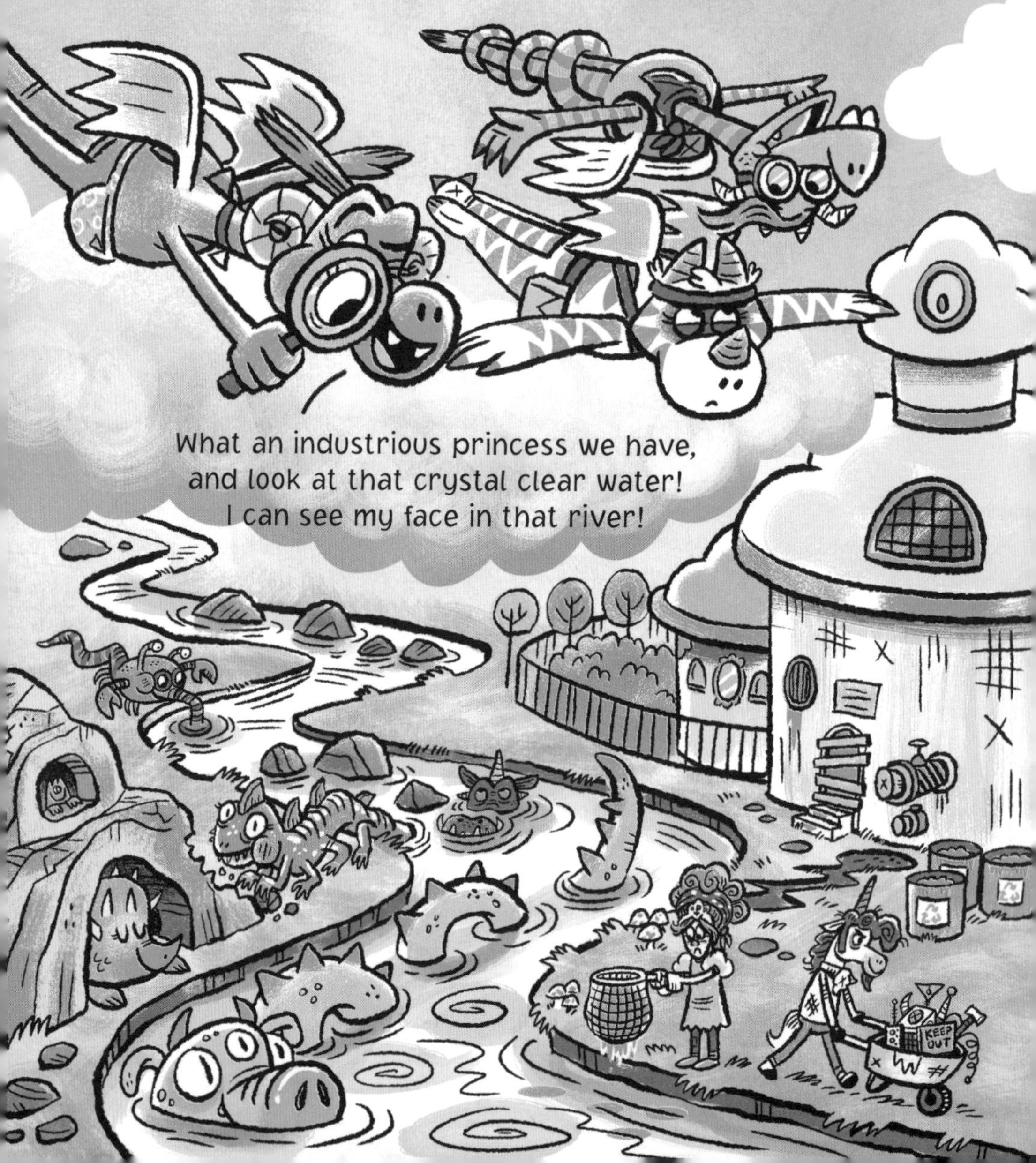
What an industrious princess we have, and look at that crystal clear water! I can see my face in that river!
KEEP OUT

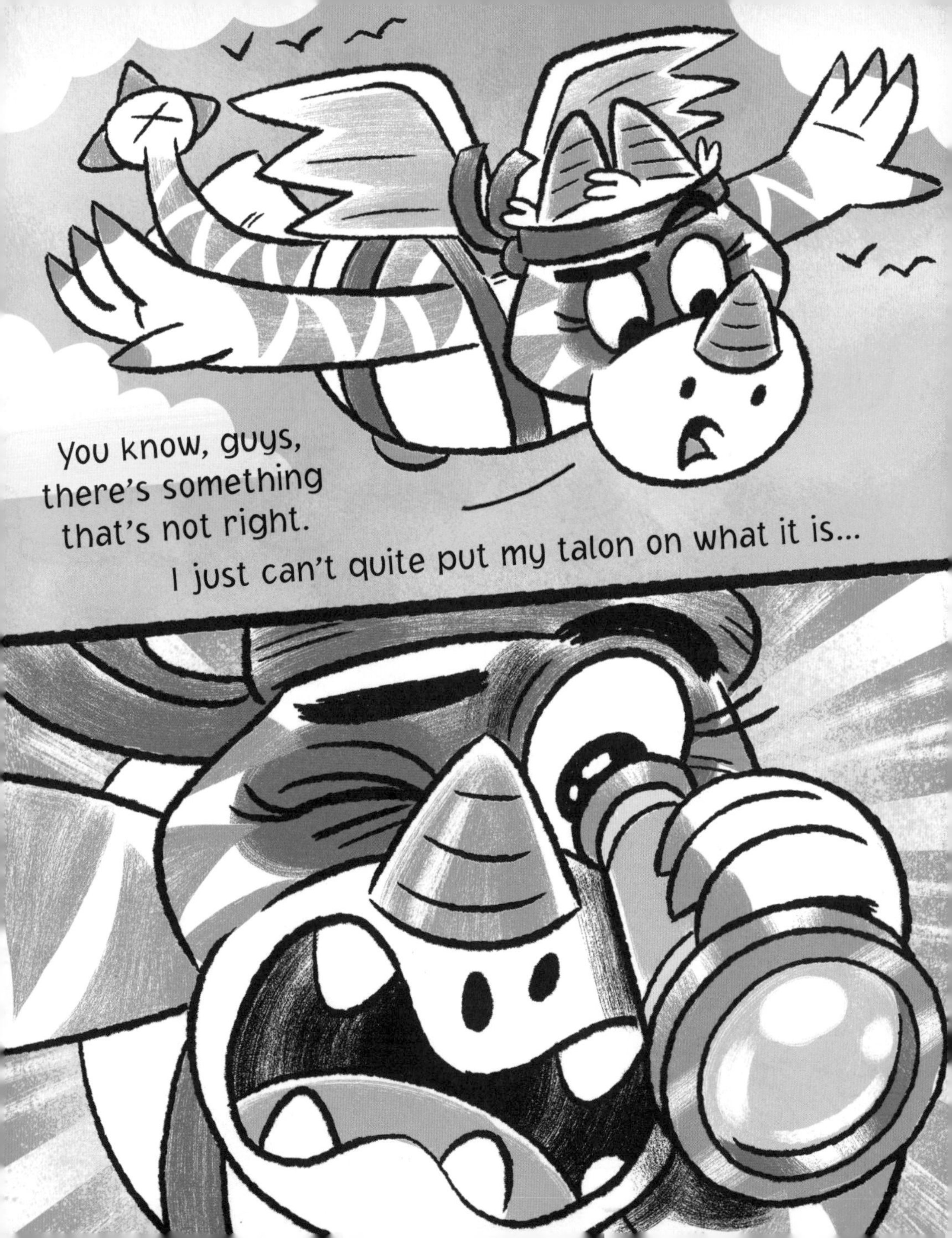
You know, guys,
there's something
that's not right.
I just can't quite put my talon on what it is...

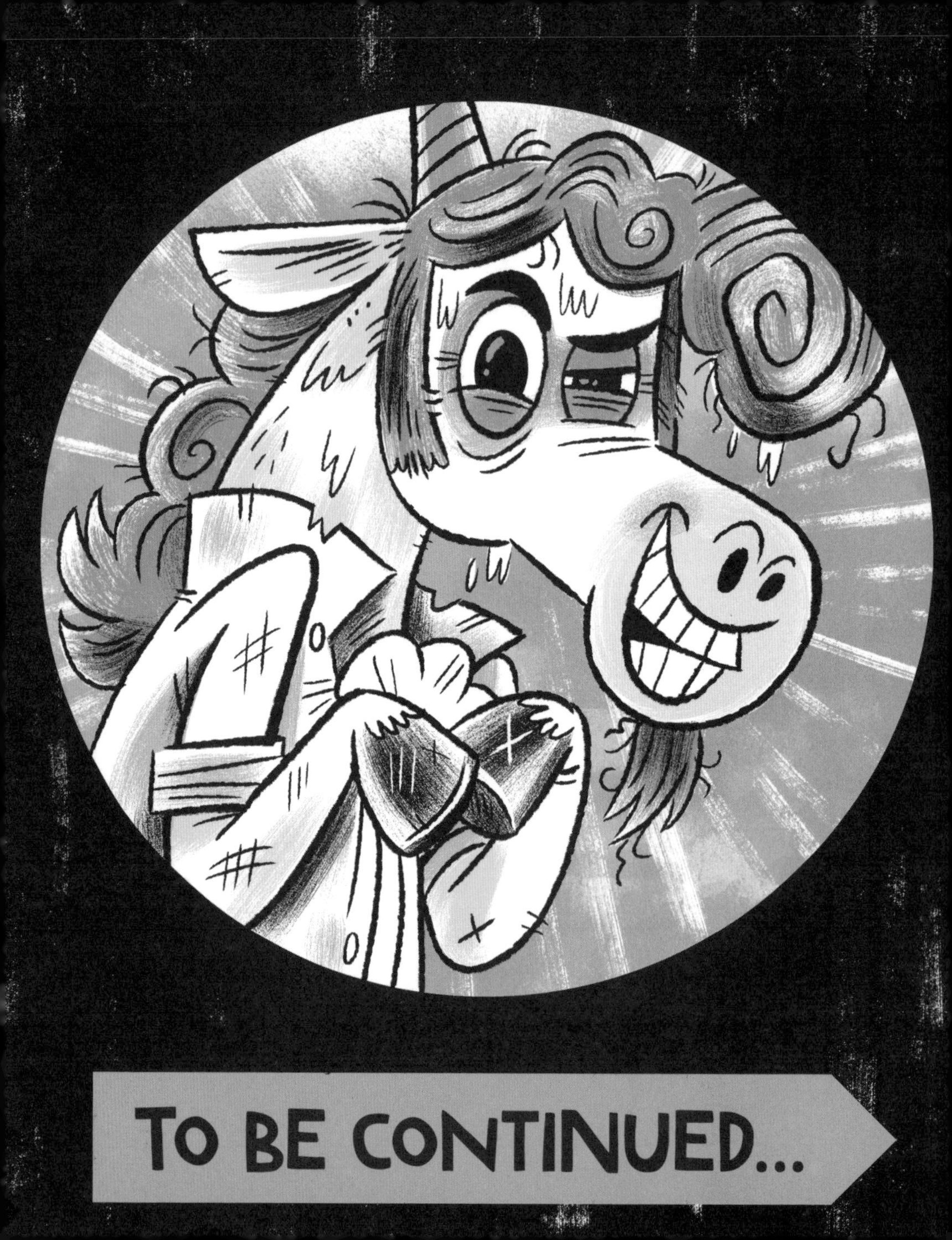
TO BE CONTINUED...